STARR BRIGHT
WILL BE WITH
YOU SOON

STARR BRIGHT WILL BE WITH YOU SOON

Joyce Carol Oates

WRITING AS

ROSAMOND SMITH

A DUTTON BOOK

DUTTON
Published by the Penguin Group
Penguin Putnam Inc., 375 Hudson Street,
New York, New York 10014, U.S.A.
Penguin Books Ltd, 27 Wrights Lane,
London W8 5TZ, England
Penguin Books Australia Ltd, Ringwood,
Victoria, Australia
Penguin Books Canada Ltd, 10 Alcorn Avenue,
Toronto, Ontario, Canada M4V 3B2
Penguin Books (N.Z.) Ltd, 182–190 Wairau Road,
Auckland 10, New Zealand

Penguin Books Ltd, Registered Offices:
Harmondsworth, Middlesex, England

First published by Dutton,
a member of Penguin Putnam Inc.

First Printing, March, 1999
10 9 8 7 6 5 4 3 2 1

ACKNOWLEDGMENTS

Chapter One, "At the Paradise Motel, Sparks, Nevada," originally appeared, in a slightly different version, in *Murder for Love* (Delacorte, 1995), edited by Otto Penzler.

Chapter Two, "At the Golden Sands, Las Vegas, Nevada," originally appeared, in a shorter version, in *Hot Blood* (Pocket Books, 1997), edited by Jeff Gelb and Michael Garrett.

 REGISTERED TRADEMARK—MARCA REGISTRADA

LIBRARY OF CONGRESS CATALOGING-IN-PUBLICATION DATA

Smith, Rosamond.
    Starr Bright will be with you soon / Joyce Carol Oates writing as
Rosamond Smith.
        p.   cm.
    ISBN 0-525-94452-4 (alk. paper)
    I. Title.
PS3565.A8S76   1999
813'.54—dc21   98-36193
                                           CIP

Printed in the United States of America
Set in Bembo
Designed by Stanley S. Drate/Folio Graphics Co. Inc.

PUBLISHER'S NOTE
This is a work of fiction. Names, characters, places, and incidents either are the product of the author's imagination or are used fictitiously, and any resemblance to actual persons, living or dead, events, or locales is entirely coincidental.

This book is printed on acid-free paper. ⊗

for John Hawkins, long a secret sharer

I resolved in my future conduct to redeem the past.

—Robert Louis Stevenson, *Dr. Jekyll and Mr. Hyde*

How many of you pigs. Emissaries of Satan. Adulterers in your hearts & fornicators. How many rapists & despoilers of the innocent, how many creatures groveling in lust. How many of you deserving of God's wrath STARR BRIGHT might have killed & chastised had I not been run to earth before my time I cannot know for such knowledge is withheld from us in the wisdom & comfort of the LORD GOD. AMEN

I

1

At the Paradise Motel,
Sparks, Nevada

In the desert, through shimmering planes of light, the hazy
mauve mountains of the Sierra Nevada in the distance, autumn sunshine fell vertical, sharp as a razorblade. The sky was a
hard ceramic blue that looked painted and without depth as a
stage backdrop. "Starr Bright" woke startled from her druggy
reverie of the past several hours wondering where she was, and
with whom. A familiar-unfamiliar succession of motels, restaurants, gas stations, enormous billboards in Day-Glo colors ad-
vertising casinos in Reno and Las Vegas—but it was CITY
LIMITS SPARKS, NEVADA they were entering, Billy Ray Cobb
behind the wheel of his classy rented platinum-gray Infiniti
with the red leather interior smelling of newness. "Starr Bright"
removed her smoke-tinted designer sunglasses with the dazzling
white frames to see more clearly, but the glare was blinding.
Her eyes felt naked, exposed. She wasn't a girl for the harsh
overexposed hours of morning or afternoon in the desert, her
nocturnal soul best roused at twilight when neon lights flashed
and pulsed into life. *But why am I here, why now? And with whom?*

Not knowing she was awaiting God's sign.

Proud and perky behind the wheel of the Infiniti like an
upright bulldog was Mr. Cobb of Elton, California, an electrical
supplies manufacturer's representative—as he'd introduced himself the previous evening at the Kings Club. A sporty fun-loving

5

loud-laughing man of any age between forty-five and fifty-five who perspired easily, with a thick neck, heavy-lidded bulldog eyes and wattles and a damp, hungry smile punctuated by chunky teeth. He wore casual vacation clothes—this *was* his vacation, after all—an electric-blue crinkled-cotton shirt monogrammed *B.R.C.* on the pocket (so maybe "Billy Ray Cobb" was his name?), checked polyester trousers creased tightly at the thighs, a "Navajo" hand-tooled leather belt with a flashy brass buckle into which his soft, prominent belly pressed. A black onyx fraternity ring on his right hand and a gold wedding band on his left hand, both rings embedded in fatty flesh. Almost shyly he asked, "Had a little nap, Sherrill, eh?" Or, his breath quickened as if he'd run up a brief flight of stairs, he sounded shy. Then boasting, "Well, we made good time. Two hundred twenty miles in under three hours."

"Starr Bright" perceived that Billy Ray Cobb was one to crave praise from a woman like a dog craving tidbits at the table—no matter what tidbits, however dried out or tasteless or not even food at all, rolled-up paper napkin pellets would suffice. In her sexy throaty voice she murmured, "Hmmm, yes. Fan-tastic."

Seeing how Mr. Cobb was peering eagerly at her she quickly replaced the dark glasses. *Don't stare at me God damn you don't you stare at me.* But of course she was poised, at ease, gave no sign of annoyance. "Starr Bright" was always elaborately made up; her heart-shaped face a flawless cosmetic mask like something hardened to a single substance, a single texture. She knew she looked good, and more than good, but in this damned white-glaring desert sun she might look, if not her age precisely, for "Starr Bright" never looked her age, but maybe thirty-one or -two, not twenty-eight as she'd led credulous Mr. Cobb of Elton, California, to believe.

So far as he knew she was "Starr Bright"—an "exotic interpretive" dancer at the Kings Club, Kings Lake, Nevada. An independent young woman with a flair for the performance arts—not just dancing but singing as well (she had a lovely trained mezzo-soprano voice). Before Kings Lake she'd worked in Lake Tahoe, California, and before that in Los Angeles, San Diego and Fresno; before that, Miami and West Palm Beach, Florida. And there'd been an interlude in Houston, Texas.

Before that, memory faded. Like once-colorful travel posters on a wall frayed and weatherworn with time until one place looked very like another.

It was not yet 6 P.M. And bright as noon. Yet Billy Ray Cobb was eager to check into a motel. Pawing and squeezing "Starr Bright" as he drove the Infiniti, now slowed to forty miles an hour along the crowded two-lane highway; he was panting and florid-cheeked. *Stop staring at me God damn you.* His sporty-macho smell was mixed up with the aggressive smell of the red-leather interior; the air-conditioning hummed like a third presence. "Starr Bright" was flattered by her new admirer's sexual attraction to her, his look of awe commingled with frank doggy desire, or should have been; but it was a bummer, his wanting to stop so soon. "Just that I'm crazy about you, baby," Mr. Cobb said, a whining edge to his voice as if he suspected that "Starr Bright" might not believe him. "Like last night, you'll see."

"Hmmm."

Did she remember last night, no she didn't remember last night.

Wouldn't remember tonight tomorrow night, or so she hoped.

Her father's long-ago voice gentle in wisdom *You won't remember tomorrow what seemed so important today.* But he'd meant worldly vanity, tinsel hopes. Not being fucked like a dog in heat.

So: Billy Ray Cobb did not drive on to Reno as "Starr Bright" had been led to believe they would; and from Reno to Las Vegas.

Might it have made a difference if they'd driven on to Reno?

Only a half-hour drive, more desert but it would have flashed by glittering like mica.

God damn you: no. But her face betrayed no unease, not even annoyance as, impulsively, Billy Ray Cobb swung the Infiniti into a motel that was one of dozens or possibly hundreds of "bargain-rate" motels along the Sparks-Reno strip, just inside the Sparks city limits. PARADISE MOTEL   BARGAIN ROOMS & HONEYMOON SUITES!   VACANCY!   HAPPY HOUR 4–8 P.M. EVERY NITE! "Starr Bright" narrowed her aching eyes trying to recall if she had been here before. Maybe yes, maybe no. It was all vague. Billy Ray Cobb was chattering excitedly and she was murmuring "Hmmm, hmmm—" in her throaty just-mildly-bored exotic-performer's voice.

If "Starr Bright" was bitterly disappointed in the Paradise Motel, in Sparks, Nevada, having envisioned a first-rate casino-hotel in Reno for the night, smelling beforehand the insecticide-odor of the shabby room, she gave not the slightest clue. She was not that kind of girl.

With her ashy-blond hair cascading to her shoulders and her strong-boned classic face and her long dancer's torso and legs, certainly "Starr Bright" was accustomed to the close scrutiny of men; and knew to keep her most mutinous thoughts to herself. Never to bare her teeth in a quick incandescent flash of anger; never to frown, or grimace, bringing the near-invisible white lines of her forehead into sharp visibility. Never to raise her carefully polished thumbnail to her teeth like an unhappy adolescent girl and gnaw at the cuticle until she tasted blood. *Never never never so long as you are "Starr Bright."*

While Mr. Cobb checked the two of them into the Paradise Motel, "Starr Bright" strolled restlessly about the poolside area, an interior courtyard flanked by thin drooping palm trees that looked brittle as papier-mâché. A six-foot concrete wall painted Day-Glo orange blocked the view of an adjacent motel and cars, buses, motorcycles and campers moving relentlessly along Route 80, but could not keep out the steady noise of traffic. The kidney-shaped pool, in which several near-naked swimmers splashed, smelled sharply of chlorine. And there was the familiar odor of insecticide pervading all. "Starr Bright" glanced quickly about to see if she recognized anyone at poolside—if anyone recognized her—for, having been acquainted with so many men, over a period of years, she must always be vigilant.

In fact, eyes had drifted casually onto her. Strangers' eyes, both male and female. But that was to be expected: "Starr Bright" was used to the attention of strangers and would have been discomfited if no one noticed her, so leggy and glamorous in this third-rate Paradise Motel.

No one seemed to recognize her, however. Nor did "Starr Bright" recognize anyone.

Thank you, God!

Uttered quickly and shyly in her inward voice, her head bowed. As one might murmur words of gratitude to an elder, not wanting to be heard, exactly. Not wanting to call attention to oneself.

Of the ten or twelve guests in the courtyard, most had positioned themselves luxuriously in the waning sun: visitors to the Southwest, obviously. "Starr Bright" heard a foreign language being spoken—German, she guessed. Why would anyone come so many thousands of miles to spend even a single night *here*? And others were midwesterners, oily gleaming bodies in scanty bathing suits, bathing suits straining against flesh, young firm flesh and aging raddled flesh, dreamily shut eyes reckless in the sun's killer rays. Of course, they'd smeared on "suntan lotion"—"sun block"—in childlike trust that such flimsy protections could shield them from cancer. There were pastel-bright drinks with melting ice cubes in tall glasses, empty beer, Coke and Perrier bottles accumulated on the wrought-iron tables. From overhead amplifiers, rock-Muzak made the air vibrate; the pulse quicken. "Starr Bright" felt a wild impulse to dance. She was worn out from the drive, she'd taken her meds for a placid low-voltage buzz, yet the music excited her; that heavy erotic beat, the slamming percussive rhythm. After the initial attention she'd received she was now not being noticed: why? *Look at me, here I am, why are none of you looking at me? Here is "Starr Bright"!* She was wearing a tight silky-black miniskirt that came barely to midthigh, and a gold lamé halter top that fitted her good-sized breasts tightly; her long blond smooth-shaven legs were bare; her feet bare in cork platform heels. A thin gold chain around her left ankle, a tiny gold heart dangling. Pierced earrings that fell in glittering silvery cascades nearly to her shoulders, a half-dozen rainbow-metallic bracelets tinkling on each arm. Crimson lips moist as if she were quick-breathing, feverish. And the glamorous designer sunglasses that hid bruises, or the shadow of bruises, beneath her eyes. *Why will you not look at me? I am more beautiful than any of you.*

"Starr Bright's" first celebrity came early, at the age of thirteen, when she'd won first prize in a children's talent competition in Buffalo, New York, singing "I'm Always Chasing Rainbows." She'd been dazed by the sudden applause, a cascade of applause, strangers' faces beaming and their lifted, clapping hands and the blinding heat of the spotlight on her so she'd felt naked, yet blessed.

They love me. These people I don't know—they love me.

How long ago? Don't ask.

When they stop staring, and their eyes go through you, one of the older dancers at the Kings Club had told "Starr Bright," you're in deep trouble. You're on your way to being dead meat. So be thankful for the rude stares. Those pigs are money in the bank.

"Starr Bright" didn't want to think they were pigs exclusively. She'd had many admirers, and many of these were gentlemen—almost. Billy Ray Cobb for example. The kind of well-intentioned guy, if you got to know him when he was sober, gave him half a chance, he wouldn't be half bad.

Strange how, after their initial interest, the poolside loungers at the Paradise Motel didn't seem to notice "Starr Bright." Even a fattish man sprawled in a canvas chair had returned to his copy of *USA Today*. Which was God's sign, too, as "Starr Bright" would afterward realize. Not knowing at the time the import of such signs just as she did not know but would subsequently learn from newspapers and TV that Billy Ray Cobb was signing them into the Paradise Motel as *Mr. & Mrs. Elton Flynn of Los Angeles, CA.*

In the pool there was an outburst of noisy-splashy activity. A voluptuous young woman in a tiny yellow bikini was squealing and kicking, hugging an inflated air mattress striped like an American flag to her breasts, as a tanned muscled young man tickled her; their cries and laughter pierced the air. What exhibitionists! Both were good-looking, with well-developed bodies; youthful, *young*—in their late twenties perhaps. "Starr Bright" stared at them covertly, in envy. But she was disapproving. So close to naked, their bodies gleaming and squirming and thrashing, so vulgar!—the girl and her boyfriend were almost making love in the pool, in plain sight. Bright water heaved and rippled about them. Others at poolside stared openly, gaping and grinning; the lovers behaved as if they took no heed, though obviously delighting in being watched. *Yes, look at us, how happy we are, how beautiful we are, how we deserve happiness because we're beautiful, young and beautiful, what pleasure our bodies take in one another, aren't you all jealous? jealous? jealous?* The girl's shapely arms flailed in a pose of helpless alarm, her heavy breasts nearly exploded out of the skimpy bikini bra, her strong legs thrashed and the young man pushed himself boldly between them, aiming a biting kiss at her throat, as the striped air mattress slipped from them and they began, wildly squealing, to sink beneath the surface of the water. Amid the splashing, paddling, squealing "Starr Bright" pursed her lips and looked quickly away.

It was at this point that Billy Ray Cobb caught up with her.

He'd been lugging suitcases, and set them down on the puddled concrete; he was panting, and a vexed little frown gave his face a pouty, petulant cast. He closed his fingers around "Starr Bright's" left wrist. Saying two things to her in a lowered jocular voice and afterward she wouldn't be able to recall which he'd said first. One was, "Wondered where you'd got to, sweetheart," and the other was, with a smirk, "Looks like the fun's already started, eh?"

Not in her slightly scratched leather Gucci bag, a Neiman-Marcus gift from an admirer now forgotten, but in her midnight-blue sequined purse crammed with wallet, cosmetics, amphetamine and Valium tablets, did "Starr Bright" carry what she called *protection*. A pearl-handled stainless steel carving knife with a slender five-inch blade. Very lightweight, very trim. Kept wrapped in tissue at the bottom of the purse, its razor-sharp blade not yet put to the test. *Protection* she thought it, not a *weapon*; still less a *concealed weapon*. So far as she knew, without making inquiries ("Starr Bright" was not one to make inquiries about such things), carrying such a knife on one's person was not illegal, in the states in which she'd been traveling; this was after all a carving knife, a kitchen knife, readily enough purchased in any household supplies store. A knife for preventative purposes, not for any act of aggression.

    Protection after she'd been accosted and arrested in a cocktail lounge of a luxurious Hyatt Regency in Houston, Texas, by two plainclothes vice squad detectives who'd detained her in "custody" in a squad car for hours during which time they'd forced her to commit upon their pig-persons sex acts of a repulsive nature, under threat of charging her with "public soliciting" and "resisting arrest." *Never again will "Starr Bright" be humiliated, never again will "Starr Bright" service pigs on any terms but my own.*

That night "Starr Bright" dreamt so strangely!—obsessively, in anguish, of the motel pool, and the air mattress floating in the pool.

She'd scarcely seen the mattress, had little impression of it except it was made of plastic, red, white and blue stripes, about five feet long, not a child's but a grown-up's plaything; a mattress to float on, basking in the sun; an object of salvation if you were in water over your head and couldn't swim.

No death worse than drowning, a slow choking agonizing death and your life flashing before you like a crazed film reel.

"Starr Bright" wasn't much of a swimmer, water frightened her. The transparency, the eerie buoyancy that can't be depended upon; the disequilibrium when you tried to walk, in shallow water, or in the surf; the loss of control. Though, of course, she'd always liked to lounge beside pools and on attractive beaches: "Starr Bright" in eye-catching swimwear; "Starr Bright" lavishly oiled against the sun's rays; a wide-brimmed straw hat on her head, dark sunglasses protecting her sensitive eyes. She was a beautiful shapely blonde of the type seen at such places, or in advertisements of such places: luxury suited her, she was a luxury item herself. But water frightened her, the thought of trying to swim, having to swim to save her life, gave her a taste of panic cold and metallic in her mouth.

In her druggy dreams that night how cruel to find herself naked in the tacky motel pool, not a glamorous sexy figure in her sleek black bikini but a helpless flailing naked figure, an object of male derision, crude teasing. She was clutching at the air mattress sobbing, gasping for breath, heart pounding as someone (a man, a stranger, faceless, squat-bodied) tried to pull her from it and into the water to drown. Like the girl in the yellow bikini she'd kicked, thrashed, flailed about, screamed; but this wasn't play, this was deadly earnest. It seemed that her assailant might be Billy Ray Cobb (except she couldn't remember his name), then he was a stranger, then there were two men—or more?—jeering at her terror, which was a female's laughable, contemptible terror, their fingers hard and pitiless as steel tugging at her ankles, her bare vulnerable legs, arms, gripping the nape of her neck to force her face into the water as cruel children do to one another. "Starr Bright" was naked, defenseless as a child, the water lapped darkly about her and was no longer the synthetic bright turquoise of the motel pool. If only she could pull herself up onto the air mattress she could save herself!—but her arm muscles were weak and flaccid, her feeble strength was rapidly fading, her mouth filled with poisonous water it would be death to swallow. And the jeering, the laughing!—the hard hurting male fingers!

Help me! Please help me! O God!

I will be your servant forever, if You save me O God!

So "Starr Bright" thrashed about wildly, flailing her arms, kicking, fighting for her life—yet she was paralyzed, and could not move. Waking bathed in perspiration, cold clammy sweat; her muscles rigid, face contorted. Waking—where? In an unknown bed, a bed of damp rumpled smelly sheets, in an unknown room that hummed loudly with cheap air-conditioning that could not dispel odors of whiskey, cigarette smoke, human sweat and semen and insecticide. "Starr Bright" was not alone but beside a stranger, a fattish naked man who lay sprawled on his back in the center of the bed, a sheet pulled to midchest, head flung back and mouth gaping, wetly snoring.

Mr. Cobb it was. Who'd been unexpectedly rough and impatient with her. The first time, at Kings Lake, he'd been shy, boyish and fumbling like a new husband; last night, reddish-veined pig's eyes contracting and his vision going inward as *Uh! uh! uh!* he'd grunted grinding himself stubbornly and then desperately and at last furiously into "Starr Bright." *But I thought you admired me, my dancing; I thought you were "crazy" about me . . .* Twenty pitiless minutes she'd clocked this copulation as she'd clocked their earlier episodes, eight minutes, twelve minutes, sixteen; a part of her brain detached and clinical despite the line of coke she'd snorted with her bulldog-jowled friend whose name, or names, kept eluding her. She hadn't even pretended to respond, her usual low throaty sexual moaning as if she were being tortured but loving it, loving it but tortured, why bother, Cobb wasn't paying attention. They'd checked in early at the Paradise Motel for this purpose, were naked in bed trying to *make love* as Cobb called it; thrashing about on top of the bed for a while; then rose to go out hurriedly not taking time even to shower and cleanse their sticky bodies as "Starr Bright" badly wanted; yes, and to shampoo her hair; it had been two days since she'd cleaned herself thoroughly and how badly she wanted to wash between her legs, her chafed tender thighs, run the shower in the bathroom as hot as she could bear it but Cobb grown suddenly bossy insisted upon going out to buy a bottle of Jack Daniel's and several grams of cocaine innocently white and powdery-granular as confectioner's sugar and so the night had shut abruptly about her like walls pushing inward, threatening suffocation. *C'mon, baby! What'd they call you—* *"Starr Bright"? Loosen up.*

Though the man was a stranger to her, "Starr Bright" seemed to know beforehand it might be a wise move to anesthetize herself. So she'd only pretended to inhale a second and a third line of coke held on a shaky spoon-mirror to her nostrils; in fact, in the secrecy of the ill-smelling bathroom, the only place she could go to hide from Mr. Cobb, she'd quickly swallowed not one, not even two, but a risky three tablets of Valium, the most she ever allowed herself in even the worst emergency situations, or when alcohol was involved. (Trying not to think of women she'd known, dancers like herself, "exotic" or otherwise who'd overdosed on drugs and alcohol, overdosed and died and their names forgotten.) So she'd been more or less dulled against Mr. Cobb's grinding, grunting and panting; his semi-flaccid penis like a hunk of blood sausage that, though limp, yet has substance, and can be made to hurt, jammed into her; his hard grasping hands like tentacles; his red-rimmed frog's eyes, his escalating demands. How quickly the man had changed: as if they'd run through a twenty-year marriage in twenty hours, Mr. Cobb aging and coarsening before her eyes. How many minutes, how many hours, precisely where they were, and why she, "Starr Bright," a top "exotic interpretive dancer" admired by other dancers for her Ice Princess glamor and her evident intelligence and sensitivity, more than once compared to the French film actress Catherine Deneuve—why she was here, in this despicable bed, in a despicable man's arms, she could not know, could not comprehend. But the Valium had kicked in, the Valium was precious as any savior, she was sinking to sleep again, shivering, cold with sweat like congealed oil, trying discreetly to keep as far as possible from the snoring man in the center of the bed. She knew from experience *You don't want to offend them, don't want to make them angrier than they are.* And sinking into sleep again, "Starr Bright" found herself another time in a swimming pool—in a distant city, in a distant time, she was a child again, nine years old, and she'd been brought to a park by an older girl cousin who lived in town, what a treat for little Rose of Sharon Donner visiting for the day, excited as always when visiting her relatives in Yewville, which seemed to her a large city of mystery and adventure. (And it pleased her, too, that for some reason her sister hadn't been included. How much more fun without Lily, who was so shy and hanging-back!) But something seemed to have gone wrong: her cousin Beverly wasn't watching her as she was supposed to, Beverly had gone off with her own friends and so Rose of Sharon in her pink swimsuit found herself surrounded in the pool by children she didn't know. *Hey who're you? Where're you from?* Older boys of eleven or twelve, skinny strangers with hair wetly rat-slick and narrowed curious eyes that Rose of Sharon believed were friendly eyes, she was a child accustomed to being admired, being liked, of the Donner girls it was Rose of Sharon and never Lily of the Valley people fussed over, poor Lily was so shy, and Sharon was so bright and bold and outgoing and pretty, naturally boys paid attention to *her.* So she told them her name, and they laughed at such a name—but nice-laughing, teasing-laughing. She told them she was from Shaheen, and they laughed saying *Where?* for Shaheen was miles away in the country, not even a town just a place. She told them proudly that her daddy was Ephraim Donner, Minister of the First Church of Christ of Shaheen, and that impressed them, she thought, that made them listen! So they invited her for a ride in their big inner tube, which was a truck inner tube, the biggest in the pool. Rose of Sharon had seen other children riding in the tube, so big, shiny-black and floppy, the center of much splashing and hilarity; it seemed to her that only privileged, favored girls were allowed to ride in this tube, head and arms thrust through the opening, legs kicking behind, so of course Rose of Sharon said yes, she hadn't even glanced around to look for Beverly, in her excitement she'd forgotten entirely about Beverly. The Yewville boys were so friendly, grinning at her so of course she trusted them, she was nine years old and a country child and the favorite of her daddy, so Rose of Sharon Donner trusted these boys though they were strangers and her mother had warned her not to play with children she didn't know unless Beverly was with her but in the giddy excitement of the pool this was forgotten. *Hey c'mon little girl! Blondie Blue-Eyes! Don't be scared!* So she let the boys push her through the inner-tube opening, she was squealing, giggling and kicking as the boys tugged the tube across the pool, and toward the farther end of the pool where the water was five feet deep and Rose of Sharon began to be frightened but the boys doggy-paddling and splashing beside her said not to be scared, not to be scared she was O.K. because the inner tube couldn't sink. The boys were ducking beneath her and jostling her, pulling at her feet, tickling at first and then pinching; poking their hard fingers into her ribs, between her legs as she began to thrash her arms and legs, panicked, helpless and sobbing. She tried to cry *No! no! let me go!* but she swallowed water, there was so much noise in the pool no one could hear her, the boys wouldn't let their pretty little blond captive go, a gang of them now was hooting and chortling tugging her across the pool into the deep water where only older children and teenagers were allowed to swim, and at last a lifeguard intervened, a teenaged girl blowing her whistle and shouting so the boys quickly shoved Rose of Sharon out of their tube and into the water and escaped, and Rose of Sharon sank swallowing water, flailing about and would surely have drowned except for the lifeguard rescuing her, carrying her out of the pool and onto the puddled concrete where she lay sobbing and coughing up water, stricken as a wounded animal. And so ashamed! so humiliated! When she'd thought the boys had liked her so much! Her cousin Beverly was squatting over her, guilty, frightened, saying how sorry she was, how sorry she was please not to tell on her, begging Rose of Sharon not to tell either of their mothers ever, and so the nightmare was ended, and Rose of Sharon never told. For to tell would be to admit how she'd been tricked, made a fool and humbled bawling like a baby among staring strangers.

Except: the nightmares of childhood never end but continue forever beneath the surface of memory as beneath the surface of choppy murky water. So long as memory and life endure.

So it was that "Starr Bright" woke agitated and confused, half-choking out of her drugged sleep another time. She was not "Rose of Sharon Donner" now and had not been "Rose of Sharon Donner" for a long time. Luminous red numerals floating in the dark beside the bed indicated 4:46 A.M. There would be no more sleep for "Starr Bright" that night.

★   ★   ★

Through discolored venetian blind slats a fluorescent-crimson neon sign flashed in rumba rhythm. PARADISE MOTEL. PARADISE MOTEL. Quietly "Starr Bright" slipped from the damp smelly pigsty of a bed and discovered herself naked. Naked! Shivering in the drafty refrigerated air though her body was covered in sticky sweat and there was a burning sensation between her legs. Dared not waken the man, what was his name, Cobb. Had to escape from him, a dangerous man, cruel, surprising how he'd changed after a few drinks, snorting coke and he'd become a real bulldog, he'd hurt her, bruised her breasts he'd said were so God-damned beautiful they drove him crazy with wanting to suck suck suck the first time she'd undressed before him in the privacy of his Kings Lake motel room, but this time he'd been a different man, squeezing and pinching her breasts, bruising the insides of her creamy-pale thighs, grinding his only part-erect penis into her grunting *Uh! uh! uh!* as if he'd wanted to kill her, eyes bulging and pink-flushed face swelling like a balloon about to burst. Drunk, and high on cocaine, not a man accustomed to cocaine, he'd turned into a bully, a pig, and he'd lied to her, too, promising she could bathe herself, wash her sticky hair, like all of them he'd lied to her, he had no pity for her suffering.

Must change my life. Help me O God. I'm run to earth.

For God had sent her the miracle-dream, a dream of her lost, repudiated childhood. She had not had the drowning-dream, as she called it, for eight years or more. Since West Palm Beach. Or had it been Miami. *A sign of Your terrible love.*

Quickly, fumblingly, "Starr Bright" dressed herself in the dark palely raddled by flashing crimson neon from PARADISE MOTEL PARADISE MOTEL outside the window. Stepping into the torn black lace panties Cobb had ripped from her, struggling into the absurdly tight skirt, the phony-gold lamé halter. And where were her shoes? and her Gucci bag? and the blue-sequined purse?

One day they would ask why hadn't she fled Billy Ray Cobb and the Paradise Motel. Why not run out of the room, why not run for help into the motel office, bright-lit and open for business at 4:46 A.M. as at 4:46 P.M. For indeed "Starr Bright" might have done so, seeking refuge on foot in Sparks, Nevada, a police station perhaps, except she feared and loathed the police, above all you can't trust the police. Nowhere to go, *run to earth.*

When God sends His sign, it's after you are run to earth. And beaten, broken utterly. So you cast your eyes upward to Him, there is no one but Him.

There stood "Starr Bright" hastily clothed now pausing to look through Cobb's clothes flung onto a chair. The fake-Navajo belt with the brass medallion buckle. The monogrammed shirt smelling of sweat and deodorant, the polyester trousers. By the rhythmically flashing light she could see only well enough to go through the trouser pockets, remove the wallet thick with bills and credit cards, the keys for the rental car. Hands shaking but determined. And there on a table the almost-empty whiskey bottle, somehow she'd taken hold of it, and she raised it to her mouth and drank impulsively, regretted it immediately as she began to cough and Billy Ray Cobb's snoring ceased and he woke and sat up muttering, "Eh? What? Who's that?"

There followed then an episode distended and distorted as in a dream never to be recalled precisely by "Starr Bright" except in quick-jumping flashes, images.

She told the groggy suspicious man it was just her, it was just "Starr Bright" and he should go back to sleep, but Billy Ray Cobb had flared up in anger swinging his bare legs out of bed, demanding to know, "Baby, why're you *up*? It's fucking *night*." And she'd tried to hide the wallet and car keys inside her clothes, turned from Cobb, saying she needed to use the bathroom. But by now Cobb was on his feet. You wouldn't have believed a man his age, his size and fattish condition could wake up so quickly, must have been adrenaline charging him, swaying but belligerent demanding to know what the hell was going on. He was just a little taller than "Starr Bright" in his bare feet, no more than five feet nine but he outweighed her by one hundred pounds. Saying, advancing upon her, "Yeah? Happens the bathroom's in this direction, sweetheart. Or were you gonna take a leak on the floor?" And "Starr Bright" was stammering trying to explain she wanted to take a shower, needed to take a hot shower, wash her hair, couldn't sleep smelly and dirty as she was and Cobb interrupted, "Shower in the middle of the fucking *night*? You expect me to believe that?" She was about to make a run for the door though knowing the door was chain-bolted and double-locked and she wouldn't have had a chance to escape and by this time he'd seen the wallet and car keys in her hand, and grabbed her, limp and weak as a rag doll she was as he shook her, slapped her, "What the fuck, bitch? Caught you, eh?" getting a hammerlock on her and grunting dragging her toward the bathroom. "You say you want a shower, eh?—dirty hair washed? Dirty cunt washed? How's about in the toilet bowl? Think you can put something over on *me*! Make an asshole out of *me*! You're messing with the wrong man, bitch!"

"Starr Bright" was on her knees. Cobb was slapping, punching her furiously, an undertone of shame in his voice, "—Telling me all that shit last night and I fell for it! What a sucker! Shoulda known you whores are all alike, don't deserve to live! Going into my wallet! Can't wait till morning to be paid!" and he'd picked up his wallet where it had fallen to the floor and extracted a handful of bills tossing them into the air in derision and pushing "Starr Bright" down on hands and knees where they fell, saying, "Crawl for it, bitch, pick 'em up, bitch, pick 'em up with your cunt," and when she refused to move he pushed her down and straddled her, heavy sweating naked body on her back, penis and testicles flopping against her back, "Hey, you like it, babe! You know you like it! 'Starr Bright'— what a crock of shit! Phony bitch, all of you phony bitches, whores! Don't deserve to live, you contaminate the world for decent women." He snatched up his belt and began to strike her with it, the brass buckle against her legs, thighs, buttocks, he was laughing, "Giddyup, horsey! Giddyup, horsey! You like it, eh?—cunt? Sure you do," and when "Starr Bright" collapsed beneath his weight Cobb ground himself into her, penis like a steel rod now, hardened with fury, loathing, the wish to hurt, and the rattling air-conditioning muffled their cries if anyone had been listening, if anyone had cared to listen here at the Paradise Motel, Sparks, Nevada, but of course no one did, as Billy Ray Cobb hooted and laughed and collapsed onto her, and lay heavily panting, unmoving for several seconds. When he rose from her, "Starr Bright" lay limp on the floor.

Cobb was immensely pleased with himself, you could hear it in his voice. Not just he'd punished a thief but he was right to do so, it was a good deed he'd done, her punishment deserved. And more: "Now get out of here, 'Starr Bright.' Before I get mad." He prodded her with his foot, he grabbed her by the hair, teasing, "Before I do something can't be undone," teasing, "Don't play no more games with me, cunt, like you're hurt or something. Like you're so sensitive or something. This room *I'm* paying for, get *out*." Forcing her to crawl in the direction of the door, through the scattered bills, his fingers gripping the back of her neck. How triumphant he was, how triumphant other men had been at such moments, waves of animal heat rippling from his body that was covered in coarse graying hair like wires. Saying again she didn't deserve to live among decent women, lucky he hadn't broken her jaw, "Starr Bright" fumbled for her sequined purse lying on the floor and he said, "Yeah! Right! Take your trash with you! Stinking up the room." He unbolted and unlatched the door, opened it as "Starr Bright" managed to stand, her clothes torn, her nose bloodied, Cobb sighted her cork-heeled shoes on the floor and snatched them up and tossed them out the door, "Trash! Stinking! Get *out*!" and when "Starr Bright" failed to move quickly enough he gripped her again by the back of the neck about to fling her through the doorway after her shoes but in that instant no longer dazed and fumbling *for God gave me strength, guided my hand according to His desire* "Starr Bright" had the knife out of her purse, held it with desperate tightness and drew its razor-sharp blade swiftly across Cobb's throat and he cried out more in astonishment than in pain as at once he began to bleed profusely, a virtual fountain of blood springing from his throat, he clutched at it trying to stem the flow, his clumsy sausage-fingers trying to repair the terrible damage in his flesh, and "Starr Bright" leapt free of him as he fell, sinking to his knees, murmuring with what remained of his voice, "Hey, what—? My God, help—help me—"

No help. None. No pity, and no mercy for she'd been bled dry of such herself. Run to earth, and broken utterly. And suffused with God's will. *God gave me strength, guided my hand* and so it was, and so it would be. So "Starr Bright" calmly watched Billy Ray Cobb die as you would see a task through to its necessary and inevitable completion. As you would not even wish to hurry such a task, surrendered to a greater will. *Thank you God. Thank you God. Thank you God.* The quivering pig-body amid a gathering pool of pig-blood dark as oil staining the cheap nubbed carpet in the flickering crimson-neon winking from the window.

Why "Starr Bright" dipped her forefinger into the pig-blood, to test its heat perhaps, to test its viscosity, she would not know and would not afterward recall. Whispering aloud, in wonder great as the dying man's before God's wrathful throne, "Now you see! Now you see! Pigs and fornicators!"

★   ★   ★

In the light of early morning, not yet dawn, an eerie calm prevailed. It was the silence of the West, the vast empty desert, the vast empty Western sky, the silence of unclocked time. In the courtyard of the Paradise Motel the kidney-shaped swimming pool was deserted, looking smaller even than it had looked the night before. And there floated the inflated air mattress, not striped like the American flag as "Starr Bright" had thought, but only red and blue stripes. A toy for adults, something demeaning and sad about it floating on top of the insect-stippled turquoise water that was like a skin stretched out over something living, invisible and inviolable and unknowable.

At 5:47 A.M. and in no apparent haste, "Starr Bright" quietly departed room 22 of the Paradise Motel; shut the door behind her, and crossed the empty courtyard to the parking lot at the rear of the motel; unlocked the platinum-silver Infiniti sedan with the Nevada rental license plates; placed her Gucci bag on the passenger's seat, and her midnight-blue sequined purse on top of the bag. Had there been an observer he would have noted a tall, poised, coolly attractive blond woman in white linen trousers, a pale blue silk shirt, practical flat-heeled sandals. Oddly, she was wearing gloves; and though the sun had not yet risen, her eyes were hidden behind dark, smoke-tinted glasses. Her ashy-blond hair, still damp from the shower, had been brushed back neatly from her face and fastened into a chignon. She was stylishly attractive but not glamorous; her flawless cosmetic mask was subdued in tone, her lipstick beige-pink; she might have been an executive's assistant, or a professional woman herself, alone on holiday. Certainly she appeared utterly natural departing the Paradise Motel at this early hour, showing no sign of agitation, nor even of unease. *As if Starr Bright had been here before. In His sign. And all has passed in a whirlwind in His terrible justice and mercy.*

In the eastern sky, beyond the fake-Spanish facade of a neighboring Holiday Inn, dawn was emerging out of an opalescent darkness of massed clouds. A fiery all-seeing eye. Beneath the scrutiny of this eye "Starr Bright" drove the Infiniti out of the parking lot and on Route 80 turned left and steadily east and south she would drive on that road and on Route 95 curving through the desert planes arriving later that morning in Las Vegas where amid a vast sea of sun-glittering vehicles parked at the Mirage she would abandon the Infiniti. She meant, for as long as she could, to keep that fiery eye before her.

2

At the Golden Sands,
Las Vegas, Nevada

She was here, somewhere. He'd know when he saw her and maybe, even, she'd know him.

He carried himself through the crowds with the cocky air of a man bearing a secret too good to keep for long. Sucking a cigarette, licking his upper lip with his tongue as if savoring it, eyes roving, searching. He wore $150 cowhide boots with a substantial heel, designer jeans, a sporty wide-shouldered Italian-style gunmetal-gray silk-cotton-and-polyester jacket and a black silk shirt open at the throat. He was, with the heels, almost five foot ten; muscular through the chest and shoulders (a former athlete, maybe? high school football?); his flesh just slightly soft, going flaccid at the waist (but the stylish jacket hid that); his hair, receding sharply at the temples, was brush-colored and wiry and had been combed at artful angles to minimize hair loss. With his close-set watchful eyes and sharp-boned western-looking face he resembled a hawk ever vigilant for prey. Here in Vegas for the weekend he was thinking he deserved a good time, deserved some God-damned happiness like anybody else and he meant to get it.

In the Barbary Coast casino into which he'd stepped out of a sun-glaring temperature of 97°F a blast of refrigerated air caressed his forehead like a woman's soothing fingers. *Mmmmm* he liked the sensation, he believed it was his due.

Back home in Sumner County, Nebraska, he had a life known to many; a "career"; an identity linked primarily to the career. He was proud enough of this without being blind to the fact that probably he'd never be promoted much beyond his present rank. When thinking along these familiar lines he was in the habit, when alone, of shrugging and muttering aloud, "So? What the hell." Smiling a quick pained smile as if some asshole had told a joke meant to be hilarious and, sure, Ernie Fenke was a good sport, he'd laugh.

It wasn't the first time he'd flown to Vegas for a weekend. And this time a three-day weekend, end of October. Leaving the Omaha airport late on Thursday, taking a single suitcase containing his Vegas clothes which were not clothes he wore in Sumner County, Nebraska. They were not clothes his wife knew about, nor anyone in his family; he kept them in a locker at headquarters. Going to Vegas once or twice a year was his own business, nobody else's. None of his colleagues knew, either. In dreams he saw himself illuminated and virile as on a video screen. In dreams he had the power to gamble away all the cash in his pocket, reaching deep into his pockets and drawing out more, more, more, no end to the cash he had, he'd live forever. At craps, at blackjack, at poker betting ever higher stakes and winning as strangers watched in awe; beautiful women watched in awe. He worried he might be a binge gambler, maybe a binge drinker, he knew from professional experience what a deadly combination this was, what it did to even intelligent, decent people but he was too smart to allow any such weakness to overcome him. *It's just I deserve a good time, shit a man deserves some happiness doesn't he!*

His wife Lynette, poor sweet dumb girl he'd married, already pregnant, out of high school, the best-looking of the varsity cheerleaders but he'd always known how to keep her in line. Not scared of him exactly but never fully at ease, not her or the kids, never taking Ernie Fenke for granted the way the wives of most of his friends took them for granted. Why couldn't I come with you just once, Lynette would ask, and he'd tell her bluntly no, these were professional trips, not vacations; these were "conferences" and "seminars" he had to attend, not in Vegas but, for instance, Salt Lake City, another time Albuquerque, this time Des Moines—hardly places a man would choose to spend a three-day weekend. And maybe Lynette believed him, and maybe she didn't; looking sometimes as if she had more to say but hesitated to say it.

Though never once in eighteen years of marriage had he hit her, and vowed he never would, Ernie Fenke wasn't that kind of man. Not in Sumner County, Nebraska.

In Vegas he rented a car and checked in, not at one of the big hotels, but at the Golden Sands Motor Lodge on the strip, a motel of no distinction, moderate-priced with a pool he wouldn't use and where each room opened out directly onto the parking lot. Which was what you required when you required privacy. Not like the high-rise hotel, the Sahara, he'd made the mistake of staying in on his first Vegas visit six or seven years ago, bringing a girl back to his room and when things got too rough the girl had lost it and started screaming and within minutes a house dick had pounded on the door and he'd had no choice but to open it, disheveled and sweating and wearing only trousers he'd hastily yanked on, but managing to say in an offended voice, "Officer, there's nothing wrong here, just my girlfriend and me," and the detective said pleasantly, "I'll need to look around, it's just routine." And so the man had come in and looked around, sniffing like he smelled a bad odor, and the girl was in the bathroom hurriedly fixing herself up, and Ernie said, "My girlfriend is a screamer, that's all it is. Somebody called down to the desk?" and the detective said, pausing outside the bathroom door upon which, too, he knocked, "Oh, yeah? Is your girlfriend a screamer?" and Ernie said, managing to laugh, laughter like clearing his throat of clotted mucus, "Yeah, but I don't hold it against her." The girl then emerged from the bathroom, in a kimono wrapped tight about her short-legged, chesty body; she'd slapped on makeup to disguise the welts on the underside of her jaw, and she was wearing bright lipstick, and she was smiling; stiff-bleached hair falling over half her face, and her eyes glassy as marbles. "Tell this officer there's no problem, Sonya," Ernie said, and Sonya said, "Officer, no problem," with a twitchy smirk. Ernie was wondering if he should offer the detective a bill or two, fifty dollars maybe; or would that be a mistake of offering him money which was a God-damned insult—as if he, Ernie Fenke, was looking for bribes; as if he, Ernie Fenke, was in fact bribable!—which maybe in another set of circumstances he might be, but these days sting operations were so common, in the papers and on TV, so anyone who imagined Ernie Fenke was stupid enough or desperate enough to be tempted to take a bribe had insulted him doubly. So he decided no; and the girl was convincing enough; and the detective seemed to want to believe them, backing off and saying in a bored voice, "O.K., kids, but take it easy from now on." So it was O.K. but Christ he'd resented having to deal with it. He resented his privacy invaded and scrutinized by some s.o.b. private cop near enough to him in age, size, disposition and possibly income to be his twin brother. So he'd never returned to any big hotel again, much preferring the small two-story motels along the strip like the Golden Sands which was about two miles from the center of Vegas.

At Caesars Palace, at Pleasure Island and the Mirage and the Hilton and the Sahara. At craps, at poker, at blackjack and at craps again. He'd won a few bucks, and lost; lost, and won; drew on his American Express card taking a chance he'd win enough to keep going, and so he did; for five hours of strain coming out a lousy $238 ahead. And he hadn't yet hooked up with a girl, he'd been so anxious waiting to get hot, really hot; but it wasn't happening.

I need one, I need a woman. For luck.

He had a habit, not nervous exactly but half-conscious, of slipping his hand inside his jacket and rubbing his chest; touching the .32-caliber pistol he carried close beneath his heart everywhere he went as if to check yes it's there, he's O.K.

In Barbary Coast cruising the slots hawklike and alert for prey. A man handsome and stylishly dressed as Ernie Fenke with his macho swagger *Yeah, I think pretty well of myself and you would, too, in my place* shouldn't have trouble attracting desirable women, right? His hair oiled and combed to hide the balding spots, a gold chain glinting at his throat, and chest hair just visible at his opened collar. Of course there were always hookers, high-priced whorehouses outside the city limits (with shuttle service provided, he'd tried it once) but Ernie Fenke wanted something better. And deserved something better. The cowhide boots giving him a full inch or more in height, so he moved through crowds catching sight of himself in mirrors and reflective surfaces and admiring what he saw. But he was disdainful of the many homely, frankly ugly and overweight women in the casino; so many middle-aged, old and even elderly men and women playing the slots, dozens, hundreds, acres of them in Vegas, everywhere in Vegas, their clawed arthritic hands covered with liver spots and visibly trembling as if with palsy or Parkinson's and some of them blind or in wheelchairs, or both, Ernie was shocked to see such behavior among his elders, people his parents' age, damned depressing sights, and most of them smoking, too. The slots were, generally, depressing. Rigged for the house to win, for penny-ante suckers to play, lowest level of gambler. Not like the more manly games poker, blackjack and craps where intelligence and gambling ingenuity might prevail.

It was late, he was getting anxious, his eye snagged on two young women in jeans and designer blouses and too much makeup squealing with excitement as a small jackpot of silver dollars spilled out of a machine to the accompaniment of flashing red lights and hurdy-gurdy music. Ernie saw it was just a

$277 jackpot, chump change but the girls were making a show of catching the coins in paper cups, exclaiming to each other. "Hey girls, congratulations!" Ernie said, and the plumper of the two actually whirled about and hugged him, a total stranger, smearing lipstick on his cheek like it was New Year's Eve or Mardi Gras. So Ernie fell to talking with them, and bought them drinks at one of the bars, Irma and Janice who were "executive assistants" as they called themselves, meaning probably secretaries, from Topeka, Kansas, here in Vegas for the weekend. Their first time in Vegas, their first jackpot ever, oh they loved Vegas it was even more exciting than they'd hoped, there was surely nothing like Vegas back in Kansas! Breathless and giggling displaying their young bodies for Ernie Fenke and, yes, he was moderately turned on, bought them another round of drinks and listened to their chatter, then suddenly bored he said, "Hey, you gals are terrific but I gotta run. Have a great weekend," tossing bills down for the waiter and walking off knowing Irma and Janice would be hurt, disappointed. The tall homely one with the buck teeth and the shorter plumper one with the brown cow-eyes like Lynette's gazing after him wistfully as he strode off brushing his oiled hair back with deft motions of both hands.

Eat your hearts out, girls.

Enough of Barbary Coast, where his luck wasn't with him. He left, crossing the street, surprised to see it was dusk already, almost night. In the casinos, which were windowless and clockless, you were led to forget there was such a thing as time. Or, glancing at your watch, you saw it was 10:48 not knowing was this morning or night. And there's a satisfaction in that. Like the time he'd poked a girl with the .32, teasing, tickling, nudging her breasts and belly and between the legs, not rough, really just playful and even affectionate, and she'd been laughing, high and laughing and suddenly she'd stopped laughing and got scared and it came to him in a flash *You could, you know—just do*

it. And there'd be a satisfaction in that, for sure. Ending everything, not just her, whoever she was, but him, too. But in the
next moment he'd forgotten, of course—Ernie Fenke could
think of better things to do with a woman than blow her away.

He was headed for the Century, a tall golden-glimmering
tower of lights against the murky sky. Grateful the sun had gone
down though it was still muggy, hot; temperature in the high
80s; and the hazy-gritty air hard to breathe. He was excited,
edgy; he recognized the symptoms; another drink helped, but
not enough. Knowing his luck wasn't with him yet but, God
damn, he was too restless to keep from trying it; found himself
at a blackjack table where he dropped $370 in four minutes. To
prove what? When he already knew? Not lonely but keenly
feeling the absence of a woman, a good-looking sexually
charged woman at his side. A woman to bring Ernie Fenke the
luck he deserved, a woman to explore that king-sized bed at
the Golden Sands Motor Lodge with him. Not a screamer if he
could help it but how'd he know beforehand? He never did.

Wandering through the crowded noisy smoke-filled casino
with rainbow spotlights overhead, crisscrossing one another like
the tails of random comets. What a place, Vegas: a dream, but
not a dream you had to sustain, yourself: an easy dream, a pure-
pleasure dream, like a fold-out 3-D children's storybook. His
pockets were stuffed with coupons, everyone trying to give
away something, or give that illusion to bring the suckers in.
He had coupons for a half-dozen meals but hadn't sat down to
one yet; too much excitement, too much electricity in the air.
It was like being a teenaged kid again, in Vegas; horny as hell,
charged up ready to explode. In his cowhide boots, in his sexy
Italian-style jacket, his black silk shirt open at the throat he was
a predator uncertain of the specifics of his prey but knowing it
was in his vicinity, he'd locate it soon; knowing he had to eat,
and soon. Following a woman then abruptly losing interest
when he saw she was his age, at least—late thirties; following
another, fantastic ass in almost-translucent purple shorts and a

tiny halter top, punk-style dyed green hair meaning she'd be wild as hell in bed and wouldn't need to be respected, but, God damn, he lost her to a guy. Mostly the Century was packed with couples, all ages, all sizes and races; Vegas had changed in just the six or seven years he'd been coming here, more ordinary people every season, more families with kids; there were couples who reminded him of his parents and in-laws; couples who reminded him of himself and Lynette as they'd been ten years ago, or would be twenty years in the future, God! No wonder he hadn't any appetite to eat.

At last at a crowded roulette table he sighted a good-looking redhead in an eye-catching costume: sexy gold lamé minidress and high-heeled cork shoes, she appeared to be alone, though plenty of guys were noticing her; numerous rings on her fingers so he couldn't tell if she wore a wedding band, but in the case of a woman like this, what would a wedding band signify if the husband wasn't within a hundred feet of her? A divorcée, Ernie supposed; maybe spending a few days in Vegas to clear out her head; looking for a pickup, too—maybe. It was Saturday night, after all. (In Vegas it was always Saturday night except for a few depressing hours on Sunday morning.) He saw her pushing chips out, and not getting chips back; pushing chips out, and not getting chips back. He saw a hurt, stung, scared look in her face that's the look of a woman losing a bet; he couldn't see how much she'd lost, but he was glad she'd lost; when a woman wins, she isn't likely to need a man. He followed her when she left the table abruptly, walking quickly in her high-heeled shoes, her pale face slightly flushed, a breathless look to her, hoped to hell she wasn't meeting up with some guy. Red-haired and sexy and not too old for him, in her late twenties possibly; reminded him of Sharon Stone, that tough-sexy look. Like her legs would wrap around you and practically break your back and you'd love it. He didn't like it that she was tall, preferred shorter women, of course the heels added inches to her height and when she kicked them off she'd be more to his taste.

A creamy-pale face smooth as a mask, not much expression, a bright red mouth like something gouged into flesh. He followed her through the casino, in and out of crowds, possibly she was aware of him by now and not minding it that he, a good-looking guy, was following her; you don't dress like that, wear your hair tousled like that, unless you want men to look seriously at you, and think serious thoughts about you. Jesus!— that gold lamé dress that fitted her slender but voluptuous body as if she'd been poured into it! The sight turned him on, shiny gold fabric tight as a tourniquet especially at her belly, pelvis. Her legs were long as a dancer's legs, maybe she was a showgirl, or had been; long, bare, smooth legs; a thin gold chain around her left ankle. *Honey look at me: Ernie Fenke's your man.* He was disappointed, though, she'd gone to the slot machines; losing at roulette and back to playing slots, both of them sheer blind chance and slots the lowest form of casino gambling. And she wasn't having luck here, either. Slots was a sucker's game, took no brains at all, still there's always the flutter of hope you *might* win; rigged to favor the house ninety-nine times out of one hundred but you *might* win; there were wins timed regularly in a row of machines to keep the credulous hopeful; to keep the suckers going, going and gone.

Until the last quarter is gone. And the good-looking redhead was losing; playing with an air of expectation tinged with hurt; a childlike look to her glamor-face; she was playing and losing, playing and losing so Ernie felt sorry for her; it was an emotion he enjoyed, feeling sorry for women. As long as it wasn't expected of him. This woman was looking anxious now, and she was looking more and more like someone in need of company. She paused in her playing to open a blue-sequined purse to look for, Ernie guessed, a pack of cigarettes she couldn't seem to find. "Here y'are," Ernie said, his own pack in his hand, there he was smiling and available and ready to assist; the woman lifted her eyes to him in mild surprise, pleasantly, as if she hadn't been aware of him watching her intensely for the past ten minutes or more. She smiled in return, and accepted the cigarette, and said in a throaty, husky voice so soft Ernie Fenke had to lean close, inhaling her perfume, to hear, "Why, thank *you*."

So they met in the Century, in the midst of numerous strangers avidly playing slots, and became acquainted; very quickly acquainted, for in Vegas there isn't time to spare. "What's your name?" he asked, and in her soft-sweet-sexy voice she said, "Sherrill," and he said, " 'Sherrill'—I like that name. Sherrill what?" and she said, "Sherrill Dwyer," so easily and looking him full in the face so he believed absolutely she was telling the truth. He grabbed her hand and shook it, squeezing the soft, rather cold fingers hard, "I'm Earl Tunley," which was the name of a right-wing state congressman from Sumner County, Nebraska, and she said, " 'Earl'—I like it, I've never known any 'Earl' close up," and he said, "There's always a first time, Sherrill, right?" and they laughed together as if this was quite a joke. And he saw that Sherrill Dwyer's eyes were a cool bluish-gray, like pebbles washed by rain; he saw without exactly noting that he saw, in the excitement of the moment, white near-invisible lines radiating outward from the corners of her eyes. He smelled something metallic and ashy beneath the ripe-peaches scent of her perfume. He liked what he saw, and what he smelled, and the effect she was having on him, a sexual stirring he understood to be the stirring of his luck, returning to him. He asked would she like a drink, and she said yes; and later he asked would she like something to eat, and she said yes; it was clear they got along, Earl and Sherrill, they liked each other a lot, understood each other it seemed; maybe even, as Sherrill speculated, they'd somehow met before, in another lifetime. Wasn't that possible? So Earl Tunley laughed indulgently and said, "Sweetheart, in Vegas anything's possible."

It was 2 A.M., a giddy crazy hour in Vegas and not really a time for serious eating. So they left most of their food on their

plates and retired to the Golden Sands, to room 19, to become
better acquainted. Ernie who was Earl bought a bottle of Jim
Beam en route and two packs of Camels and they were feeling
good, keyed up and amorous and grateful to have found each
other. Their first time in bed, to be specific on top of the king-
sized bed, was so great so terrific so fantastic it truly did seem,
as Sherry insisted, they'd known each other in another lifetime.
And Earl sighed yes, could be. Lying then naked and luxuriant
smoking cigarettes, sipping whiskey out of tumblers, still too
excited to sleep. In Vegas, who wants to sleep? Earl Tunley was
saying he was from Council Bluffs, Iowa; owned a TV and
video store; Sherrill who'd become Sherry in his arms, blowing
in his ear and moaning in sexual heat, described herself as a PR
girl from Fresno, California, between jobs. She was staying in a
motel farther out on the strip, not liking the congestion of the
big hotels—"And all these crude guys hitting on you." Earl
wasn't a married man any longer, he'd been married for almost
ten years and lucky he and his wife hadn't had any children so
he was spared child support and his ex-wife was remarried so
she was out of his hair permanently; and what about her,
Sherry?—and glamorous red-haired Sherry said, sighing, for a
fleeting moment sad, that she'd been married, too, at the age of
eighteen; but it had ended a few years later, and she tried never
to think about it. She said, "I was just a child, back in—this
small town in Pennsylvania no one's ever heard of. I thought it
was true, deep love Michael and I felt for each other but it was
a delusion, oh I was flattered this rich man's son, who'd been a
football hero at our high school a few years ahead of me, was
crazy about *me*." And she wiped carefully at her eyes, not wanting the silvery-blue eye shadow and the inky black mascara to
run; perhaps the makeup was waterproof, since it didn't run.

In a playful growling voice Earl who was Ernie, unless he
was Ernie who was Earl, said, "Sweetheart, anybody'd be crazy
about *you*." And it was time to make love again. Jesus, he was
feeling good!—feeling his old luck return, coursing through his

veins, into his cock, like molten gold. Whoever he was, Earl, Ernie, Tunley, Fenke or somebody not yet known he was grateful to this terrific woman, and he was the kind of good-sport good-hearted basically generous guy to show it. Only watch.

*   *   *

Am I afraid?—I am not.
Am I despairing?—I am not.
For You have given me a sign, & Your blessing. & I am patient, I have learned to bide my time.
The next man, maybe. Always there was the promise of the next man. When she danced, always there was the promise of being singled out, raised above the others, a photo-feature in a newspaper, or in *Nevada by Night*: "Starr Bright." Always the promise of a really serious male admirer who would love her for herself alone and wish to marry her.

Now, no longer dancing, lacking that arena for display, "Starr Bright" was temporarily disadvantaged. And her money was rapidly running out.

Not just money for food, for necessities and a decent place to stay, but money sufficient to maintain "Starr Bright's" cultured-classy appearance; the crucial "Starr Bright" appearance that made all the difference. For you can't attract the attention of a worthwhile man unless you look good; and looking good, even if you're a beautiful woman, doesn't come cheaply.

Where had the money gone?—*her* money she'd earned. She'd counted $692 from the man's wallet before tossing the wallet away in a developer's landfill off Route 80 where no one would ever find it; $692 which should have been enough to stake her for a while, staying at the cheapest motel in Vegas she could tolerate, and mainly playing the slots which was minimal risk with the possibility of a big jackpot; in fact she'd won a $444 jackpot at Vegas World on her second night but hadn't been able to repeat the win; believing that her luck was building up, gradually building up like steam pressure that had to explode eventually. When the slot machines disappointed, she'd tried blackjack, roulette, keno and the Nevada State lottery, praying *Just this once, O Lord, and I will never ask another favor of you.* And perhaps she believed this, and meant it. As years ago, when they were little girls, she'd cajoled her sister Lily into praying with her, reasoning that double prayers had double power.

One of "Starr Bright's" problems was that if she'd been drinking she was susceptible to wild mood swings. She was susceptible to behaving impulsively. Bursting into tears—tears of happiness?—when she'd won the $444 in silver coins. And later that night meeting up with a sobbing fat woman who'd lost all her money in the casinos and said she had nowhere to go and the woman's name was Lilia (which could not have been a coincidence, could it?) and "Starr Bright" had peeled off three crisp $50 bills to press into the woman's hand. And the woman had stared at her in disbelief, and stammered thanks, and blessed "Starr Bright" as an angel of mercy sent direct from God.

Just this once, O Lord. And I will never sin again.

Though knowing that God disapproved of gambling. Disapproved of these sinful cities of the plain, Sodom and Gomorrah. As in her innermost heart she disapproved. For hadn't she been brought up in a devout Christian household to love God and her savior Jesus Christ above all earthly vanities; brought up to know that the wages of sin are death. But: there are times of upheaval when you have no choice except to gamble, gamble your very life, you're desperate and run to earth and this was one of those times, He would understand, surely He would understand. A God of wrath but also a God of mercy and forgiveness.

For this was the one true fact: He was always guiding her hand.

"Starr Bright's" trembling hand gripping the razor-sharp carving knife that was her secret protection.

For if He had not guided her hand, how could she have acted? How could she have defended herself against her violator?

As, that morning in October, she'd driven in the rental Infiniti from Sparks to Reno, from Reno to Vegas, how many solitary hours in the desert singing hymns at the top of her lungs she hadn't sung in more than twenty years, singing a tune of her childhood:

> "Starr Bright will be with you soon!
> Starr Bright will be with you soon!
> Starr Bright, Starr Bright!
> Starr Bright will be with you soon!"

And laughing, and talking to herself, and already she'd begun to forget; what had happened in the Paradise Motel she'd begun to forget; for forgetting is part of healing, and God's grace is to heal. At dawn as the fiery eye emerged from the dark side of the earth she'd known that she would be guided, she would not come to harm. A wind rose out of the desert blowing dust and tumbleweed across the highway and she'd arrived in a gritty cloud obscuring the sun. Calmly locking the Infiniti with a gloved hand and tossing the keys beneath the car and walking away unobserved carrying her Gucci bag and other items, traveler's items, through the sea of vehicles parked at the Mirage. *And I saw a sea of glass mingled with fire and knew I had come to the right place.* In this Sodom and Gomorrah of the desert "Starr Bright" stepped into a dream, but it was not a dream of her own, it was not a dream that depended upon her to sustain it, it was a dream already existing, in which she could hide, as a hunted creature can hide in the wilderness; she'd been in such cities before, and knew the solace of such anonymity. And in a women's rest room at the Mirage she'd changed certain of her outer garments and fitted her beautiful red wig exactly to her head, it was a finely woven $300 human-hair wig she'd purchased for professional reasons in Miami that had the power to change her appearance, and her personality, utterly. And so if pigs' eyes moved onto her snagging onto her they were not eyes to capture *her*.

Thank you O God for this safe passage.

Strange then the next morning to read in the tabloid *Las Vegas Post* the banner headline

BLOODY RITUAL EXECUTION
"PIG DEATH" IN SPARKS MOTEL ROOM

because already she'd forgotten so much. Because already she'd begun to heal. Like the ugly welts on her breasts and her belly and between her legs that were beginning to heal, with God's grace. Like the bruises at the nape of her neck and at the small of her back where he'd straddled her. It was an ugly, lurid but fascinating story the *Post* had featured on its cover and inside front pages. How many times such had happened, and would happen. In the desert, beneath the vast empty sky into which you might fall, fall forever. A DO NOT DISTURB sign had hung outside the door of a motel room for a full day, the blinds of the room had been closed tight and the customer's car was gone from the lot and there appeared to be no activity and at last a maid unlocked the door to discover to her horror what waited inside to be discovered. *A forty-seven-year-old California man lying in a pool of congealed blood. A corpse bloodied, mutilated, naked. His throat slashed so he'd bled to death and there were multiple stab wounds in the genital area and there was blood splattered everywhere, even on the ceiling. And on the wall beside the bed in eight-inch bloody letters*

DIE PIG FILTH
DIE SATAN
✦

The murdered man had been identified as "William Raymond Cobb of Elton, California." His wallet and rented car, a

new-model Infiniti, were missing, and Nevada State police
were searching for a female companion with whom he'd registered in the motel as "Mr. & Mrs. Elton Flynn of Los Angeles."
A photograph of Cobb reprinted in the paper had not resembled anyone "Starr Bright" could recall. She was certain she'd
never seen this man; she'd never seen any bloodied wall. *The
maid must have written those words on the wall, & the star-sign to cast
suspicion onto "Starr Bright."* As in a vague, shifting dream she
could remember a swimming pool filled with bright turquoise
water that stank of chlorine, and she could remember a child's
plastic toy or inner tube floating in the pool; but she couldn't
remember any "William Raymond Cobb" and doubted that
she had ever been in such a man's proximity. At Kings Lake, as
elsewhere, so many men had introduced themselves to "Starr
Bright," how could she remember them all? And why should
she remember them all? She studied the face squinting up at her
out of the cheap tabloid paper, a jowly middle-aged face, a
coarse male face, a face "Starr Bright" might pity as one might
pity the face of a victim of any brutal or humiliating misfortune.
*God, have mercy on this sinner. If You deem such a sinner worthy of
Your mercy.* "Starr Bright" was skeptical that, as the article
claimed, Cobb had been married for twenty-two years; and was
"survived by" a wife and children, a brother and a sister.

The desk clerk at the Paradise Motel told police that it had
been obvious to him that "Mr. & Mrs. Flynn" hadn't been
married. As if it mattered! The man had behaved nervously and
guiltily, making awkward jokes; must've been twenty years
older than the woman; the woman was beautiful, glamorous;
looked like a supermodel, or an actress, or a hooker—"but a
high-class hooker." Another witness, staying at the motel,
claimed she'd seen the woman swimming in the pool, wearing
a tiny yellow bikini; the woman and Cobb were swimming and
splashing in the pool, drunk; later, in the cocktail lounge, the
couple had been observed quarreling by several persons, including the bartender. The desk clerk described the missing woman

suspect as platinum blond, approximately twenty-three years old, stylishly dressed; about five foot five, weighing maybe one hundred pounds; the bartender, who was a woman, described her as "dishwater blond" with a "coarse skin," thirty-five at the youngest, heavily made up, five feet eight or nine and weighing possibly one hundred twenty pounds. Other witnesses recalled her seeming drugged, or drunk; as friendly and smiling; as not friendly at all but stiff, icy-cold—"Looking at you like she'd like to slit your throat."

"Starr Bright" laughed angrily. A tower of Babel, a crowd of false witnesses, she would pay them no further heed.

But for curiosity's sake, and as memento of her Nevada visit, she tore out the pages from the *Post* containing the account of William Raymond Cobb's murder. And carefully folded them, and placed them inside the slightly tattered silk lining of her Gucci bag; with a bulky brass belt buckle wrapped in toilet paper. And she counted the cash in her possession that bright-glaring October morning: $692.

Next day, the *Post* published a police artist's drawing of the "female suspect" who'd shared a room and a bed with Mr. Cobb of Elton, California, and who was now missing. An ugly picture, "Starr Bright" thought: a stark, staring hungry face, oversized lips and tousled showgirl hair, of any age between twenty-five and forty. *This is not me, nor anyone known to me.* What relief in such knowledge!

The dead man's rented car had been discovered in the parking lot at the Mirage; a Reno woman, a psychic who'd worked with Nevada State police in the past, claimed she'd had a vision of the suspect dead herself at the bottom of a ravine in Red Rock Canyon, but a search in that desolate area had turned up nothing; there had been, and would be, numerous scattered sightings of the suspect through the Southwest, as far away as Nogales, Arizona, and San Diego, California; but nothing came

of these leads; police were reported "continuing with their investigation" but no arrest had been made.

Not me, nor anyone known to me.

In her red wig, her miracle-wig that altered her appearance
and her personality entirely. "Sherrill" she was now, or
"Sherry." And "Starr Bright" in hiding secret as the dark side
of the moon.

Except most of the money was gone. Not only the fat
woman sobbing her heart out in a women's rest room but wait-
resses, waiters, the motel maid who was a Hispanic girl of about
sixteen, and pregnant—these parties "Starr Bright" couldn't resist tipping, sometimes with $5 bills. So the money was going,
down to $37 the night she met up with the man who intro-
duced himself as Earl Tunley.

Trying not to be scared, living as she was from day to day,
hour to hour. The slots, blackjack, roulette and keno and the
lottery and again the slots. Waiting for her luck to change.
Waiting for a man, the right man. Waiting for a sign. And there
was Earl Tunley so powerfully attracted to her, she saw desire
shining in the man's eyes suffusing her like flame. Hadn't she
reason to believe her life might be changed for the better.
Hadn't she reason to believe her bad-luck streak had ended.

Wanting to believe that Earl Tunley in his cowhide boots,
black silk shirt and Armani-style jacket, Earl Tunley with his
hot, quick hands and mouth was truly from Council Bluffs,
Iowa; for she had the idea that a man who sold TV and video
equipment in Council Bluffs, Iowa, was a man you could trust.
And he'd promised to stake her "as much as required" and this,
too, she wanted to believe.

Except hadn't there been, from the start, something swag-
gering and authoritarian in his manner? As if, somehow, she'd
met this man before?

After their fantastic lovemaking, there she lay naked and
content in Earl Tunley's king-sized bed in the Golden Sands
Motor Lodge lazily stroking Earl Tunley's chest, running her

long polished fingernails through his steely-gray chest hairs and stroking the glittering gold chain he wore around his neck which looked like the real thing, 24-carat, and she'd thought with girlish naïveté *This one, this one maybe I could love, maybe* seeing in her mind's eye dimmed and confused by alcohol and by the late hour something looming chalky white, a dreamy image of Council Bluffs, Iowa. And her new lover was smiling saying, "You want it, sweetheart? Take it." And for an instant she thought he was serious, then she realized he was being sarcastic; and she said quickly, "Why no, Earl," and he said, "Sure, sweetheart. It's yours." He fumbled to undo the clasp and she stopped his fingers and said in a husky, earnest voice, "Earl, no. I don't want a single thing from you, ever—except a little more loving." So he shrugged and said, "Well, O.K.," staring at her smirking *Sure you want my gold chain, sweetheart. You know and I know you want all you can get from me, right?* But she'd pretended not to know, and kissed him, and ran her hands rapidly over his muscular body, stroking his clammy-cool penis reverently until he groaned forgetting any sarcasm, any doubt of her motives, and it was all right between them again. Or seemed so.

"Oh, lover. Oh my God—"

Later in the bathroom, readying herself for another stint of casino gambling (though in fact she'd rather have soaked in a hot tub and gone to bed to sleep, alone) she realized that ugly moment between "Sherry" and her new lover had been her own damned fault. She'd made the guy anxious alluding to a former husband—a "boyfriend"—God knows, men are worried about their sexual performances, this one had tensed up at even the hint she might have been comparing him to some teenaged "football hero" stud. That was it!

An error "Starr Bright" vowed never to make again with Earl Tunley, or another.

★   ★   ★

JACKPOT!
$1000 SILVER DOLLARS JACKPOT!

"Oh, Earl! Look!"—as the slot machine released a cascade of silver dollars like madness.

Laughing, incredulous, cigarettes clenched between their lips, they held CASINO AMERICANA buckets to the machine's opening, to catch the miraculous coins. "Baby, you've got the touch. Congratulations!" Earl said, kissing her as a small crowd of onlookers cheered and applauded. Envy shining in their eyes, "Starr Bright" could see even in the midst of her exhilaration. Envy not just that "Starr Bright" had won a $1000 SILVER DOL-LARS JACKPOT—the machine lighted up red, white, and blue like a berserk American flag, hurdy-gurdy music playing loudly—but that she was a beautiful glamorous sexy redhead in a gold lamé dress tight as a tourniquet across her breasts and pelvis and she had a lover, good-looking, manly, a gold chain glinting around his neck, clearly crazy for her. *Thank you God thank you God thank you God.*

"Now, let's play craps. Slots is small-time."

"Oh, but Earl, honey—"

"Baby, don't worry, I'll stake you—five hundred dollars. The one thousand is all yours."

"But, Earl, craps scares me; you can lose too much too fast. I trust the slots."

"Baby, I told you: slots is small-time. Craps is the real thing."

Earl had staked "Starr Bright" for the slots; she'd played as many machines simultaneously as she could manage, while he looked on indulgently, supplying them both with drinks, ciga-rettes. Now it was 3:43 A.M. in the casino at the Americana amid lavish neon-flashing red-white-and-blue American flags, eagles, replicas of Uncle Sam and Abraham Lincoln, George Washington, John F. Kennedy gazing out over the swarming sea of gamblers. "Starr Bright" had been playing the slots only twenty minutes when she'd won the jackpot and she owed her good luck to Earl Tunley, leaning now against the man, twining herself around him inhaling his rich ripe manly odor liking it that people were watching them, sad-faced fattish women with too much makeup who hadn't ever won a jackpot and hadn't any man to love them like Earl Tunley. "All right, lover," she said, sighing, hugging the bucket of gleaming new-minted silver coins, "—you know best."

So they left the slots, and went to play craps; "Starr Bright" dazed with excitement, exhaustion; smiling upon everyone she saw; in a state of bliss. Her lover Earl was excited, too; edgy, positioning himself at the craps table with "Starr Bright" beside him, at his left elbow—"Now don't budge. You're my good luck, baby." Calling her "baby" so frequently now she guessed he'd maybe forgotten her name.

Earl pushed out $300 worth of chips and got into the game immediately. And when "Starr Bright" opened her eyes again he'd won: chips were being pushed in his direction. "Starr Bright" kissed him, crying, "Terrific, lover!" But Earl scarcely paid attention, gathering in his new chips and mingling them with the old. He counted out $500 worth of chips for "Starr Bright" and told her to do what he said; they'd both be betting, and he intended to win, big. "Starr Bright" pretended enthusiasm; she'd been drinking whiskey sours, on a near-empty stomach; she smiled, smiled and looked gorgeous which was what a gambling man required, a great-looking redhead beside him at the craps table. "O.K., baby," Earl said, drawing in a deep, exhilarated breath, like a man on a high diving board, "—bet *pass*." When "Starr Bright" hesitated, Earl closed his hand over hers and pushed out a pile of chips. The principal player at the table was a fattish flush-faced man with startling blue eyes; he was the one who wielded the dice, and all eyes avidly fastened upon him as he shook, and rolled—and whatever it was, half the players at the table seemed to have won, along with him; and half the players seemed to have lost. Earl grunted with satisfaction, squeezing "Starr Bright's" hand so hard he nearly crushed the bones, so she figured they'd won. How much? It looked like a lot.

At 4:10 A.M. it was Earl Tunley's turn to shake the dice. "Starr Bright" had been drifting off, woozy and blissful in her private space thinking *My jackpot! My 1000 silver dollars!* She hated craps, a fast cruel confusing game involving numerous players, side bets on bets, "points" that were made, or lost; the rapid motion of dice, chips, dice, chips was too much for her eye to follow; the pattern of numerals and figures on the table-top, the calm expressionless manner with which the uniformed casino girl (beautiful, years younger than "Starr Bright") raked in piles of chips with a little Plexiglas rake, taking hundreds or even thousands of dollars from losing players without a blink of an eye—God, what a cruel game! "Starr Bright" followed Earl's directions betting he'd make his point, she wasn't aware of how much she was betting only that he'd staked her and she couldn't lose, could she?—the bucket of silver dollars was at her feet. She wanted him to love her, she'd experienced, almost, a glimmer of emotion, and of sexual excitement, in his arms, in his king-sized bed at the Golden Sands Motor Lodge. There was something consoling about Council Bluffs, Iowa—wasn't there? *A pig like any of them, a mask of Satan. You know.* Earl was nudging her impatiently to place a bet, "Everything you have, baby," and "Starr Bright" said in a pleading little-girl voice, "Oh, Earl honey—*everything*? I'm scared to go all the way." Earl's face shone with an oily perspiration and the gold chain glittered around his neck like a living thing. His eyes were red-veined, but sharp. He was saying, boasting, "Redheads are my good luck," loud enough for other players, men, to hear. "Starr Bright" saw both her hands, trembling just visibly, push out a messy pile of chips onto the pass line. How much? How much was she risking? Grandly, Earl shook the dice, shook and rolled and all stared as the dice turned up four and three.

"Seven! Won!"

Earl was grinning, excited as a kid. The casino girl scarcely gave him a glance as she pushed a large pile of chips in his direction. Cool as swabbing down an emergency room splattered with blood, "Starr Bright" thought. That was the kind of professional hauteur you needed to be an exotic dancer, too.

Thank God, they'd won. Five thousand? Or more? Earl gulped down the remainder of his drink, sex-moaned in "Starr Bright's" ear, "Oh baby, baby—" but didn't otherwise pause. No time to rest, no time to catch his breath, Earl wanted to stay in the game now he was hot. "Starr Bright" was beginning to feel faint. Not long ago she'd been a terrified passenger in a Porsche being driven at one hundred miles an hour along a rain-slick highway and it was the identical sensation—exciting, exhilarating, but crazy and dangerous. Too much too fast.

By 4:35 A.M. they'd won—what? Thirteen thousand, Earl was saying. He was counting his chips, muttering to himself, grinning and wiping his damp face; his eyes were glassy and bright and his lips slack, loose. There was something about him "Starr Bright" could almost identify, some characteristic, trait— but what? As if she'd met him before this night, or someone very like him. He was looking flushed with success. He hadn't wanted to take time to shower or even wash himself after they'd made love, eager to get back to the casinos, and now a powerful odor wafted from him, "Starr Bright" hoped no one else at the table could smell it—male sex, male heat, male passion. *A filthy pig like any other. You know.* She had to admit, winning made a man sexy; winning made a man desirable; this was a man she could love, maybe. Except he'd developed a habit of nudging her in the breast saying, irritated, "Stand still, right here, don't be moving around, I told you. You're my good-luck piece of ass." And he laughed loudly, and "Starr Bright" tried to smile. He was shaking dice again, he'd pushed out half his enormous pile of chips and wanted "Starr Bright" to bet he'd make his point so vaguely, blindly she pushed out half her pile of chips, too.

Thinking *God, don't let us lose. Let him love me.* A dazed-groggy prayer that was the same prayer mouthed everywhere in Vegas by hundreds, thousands of anxious gamblers every second of every hour of every day.

Another time, Earl Tunley rolled and won.

Following this things became even more confused. A roller coaster going faster, faster, faster. They'd won $12,000? 15, 20? Her lover from Council Bluffs, Iowa, and glamorous sexy red-haired "Sherrill Dwyer" from—somewhere in California. Earl was saying, gloating, "Jesus, I'm hot. Back home they can kiss my ass. A man needs respect and this is *it*." He'd been squeezing "Starr Bright's" upper arm, there were red welts in the flesh. Now that she had money again, she could repay the loan from her sister—what had it been? $500, not much—she'd had the feeling that her sister's husband, whose name she couldn't remember, resented the loan, or loans; well, fuck him! Lily's sister Sharon always repaid her loans and with interest, too.

"Starr Bright" must have been easing away, her feet aching in the ridiculous high-heeled shoes that pinched her toes forcing the weight of her body into a tiny pointed space, for Earl Tunley gripped her arm again and smiled hard at her and repositioned her at his side. "Now stay still, baby. We're going for broke." "Starr Bright" winced, "Please, Eddy—that hurts," and Earl said, his voice slurred, " 'Ernie' you mean—no: 'Earl.' You mean 'Earl.' " And "Starr Bright" said quickly, " 'Earl'— that's what I said, honey. 'Earl' is your name," and Earl laughed harshly saying, "Fucking 'Earl' is my fucking name, not fucking 'Eddy,' " his laughter explosive as a sneeze. He took up the dice again exuberantly and "Starr Bright" murmured, "Here we gooo! Sky's the limit!" and planted a kiss on his burning cheek; but instead of rolling the dice as everyone expected, Earl turned to her, his lips drawn back from his teeth in a savage grin, and said, "Watch it, cunt. I'm warning you." So "Starr Bright" went very still, and contrite. And Earl rolled the dice, and came up with a number that wasn't good, muttered, "Shit," so "Starr Bright" thought in a panic they'd lost, but, as it turned out, he

had another roll and another chance, and this time he rolled—
two sixes. And this wasn't good, either. "Starr Bright" said in
a giggly-drunken little-girl voice, a voice meant to dispel the
sickening sensation in the pit of her belly, "Oh, damn! You'd
think a twelve would be better than an eleven, wouldn't you?"

But no one laughed. Glazed-eyed Earl didn't hear.

No pause in the game. Not a heartbeat. A few of the players
avoided Earl's eyes out of brotherly sympathy perhaps. "Starr
Bright" stared as the casino girl coolly raked in Earl's big pile of
chips—and "Starr Bright's" without an eyeblink. How much
had they lost? "Starr Bright" was whispering, "Oh, lover.
Ohhhh." She meant to console him slipping her arm through
his but he shook her off, uttered something she didn't catch,
stooped to take up the bucket of silver dollars from the floor
and as "Starr Bright" stared uncomprehending after him he
went to a nearby cashier's counter to cash the silver dollars into
chips. And came back, grim, determined, sweat gleaming on his
face like congealed grease, and the look in his eyes warning her
not to fuck with him. "Starr Bright" tried to protest faintly,
"Earl, honey, those silver dollars were mine, you said—you
promised," and Earl repositioned her at his side and said, "Just
stand still, baby. And shut the mouth."

So Earl bet one thousand dollars' worth of chips on a single
roll and "Starr Bright" hid her eyes behind her trembling fingers praying *God oh God!* though seeming to know the prayer
was helpless to intervene. And even as Earl threw the dice, sent
them flying and bouncing across the table, "Starr Bright" must
have suffered a moment's weakness, a mini-blackout—falling
against him, so that, even as he lost the roll, he'd turned to her
and slapped her across the mouth, the movement of his hand so
swift that no one at the table saw, or seemed to see; and "Starr
Bright" herself could not comprehend what had happened, except her lower lip throbbed with pain and began to bleed. Earl's
face had gone the color of bread dough and his bloodshot eyes
glared. "Cunt, I told you not to fuck me up," he said, advanc-

ing upon her as others at the table scrambled to get out of the way, leaving "Starr Bright" to her boyfriend's mercy, "—didn't I tell you *not to fuck me up.*"

"Earl, I'm sorry—"

"Y'know what you cost me, cunt?—*twenty-seven thousand dollars!*"

Abruptly as if he'd emerged from out of a trapdoor a casino security guard appeared, a hefty black man of few words, "That's enough, mister, come this way please," and before they knew what was happening they were being escorted politely but unerringly out of the casino. "Starr Bright" supposed that the girl at the craps table had summoned the guard with a secret buzzer. Earl was sullen, blustering and intimidated, his words slurred, "Butt out, asshole, this is a private discourse, this cunt cost me a bundle," and "Starr Bright" was trying earnestly to explain, "Sir, he doesn't mean it, he's my friend, he didn't hurt me, he's excited 'cause he just took a big loss," and Earl said angrily, "Shut it!" and "Starr Bright" said, "Really, sir, he's the sweetest man, he never meant—" But the robotlike guard who was six foot five, two hundred fifty pounds and dark-skinned as a polished hickory nut seemed scarcely to hear as if this, his task, was too familiar and too boring to require from him more than a few clipped words mechanical as a recitation, "Thank you for patronizing the Casino Americana and perhaps another time you will revisit us under more favorable circumstances." When Earl hesitated at the exit, the guard hoisted him into the revolving door and gave the door a fierce spin and a moment later Earl and "Starr Bright" were out in the warm, faintly sulphurous night.

Earl said, aggrieved as a lost child, wiping his face on the sleeve of his Italian-style jacket, "Craps is my *game.* I was *w-winning.*"

"Starr Bright" slipped her arm around his waist (which was warm and rumpled as damp laundry) and said, soothingly, "That's right, Earl, you *were* winning. You *were.* You can win again. You can draw on your American Express card, can't you, lover? Sure you can."

Because I had hope, still, that he would love me. I would love him.
   Because I was afraid to be alone that terrible night.
   Because I wanted the $1000 he owed me.
   Because I knew that my heavenly father would watch over me in time of peril.

*   *   *

And at first it had not seemed an unwise decision. She had not seemed in immediate danger.

Taking a cab back to the Golden Sands Motor Lodge because the man who'd introduced himself to her as Earl Tunley wasn't in any condition to drive. Stumbling into the dim-lit room that smelled still of their bodies, and stained bedclothes; fecund odors of sweat, semen, damp wadded towels and insecticide. Always the odor of insecticide. And Earl was amorous in his misery, wishing not to think of the many thousands of dollars he'd lost which seemed to him in his confusion to have been his money from the start, stolen from him by the cruelty of chance and a woman's blundering. Kissing "Starr Bright" roughly with his tongue, burying his hot face in her neck and between her breasts and moving his hands swiftly and hungrily over her. Like a drowning man he groaned, "Oh baby, baby—"

"Starr Bright" eased her neck and head away from her lover's fumbling caresses, cautious he might dislodge her wig; the human-hair miracle-wig that fitted her head snug as a bathing cap. He'd slapped her pretty hard there in the casino and her lip was swelling but in the urgency of the moment she wasn't thinking of it; anyway, other men had struck her and she'd survived; and maybe deserved being struck now and then for *you're a cunt, you know it* and she guessed she knew and accepted this judgment for hadn't she abandoned her own baby years and years ago, wished even to drown her own baby years and years ago and the very memory by now vague and faded like a Polaroid snapshot too long exposed to light. But, oh God: if he would let her alone and she could shower and cleanse herself and fall into bed and sleep, sleep. The sweet sleep of dreamless sinless oblivion. The sweet druggy-alcohol sleep like dying. And next day he could withdraw cash with his credit card and they would hit another casino, another craps table, and just maybe win, and win big. Because it did seem plausible to her that Earl Tunley deserved to win back the $27,000 he'd lost; he'd been winning, he'd been on a roll, and it had been taken from him unfairly. For this was gambler's logic and it was "Starr Bright's" logic in her innermost heart. *That which you sow, you shall reap.*

And when her lover got back the $27,000 that was rightfully his, she would share in it, too.

It seemed to be dawn. Hazy tendrils of flame in the eastern sky. The venetian blinds of room 19, at the far end of the long graceless concrete-block Golden Sands Motor Lodge, were tightly drawn. On top of the TV was a nearly empty bottle of Jim Beam, and greedy Earl Tunley snatched it up and gulped its contents like a thirsty man. And "Starr Bright" sighed, and was going to make a practical suggestion about a little sleep, and suddenly Earl turned on her, cursed her, "—told you not to fuck me up, didn't I?" and when she protested he grabbed her, and they struggled, and he said, grunting, "—could smash your face, cunt—make you ugly like you deserve! Strangle you—" and she was too terrified to scream for help, knowing that no one would hear, no one would wish to hear, and she was too weak suddenly to defend herself as the man pushed her backward, threw her onto the rumpled bed, and reached with grasping fingers up inside the tight lamé skirt to take possession.

God help me.
Waking with difficulty, her head aching, pounding where

he'd struck it repeatedly against a wall. Slowly she disentangled herself from the snoring man, cautious of waking him. His hairy sweaty limbs had been flung over her, pressing her to the bed; his heavy torso, slack belly. And how heavy his head, his eyes shut upon a thin crescent of white like mucus. Eddy? Earl? Though knowing he had surely lied to her she saw again a fleeting vision of chalk-white cliffs—Council Bluffs, Iowa? Her mouth throbbed with pain, the lower lip was grotesquely swollen. Like a bee sting she'd had as a child, and her sister Lily had said *Oh I wish the nasty bee would sting me, too!* Her left eye, too, was swollen—he must have punched her there. And the nipples of both breasts had been pinched, hard. He hadn't removed her dress but had pushed it up to nearly her armpits. He'd threatened to kill her if she screamed and perhaps he had killed her, it was not "Starr Bright" but her child-spirit Rose of Sharon who awakened in her now. *Because the spirit cannot be extinguished, the spirit liveth and abideth forever.*

The man stirred, groaned as if in pain—but didn't wake. A wet whistling snore issued from his slack mouth. Except for black silk socks on his feet, the lower half of his body was stark naked; his shirt was unbuttoned and open upon a fattish-muscular chest covered in isolated wirelike hairs. The skin was creased, the color of rancid lard. No beauty here. Only the glittering gold chain around his neck.

Recalling with shame how he'd jeeringly offered her that gold chain. As if he'd thought her a prostitute. Why hadn't she fled him, then!

Pig, fornicator and despiser of women.

Emissary of Satan.

"Starr Bright" extricated herself from the man who'd raped her, beaten her, threatened death. It was just 7 A.M. She'd been unconscious for more than an hour. A fierce fiery light penetrated the slats of the window blind and the crack beneath the door. "Starr Bright" tried to smooth down her dress, which was badly stained, torn at the shoulder. In the bureau mirror she saw her wavering, cringing reflection. Yet the red wig was still in place. Her makeup had been rubbed virtually off, her face was white, pinched-looking, sickly; her left eye blackened, her lower lip swollen to twice its normal size. *Is that me? Is that who I've become? God, have mercy . . .*

"Starr Bright" would have slipped from the room and left behind the snoring man except: headed for the door, she stumbled upon the man's jacket on the floor, and stubbed her toe against something heavy in an inside pocket.

She investigated, and discovered—a pistol.

A pistol! It shone like blue steel, with a short barrel of about four inches; compact, and deadly. "Starr Bright" stared at it in astonishment. She knew little about guns, she'd held a gun in her hand upon occasion but had never fired one and could not have identified this except to know that it was a revolver, each bullet in its chamber in the revolving cylinder. What a good clean metallic smell.

Its make was Ruger. Of this, she'd never heard.

As soon as the pistol was in her hand, "Starr Bright" felt a deep suffusion of relief. Though her hand visibly trembled, and her head and body were encased in pain. She understood that the child Rose of Sharon would be protected now, inviolate. "Starr Bright" knew that the man could not hurt her now. God had gifted her with unexpected power over the man.

"Thank you, God! Praise God!"

In other pockets of the jacket she discovered the man's wallet, and a badge, and a law officer's ID, with a photo: ERNEST D. FENKE   DEPUTY SHERIFF   SUMNER CO.   NEBRASKA.

"Deputy sheriff—!"

And now she began to laugh. "Starr Bright" hooked up with a cop! An off-duty cop, one of the enemy.

You never could predict God's designs. For the God of wrath was also a God of jokes, tricks. You had to have a sense of humor to comprehend Him.

Playful as a mischievous child "Starr Bright" affixed the

shiny brass badge to the gold lamé fabric above her left breast. It snagged in the material, but held. Wild! She stood very tall in her bare feet, tall enough it seemed to brush the ceiling of the room with her head. She was suffused with strength and joy like a sudden fountain of clear, pure water; almost, she could stand on her tiptoes, a graceful ballerina.

"Wake up."

She was standing above the snoring man, gripping the pistol in both hands to steady it. She'd released the trigger guard and cocked the hammer. She'd spoken calmly, with assurance, though very excited; when the snoring man failed to wake, she prodded his shoulder with the gun barrel. His eyes flew open, at first unfocused. Then he saw her. Saw the gun. The badge above her left breast.

She said, smiling, " 'Deputy Sheriff Ernest D. Fenke, of Sumner County, Nebraska.' You are under immediate arrest."

Fenke blinked rapidly as if a bright light was being beamed into his bloodshot eyes. A look of incredulity tightened his features, a stab of quick fear. The worst thing that could happen to a cop had happened to him: his gun had been taken from him. He said, "H-hey! Honey! Don't kid around with that—"

"Deputy Fenke, get up."

"Jesus, look—honey? Give that gun to me, it might go off and—you wouldn't want—"

"So you're a cop? That's your secret? 'Deputy Fenke of Nebraska'? Why'd you lie to me?"

"Please, honey—"

"You get to carry a gun, eh? Deputy Fenke? Persecute people? How many people has this gun killed, Deputy Fenke?"

"N-nobody."

"You're a liar." "Starr Bright" spoke with a strange sort of authority. Her voice serene, glistening. As if the deep soothing peace coursing through her had brought with it an eloquence not her own; the purity of the child Rose of Sharon, that sweet clear delicate soprano voice.

"Out of bed, and on your knees. Now."

And he obeyed her. Groveling, cowardly like all such craven men—he obeyed her. It was fitting that the man, part-naked, should tremble before the woman, his pig-eyes shining with fear, awe, trepidation; his limp fleshy genitalia like a skinned baby creature prominent between pale trembling thighs. "Starr Bright" saw the logic of it, how God had once again guided her hand in His shrewd wisdom. A man, kneeling before a woman of such power, has become, by mock-miracle, *a woman.*

"Starr Bright" said, "You raped me, and you defiled me, and you stole my money from me, Deputy Fenke—*my* jackpot, *my* one thousand silver dollars. And now you must repay me."

Fenke pleaded, "Honey, I—I didn't mean to hurt you! Ever! I thought we were—just—" He gestured toward the bed as if to say just *fooling around, screwing around—nothing serious.*

It wasn't clear whether "Starr Bright" meant to arouse such fear in the man or whether, barefoot, her gold lamé dress riding up to her thighs, the glinting badge on her left breast, she was being playful, seductive in a new way. In almost an incantatory voice she said, "Rapist. Filthy pig. And thief—common thief, Deputy! Taking my jackpot from me when you'd promised it was mine to keep."

"Honey, I'll pay you back—I was going to pay you back—"

"You were, Deputy?"

"—I was going to draw five thousand dollars on my credit card tomorrow. Get back into action, the two of us—"

"That's the truth? You lied to me once, Deputy Fenke, why should I believe you now?"

"Baby, I didn't lie to you. I was maybe drinking too much—I got carried away. I'm crazy about you."

"Yes? That's why you raped me?"

On his knees, trembling before her, the man tried to smile. A sick guilty feeble smile. Staring at "Starr Bright" with his bloodshot eyes as if trying not to see the pistol in her hands, aimed at his face; trying not to acknowledge that he saw it. He was saying, "I—didn't r-rape you, honey. That's a terrible thing to say. I would never force a w-woman—"

"No?" "Starr Bright" indicated her swollen lip, her throbbing eye. Lifting her skirt to show bruises, welts. Torn black-lace panties.

And the man gaped at her miserably. Could only shake his head as if in honest befuddlement. *I did such a thing? No!*

"Starr Bright" began an interrogation. Asking the man did he love her and he said quickly sure, oh sure he was crazy about her! She asked was she beautiful in his eyes and he said eagerly oh yes, yes she was beautiful—"Baby, you know it! You're terrific." And she said coyly, redheads were his good luck, yes? Was she his good luck? and Fenke was nodding yes, emphatically yes when in a gesture of triumph "Starr Bright" yanked off the red human-hair wig, revealing her ashy-blond hair flattened and matted, pinned in unflattering clumps around her head. And Deputy Fenke's slack pale hungover face showed yet more astonishment, incredulity.

Slyly "Starr Bright" asked, "*Am* I beautiful, Deputy?"

He'd swallowed hard, and was stammering, "Y-yes . . ."

"Starr Bright" laughed in delight. Like the cruelly prankish girl she'd been long ago. Rose of Sharon who was the unpredictable Donner sister but of course you forgave little Sharon, she was so vivacious, so beautiful. Taunting the man now, "Crazy about me, eh?"

"Yes . . ."

Laughing heartily at the look on his face. Sick sinking flailing look of a man who's trapped. It was cruel, it was heartless, such taunting, but she could not resist. "Say, Deputy, a law officer is supposed to be observant. How old d'you think I am?"

"I—don't know—"

"When you picked me up last night, put your moves on me, what age were you estimating?"

"I—don't know—"

"Starr Bright" laughed even more loudly, thoroughly enjoying this interrogation. "I'll be thirty-seven, my next birthday."

Fenke laughed nervously. "That's—not old. I'm thirty-nine . . ."

"Would you have picked me up, if you'd known my age, Deputy Fenke?"

"Yes!"

"You *do* think I'm a beautiful woman?—desirable?"

"Baby, I'm crazy about you—I said. Only please—maybe you should give me the gun now? So nobody gets hurt? And we can get dressed, and go out, and I'll get some cash, and—"

Fenke was reaching out toward her, hesitantly, in appeal; but "Starr Bright" stepped away, frowning. She waved the pistol at him.

"No! Stay right where you are, mister. Or I swear I will shoot you right in the face."

"Jesus, Cheryl—"

" 'Sherrill.' "

"—Sh-Sherrill. I meant to say."

"My name is 'Starr Bright.' "

" 'Starr'—?"

"You never saw 'Starr Bright' dance. You aren't the one—that was another one—did you know him? 'Cobb.' " For a moment she was confused in time; the men were confused, interchangeable; perhaps in fact they were the same man. It seemed to "Starr Bright" that in some mysterious way the men, or the man, knew her; and knew his ineluctable fate. So they might discuss it together calmly, as if reminiscing. "They said in the papers, on TV—'Starr Bright' slashed a man's throat and danced barefoot in his blood. Drew the sign of the star in pig's blood on a wall. I don't know if it's truth or falsehood, it was something that happened in Sparks, Nevada, at a certain hour and it was not a choice." The memory of what had happened in that other motel room in the desert was blurred as tissue in water; this man's frightened dough-face was a barrier between her and the memory. Or perhaps it was no memory at all, perhaps she'd only read about it in the *Las Vegas Post* and studied the photographs of Cobb and the blood-smeared wall. She said, smiling, "Oh, that one bled like a stuck pig, he *was* a stuck pig. All of you—*pigs.*"

"W-what are you saying, Sherrill?"

"Cobb. You know—'Pig Death.' It was written up in all the papers, it was on TV."

Fenke stared at her, his eyes glazing over in horror. In a hoarse voice he said, "You're kidding, aren't you? My God."

"Starr Bright" laughed in girlish delight. How like performing before an audience this was. She'd known, at age thirteen, this would be her life.

She told Fenke how, immediately, she'd liked him; he'd stepped forward to offer her a cigarette in a moment of need, a weak moment of hers, and she'd been grateful to him. She had a hopeful heart, she was a professional singer-dancer and yet a woman who craved love; a woman who wanted to be respected, treated right. And she'd thought, at first, for a while last night, that he was the man for her. "But then you spoiled it, Deputy. You raped me, and you defiled me. And you stole my thousand dollars."

"I—I—I'm sorry—oh God, Sherrill, I'll make it up to you, I promise—"

"You *are* sorry? That's the truth? You won't do it again?— hurt me again?"

"Honey, I promise."

"You apologize? On your knees? To me? And to all the women you've defiled in your life?" As Fenke nodded with pathetic eagerness, "Starr Bright" continued to point the pistol at his head. She said, "Your wife?—do you have a wife? Yes? Back in Sumner County, Nebraska?" Fenke nodded, his eyes snatching at hers guiltily. "You apologize to her, too? You, an adulterer? Fornicator? How many times, Deputy? You apolo-

gize on your knees to all the women you've defiled? You beg
forgiveness from them, and from God?"

"Y-yes . . ."

"And you'll pay me back my thousand-dollar jackpot?"

"Yes! I'll withdraw five thousand from my account right
now, Sherrill. Let me get dressed, and we can go out and find a
bank—"

"*Stay on your knees.* Why should I trust you, Deputy?"

"Please, you can trust me . . ."

"Why should I believe you? Any word out of your mouth?
You say you're sorry? But men are never sorry."

"Sherrill, baby, I *am* sorry . . ."

"Starr Bright" was speaking more rapidly, in her high sharp
soprano voice like flashing shears.

"Men are masks of Satan, never sorry. They can't get it up
unless they hurt women."

"No, no! I'm not like that," Fenke said desperately. "Jesus,
I got a daughter—I'm the father of a daughter. I'm not like
that."

"Father of a daughter?—*you?*"

"Please, honey, let me make it up to you? Give me the gun,
and nobody will get hurt . . ."

"Starr Bright" stood staring at the man. This part-naked
man on his knees. But his shoulders were straighter now, his
head higher. He seemed less afraid. *Father of a daughter—him?* A
terrible clarity was opening in her brain, a tiny pinprick of light
like a distant star rushing closer. Almost softly she said, "You
won't be angry with me, if I give you back your gun?"

"No! I promise, Sherrill."

Fenke reached out hesitantly to accept the gun from "Starr
Bright" and for a moment it almost seemed that she would
surrender it to him. But there was a tawny light in her eyes, her
smile slipped sideways like grease. Nimbly she sidestepped him,
and raised the pistol higher to take aim between his eyes. She

laughed. "And if I do? You won't change your mind and be cruel again? And hurt me again? And say you'll kill me?"

"Jesus, no. Honey, I was drunk. I didn't mean it."

"Because it's in your power, Deputy. You're a man, and a man's got the power. And 'Starr Bright' has no power. Only just this." She indicated the gun, smiling. "And if I surrender my power, what will stop you from hurting me again?"

"Sherrill, honey—no. I promise."

"Starr Bright" backed away to the air-conditioning unit near the window, and turned the fan to high. She switched on the TV, loud. A morning talk show dissolved in peals of laughter switching abruptly to a jingly cartoon-bright advertisement for Sani-Flush.

Fenke blinked as if she'd slapped him. "W-what are you doing?"

"Deputy, tell me: are you in a state of sin?"

"S-sin?"

"Have you been washed in the blood of the lamb?"

"I—I was baptized—"

"Baptized what?"

"Catholic."

"Catholic! You! So—you believe?"

"I . . . I believe."

"In God, and in Jesus Christ?"

"Yes . . ."

"In Satan, and in sin?"

"Y-yes . . ."

"You believe God is watching over you? At this moment?"

"Yes . . ."

"God would not allow harm to come to you, then. Unless it was his wish."

"Sherrill, please, honey. I said I was sorry . . ."

"Starr Bright" spoke rapidly, and clearly, to be heard over the noises of the fan and the TV. "A man is a mask of Satan, Deputy, and maybe can't help himself. Like a scorpion. Born in sin and travail and lust and wickedness and a love of inflicting hurt on weaker creatures. Jesus saw, and didn't judge. He said, 'Forgive, and love thy enemies as thyself.' But God says, 'I am a God of wrath, and none shall hide from my vengeance.' "

Now she was wrapping a towel carefully around the pistol, and around her hand that held the pistol. Until the tip of the barrel was only just visible.

Fenke said, in a quavering voice, "Why are you doing that, Sherrill? Baby, please—"

" 'This is the Father's will which hath sent me.' "

"Sherrill—"

"One thing about Vegas, people mind their own business. You might hear women screaming—you might hear firecrackers—might even hear guns sometimes. But people respect each other's privacy." She was advancing upon the kneeling man dancerlike, knowing how, in his terror, she grew ever taller, more radiant. The light from her face alone was enough to blind him! He tried to shield the naked part of himself with his arms, and by cringing, hunching over; bringing his thighs closer together. As if ashamed of the fleshy thing between his legs, shrunken now, of the hue and texture of a slug. "My first boyfriend, the first boy I loved, I told you his name was Michael but that was not his name. He raped me, took my love for him and defiled it. And shared me with his buddies. I was fifteen; never told a soul. Too ashamed. You count on us being shamed." She paused, breathing quickly. "A cop raped me once—more than once. In Miami, and in Houston. Cops prey on the weak because they have the power. All this fallen world *is,* Deputy, is those with power preying on those without. You made a mistake, Deputy. You stole 'Starr Bright's' thousand-dollar jackpot."

A sickly jaundice-light shone in the man's eyes. He was begging, shivering. "Please, don't. Don't shoot me . . ."

"Look, I'm a sinner, too. I am 'Starr Bright' and I am a fallen angel. My daddy warned me as a headstrong child and I failed to heed. My daddy was a man of God, a shining man of God and he spoke to his flock who adored him of the dark heart of mankind. He spoke of Jesus as his brother, and of Satan the fallen angel as his brother. The one walking at his right hand and the other walking at his left hand. I broke his heart, I betrayed my daddy's love. All the days of my life I am accursed. I have not seen that man in fifteen years. Wishing to drown my own baby girl in sickness and despair and lashing out at those who would forgive me, and love me." She wiped her tearful stinging eyes on her forearm. Her vision wavered as if about to be extinguished, then came into sharp, painful focus again. She saw the kneeling man cringe before her, yet saw his eyes ratlike and alert, waiting for an advantage. She said, slyly, "Well, Deputy—all I need is your credit card."

"Sherrill, no. I'm begging you . . ."

"For what?"

"My life . . ."

"Then down. *Down*." She was moving, dancerlike, closer to him. The high-humming air conditioner and the noise of the TV made the air jangle. If she stumbled, if she weakened—he would know. By instinct he would know. He was cringing, craven and terrified yet ratlike he would know. The fact excited her, like sex. Like sex as it had once been. In her ecstasy, in her exultation, she was drawing dangerously near to him. Whispering, "Pray for forgiveness from the Lord, and 'Starr Bright' will forgive you, too."

Fenke clasped his hands together clumsily, in an eager display of piety. His chest gleamed with sweat and his face was a mask of sweat, the creases in his forehead shining like metal.

In a stammering voice, a tremulously sincere-sounding voice, he began to pray, "Our F-Father who art in heaven—" then seemed to lose his breath, and needed encouragement, so "Starr Bright" said, "—hallowed be thy name—" and quickly he continued, "—h-hallowed be thy thy name— Thy k-kingdom—" and again he paused as if his throat had closed, and

"Starr Bright" was obliged to lead him, as, as small children, years ago in Shaheen, New York, she and her sister Lily had been led tenderly and firmly in prayer by their parents, "—thy kingdom come, thy will—" and the man eagerly repeated, "—thy w-will be done—on earth as it is in—in—"

Suddenly then making his move. Lunging at her, trying to grab the gun. But "Starr Bright" was prepared for this. Oh yes: "Starr Bright" was prepared for this. As if she'd been watching the kneeling man from a far corner of the room, or from a distant prospect of time. Noting how, his head bowed, chin creased against his chest, he'd been watching her covertly, desperately, in an attempt to deceive. "Starr Bright" gracefully sidestepped him, and pulled the trigger, sending a bullet into her enemy's face.

Point-blank.

"Didn't I warn you, Deputy! Deputy-pig!"

A single deadly shot aimed at the bridge of her enemy's nose. A bullet piercing the man's flesh, his bone, plowing into his brain in an instant. He had no time to cry out, to turn away or duck. He deserved no time to prepare himself. The towel wrapped around the gun had only partly muffled the sharp, cracking sound, but "Starr Bright" believed she was in no danger, no one would hear; God would protect her as He'd protected her all along. She stood over her fallen enemy, panting in triumph, "Didn't I warn you, Pig-Deputy! Mask of Satan! All of you!"

But Deputy Fenke had collapsed, was dying, or dead. So swiftly, it had to be a miracle. His eyes were opened in astonishment and his lustrous-glassy gaze was fixed to hers—then fading, failing like a dimming light. "Starr Bright" bent to peer closely. Where was the man's soul?—had it departed his body? Was it already gone? Gone—where?

Soft now and spineless as a creature pried out of its shell to die on dry land the man lay at her feet. Her bare feet. She stepped back, out of the flow of blood. Blood flowing darkly from the single wound to his broken face and soaking into the cheap nylon carpet of what unknown room he'd brought her to, to rape her; what unknown cheap hotel in this Sodom and Gomorrah of the desert that God might strike with lightning to annihilate should He wish at any time. "Starr Bright" was trembling, panting. Her thoughts blasted clean. *For these are the days of vengeance, that all things which are written may be fulfilled.*

3

Days of Vengeance

In Joshua Tree, California. In Tempe, Arizona. In a Malibu beach house at Thanksgiving. Things got complicated.

I don't want to kill. Not a one of them. I am not one who kills. I am Rose of Sharon, I am not one who kills.

Knowing not to travel by plane. Passing through any metal detector, sending her new suitcase through any X ray. For she could not leave her protection behind.

Angry words in blood on bloodied walls. Dancing in blood. POLICE OF FOUR STATES SEEK VENGEFUL FEMALE KILLER. "STAR" KILLER SOUGHT IN SLAYINGS. A lie, most of it. Trash to sell cheap newspapers. Dancing in blood, barefoot!

Never.

Sticky warm pig's blood, infected blood: never!

In Tempe, Arizona, purchasing at a discount mall a $6.99 Holy Bible. She was a brunette with soft-doe eyes. She was Sylvia, she was Durelle. But things got complicated. Once you toss the dice you have to play the game out.

"Starr Bright" yearned to dance again! "Starr Bright" was too young to retire! Audiences loved her, roused to cheers, whistles, applause, lust. "Exotic interpretive dance." Oh she was lonely, she grew resentful. Things got complicated.

One night swallowing painkiller capsules a man (youthful middle-aged, good-looking, TV producer separated from his family) gave her to quiet her but she vomited up, sick as a dog, the chalky clotted mess.

And laughed in bitterness, resignation. *God has His plans for "Starr Bright." No sinner can intercede.*

Their names were newsprint. Their names were syllables pronounced on TV news broadcasts. Their photo-faces which were not faces she recognized.

Masks of Satan. Not true faces.

How can you tell?—the pig-eyes.

From X in Joshua Tree, $588 which probably wasn't worth it. And the Land Rover she'd driven in a trance from Bishop, California, to Salt Lake City. A vision in the salt flats, God had drawn her. From Y, $1800. He'd given her not knowing how his life was spared. But Z, in San Diego, New Year's Eve. Things got complicated.

Eastward then by Greyhound. Not daring to board any airplane.

In the papers and TV they maligned her. "PIG DEATH" KILLER SOUGHT.

In the papers and TV they celebrated her. "STAR" KILLER SOUGHT.

Threw away her clothes, the bloodstained gold lamé dress scissored into pieces, burnt. The Gucci bag, stained shoes and lovely red human-hair wig. Designer sunglasses. Purchased Kmart clothes, a foam rubber pillow for her belly. Eight months' pregnancy. Dark circles beneath her eyes, graying-brown hair the hue of dishwater. Flat shoes, nylon stretch slacks, no rings except a cheap wedding band on her third finger, left hand. And her nails needing a manicure.

Oldish to be pregnant, maybe in her forties. A blotched face, pale pulpy mouth. Favoring her right leg, a limp.

Men's eyes drifted past her, through her. Even cops'.

Always you can rely on pig-eyes *not-seeing* what doesn't turn them on.

In a diner near Denver, Colorado. Seeing the TV news, a

flash of the "STAR" KILLER'S heavily made-up glamorous face. Sitting round-shouldered in shapeless clothes, slack face, belly and dishwater hair. In a row of Greyhound passengers that would have looked to a neutral observer companionable. Though no one knew anyone else. More coffee ma'am? the bored teenaged waitress asked and the oldish pregnant woman lifted her cup daring a small almost-shy smile *Hey I've been a pouty pretty kid like you, not so long ago,* yes she said, thanks, but the bored waitress didn't catch the smile, why bother. On the TV now the cruel likeness of beautiful "Starr Bright" had vanished, a grinning man in a checked suit held a pointer to a U.S. weather map across which eerie tendrils of vapor-smoke swirled.

On the Greyhound things were smooth and clear and dull and not complicated. But you can't ride a Greyhound bus forever.

I am not one who kills, I am Rose of Sharon who sings in the choir.

I am "Starr Bright." I am an exotic interpretive dancer. I am gifted, beautiful, glamorous, singled out for a special destiny.

How can you tell?—the pig eyes.

At the shadowy rear of a tavern parking lot in Council Bluffs, Iowa. In the guy's new-model Caddy, in the plush backseat. Things got complicated. You end up fighting for your life, defending your life. Struck, stabbed, pierced the enemy pig-flesh to defend your life. Things got complicated and went their own way not like on TV.

She took pig-money to protect herself. It was too complicated to explain and no one to whom she might explain, for God required no explanation, God guided her hand. As He had directed her not to destroy her baby rock-hard and swelling like a bulb in the earth in her belly *For through this baby you will be reborn.* And not to destroy her baby after its birth as her hands had urged, seeking to hold its small head under water *For through this baby you will be reborn.*

In Council Bluffs, Iowa. She'd wanted to see the "bluffs."

Things got complicated. Can't ride a fucking Greyhound forever.

A purchase of a second Bible. A smaller one, with tissue-paper pages. Why?—"Starr Bright" hadn't yet said.

Thirty-five knife wounds to the chest, belly, "genital area" as the newscasters fastidiously reported.

Wild! How in Malibu she'd tossed the disgusting flesh-clumps into the ocean after using them to smear, stain, spell out "Starr Bright's" curse DIE PIG on the bedroom wall. Wearing rubber kitchen-gloves of course. Learning afterward from a tabloid how the "genital parts" had washed up on a private beach close by owned by a Hollywood celebrity.

An innocent memento: platinum gold cuff links inset with pearls. No initial.

Enter into the rock, and hide thee in the dust. For fear of the Lord.

1

The Nightmare

You have to do what I say! You have to! You're my slave!
   Lily Merrick shook herself awake, terrified, from a nightmare. She was dry-mouthed as if she'd been running, panting; for a confused moment she couldn't comprehend where she was.

Pleading, "No. No. *No.*"

Heart pounding erratically. Her body, tense, tight as a fist and covered in sweat, in that state of suspension in which the muscles seem paralyzed as if under a spell. The childish demanding voice rang in her ears: an old nightmare, at one time a familiar nightmare but one she'd believed she had outgrown since marrying the man who was her husband, and moving to a house of her own. Lily opened her eyes in the dark of a room that should have consoled her with its comforting dimensions and whispered aloud, "I—am Lily Merrick. My husband is Wesley Merrick. We have a daughter Deirdre—Deedee. I am not—"

But what was it Lily Merrick was *not?*

She couldn't think. Didn't want to think.

She was a woman so upset by violence and the mere reportage of violence that she could not bear to watch much of the evening television news, nor could she force herself to read of

73

atrocities in Bosnia, Nigeria, Iraq; the vicious racial beating of a young black college student by a gang of whites on Long Island last week; a rape-murder case currently being tried in Westchester County. Virtually any details of the Holocaust. Torture and mass murder in the killing fields of Cambodia. The terrifying devastation after the bombing in Oklahoma City at which all of America had watched appalled—Lily had turned away, crying. To see that heartrending photograph of a dying baby held in a fireman's arms—she was wounded, sickened. As a citizen of the world, as a responsible adult and the mother of a fifteen-year-old daughter she understood that she had an obligation to know; to know the worst; she was married to a man who didn't flinch from the worst, or so she believed of Wes; yet evidence of man's—and woman's—cruelty filled her with dismay and horror. Exhausted her, she might have said, spiritually. *If I can't intervene, it seems wrong to know.*

Of course she wasn't that unusual, she had numerous women friends and acquaintances who felt as she did; who stayed away from violent movies, never watched offensive television programs. Lily's was just a more extreme reaction, visceral, immediate as if her own being, her very nerves, were abraded. She'd been brought up to feel sympathy for others, not detachment; she'd been brought up to abhor destructive gossip; she had no natural prurient interest in celebrities' heartbreak or scandal, of which there was, in America, an inexhaustible supply marketed by the media; she had no interest in "gory details" of any kind; never watched TV tabloid programs; a kind of glaze came over her eyes, a willful yet genuine blindness, if she happened to see, by accident, atrocity photographs in the paper: yet another bloodied body lying on a dusty road somewhere in Middle Europe; in Africa, bodies heaped like kindling; the aftermath of an IRA bombing in London. She most shrank from reports of violence against children, of which there seemed, in recent years, so much. And she was particularly sickened by individual acts of systematic, apparently pur-

poseful violence: serial killings, serial killers. This most recent
serial killer, a woman, who'd murdered as many as eight—or
was it nine, ten?—men in the Southwest and California; leaving
behind mutilated corpses, bloodied walls and satanic symbols.
What Lily knew, she'd picked up from Deedee; she hadn't
cared to watch a TV news segment on the case, or read about
it in the paper; she'd happened to pass by the recreation room
where she'd overheard her daughter and girlfriend talking, one
of them saying, "Wow. About time there's a *woman* . . . Always
some damn *man* . . ." and the other murmuring agreement, and
both girls giggling. Lily passed by calling out, "H'lo, girls!"
cheery and unobtrusive as always. Never meddled in her
daughter's business, tried not to impose her sensibility on others, yes and frankly she was grateful that Deedee had a few girlfriends to invite to the house.

Waking from the nightmare, yet lying, still, in that state of muscular paralysis. She was thinking of Deedee, and of the guilt she
felt about Deedee; that Deedee could not *know* . . . certain facts
of her parentage. One day, but not yet.
    You promised. Remember! Always.
    It was a gusty sleet-driven February night, somewhere past
midnight. Wes hadn't yet come upstairs; wasn't in bed beside
her; must have been working in his office. The man was naturally restless, insomniac; even before going into the Marines, he
said, and enduring boot camp, he'd never required more than
four or five hours sleep a night.
    "Wes! Where *are* you!"
    So Lily would give the nightmare, the experience of the
nightmare, a wifely-playful tone. That was best. As she did with
most problems, hurts, disappointments, household and professional matters of a trivial nature. Make them into entertaining
anecdotes, or jokes. She was Lily Merrick of 183 Washington
Street, Yewville, New York, an attractive small city of thirty-
five thousand people twenty miles south of Lake Ontario; resi-

dent of an old, handsomely restored colonial-style house in
Yewville's oldest residential neighborhood. She was an amateur
potter, she taught an evening class at the local community college once a week, she was the wife of . . . the mother of . . .
She knew who she was!

You have to do what I say! You have to! You're my slave!

Well, it was Wes's fault. Not coming to bed at a reasonable
time. His side of the bed empty. His warm weight beside her
missing. The sound of his breathing, his snoring. The sagging
of the mattress in his direction.

She would go downstairs to get Wes. She'd kiss him, and
chide him. "Honey, come to bed! Please." No, better for her
simply to go back to sleep, stop making such a fuss. It wasn't
like Lily to make a fuss.

Lying in an odd position on her side, cramped, uncomfortable. Her forearm was pressed awkwardly against her breastbone
and she could feel her heart still beating hard. *You have to. My
slave!* These dreams she'd been having sporadically since—
when?—sometime last fall. Remnants of old childhood nightmares. Like picking through the cluttered attic and cellar of her
parents' old house in Shaheen after her father's death. Never
know what you might find.

Lily of the Valley: her name. A silly, lovely, extravagant
name, on her birth certificate.

And her sister—*Rose of Sharon.*

Since their father had died five years before, two years after
their mother's death, Lily had lost all practical connection with
her past, rural life as the daughter of a minister of an obscure
Protestant sect; she sometimes seemed, in certain of her dreams,
to have lost her way in time. In a flurry of wonder and mount-
ing panic not knowing how old she was, in which house she
was, in which bed. Or whether Sharon was close by—her
blond curls on the very pillow beside Lily's. And hadn't she a
husband, and—*who was her husband?*

Lily supposed that, in the human brain, deep in the cortex

of memory, there is no such thing as "time"—"chronology." Everything is present tense; nothing is "past." We may be numerous selves simultaneously. Adult, adolescent, child, infant. Was she six years old, sixteen years old, thirty-six years old? Shrewdly she guessed that no one was ever *older* than his or her actual age, in dreams. Because you can't yet remember.

Lily's flannel nightgown was damp with perspiration, and her hair was heavy and warm at the nape of her neck. Her heart was still beating quickly as if in the presence of invisible danger. Outside, the wind blew, blew! A northerly wind, down from Lake Ontario, and Canada. A sound like rage, jeering. *I can get into that house of yours, that house you're so proud of. I can come through the windows that have been caulked, I can come through the walls that have been insulated.*

"No. No. *No*."

*   *   *

Lily switched on a light, saw it was 2:10 A.M.

She was standing in front of the bedroom closet looking for—what? Her robe, slippers. She couldn't seem to locate her slippers. As if someone, a mischievous child, had kicked them into the shadowy rear of the closet.

You're my slave, Lily.

Do what I say: inside. I command you.

Like bile in Lily's mouth it came to her, then: the dream, the nightmare, had been a memory of her twin sister Sharon tormenting her, more than thirty years ago.

The dreams she'd been having intermittently for weeks, that left her so dazed and exhausted in the morning—all were remnants of memories. The sweet clear cruel relentless child's soprano voice was the voice of her sister Sharon. "Sherrill." Whom Lily hadn't seen for fifteen years and hadn't spoken with since their father's death and the funeral Sharon had been so terribly, terribly sorry she couldn't attend—she'd had a "professional commitment" she couldn't break.

The sisters were twins, though not identical. "Fraternal."
I am Rose of Sharon Donner, you are Lily of the Valley Donner!
We can't ever be lonely like other people. We have each other.

But that wasn't true, once they started school. Already in junior high Sharon had been eager to detach herself from Lily. She wore her hair differently, "glamorously." She spoke, laughed, moved her body differently. On the sly, she wore bright lipstick. The sisters weren't mirror-twins and didn't in fact closely resemble each other. Sharon's hair was ashy-blond, Lily's a darker blond; Sharon was an inch taller than Lily, though always more slender; Sharon was the "pretty one"—the "one with the boyfriends." It came to seem by the time they were in high school that Sharon was an older sister of Lily's and this was an assumption Sharon was keen to promote. *Just say we're sisters if anybody asks, I'm older and that's a fact. We don't look anything alike!*

Never caring how she hurt Lily's feelings, never much aware of others' feelings. Disappearing into Manhattan to pursue her "career" and no looking back except when she wanted favors from the family. Pursuing the kind of people, powerful, well-to-do, exclusively male, she believed could advance her in her career. Falling in love with the wrong men again, and again.

Sharon had returned home only a single time, since leaving to become a model. And then only for a reason. *Lily, promise me. You are the only person in the world I can trust. The only person I love.*

Then she'd gone away again, of course. She'd been out of touch with Lily at the time of their mother's sickness and death; hadn't come to their father's funeral; when Lily got married to Wesley Merrick, Sharon hadn't even sent a card. It bewildered and exasperated Lily that her own sister had no interest in, not the slightest curiosity about, the man Lily had fallen in love with and married.

And Deedee. How bizarre, Sharon's attitude toward Deedee. As if she'd forgotten the child altogether. When she called home, which was infrequently, hardly remembering to ask about her. *Oh, yes—and how's my little niece? With the exotic name—"Deirdre"?*

Lily had learned not to be hurt by her sister. Which is to say, Lily had learned long ago not to expect anything other than hurt from her sister. She would have thought that she'd eased Sharon out of her mind entirely. She would have thought that she was free of their shared past.

Except, what to make of these disturbing dreams? Beginning last October and continuing through the winter, until this very night. Riddlesome dreams, prankish dreams. Dreams that left a brackish taste at the back of her mouth. Lily knew the Goya engraving, "The Nightmare": an ugly creature squatting on a sleeper's chest. So were her nightmares ugly creatures burrowing their way up out of her body, squatting on her chest and gloating. *You have to, you're my slave! I command you.* The creature was her sister Sharon as a young child. As if somehow she and Sharon were still children, somewhat lonely children, no sisters or brothers except themselves living with their parents in a ramshackle farmhouse in Shaheen, less than one hundred feet from their father's church and the hilly cemetery of plain stone markers and crosses behind it. *You know what that is?—a boneyard. You know who's there?—dead people. That's a nasty place.*

Before they'd been bused to town schools, Sharon hadn't any outlet for her energy, her amazing vivacity. So she'd "teased" Lily as their mother called it, unwilling to concede that one of her girls was tormenting the other with the relentlessness of a pilgrim. The nightmare that had wakened Lily this night was a confused, heightened memory of the cemetery; the wooden storage shed behind the church where groundskeeping equipment was kept; a dank shadowy ill-smelling place into which Sharon had forced Lily upon more than one occasion when they were playing together. *Inside! Go inside! On your hands and knees like a puppy-dog!* And there was the yet more dank and ill-smelling cellar of the church, a virtual tomb of oozing rocks, cobwebs and rot where of course the girls were forbidden to "play." *Slave, I command you!* It was meant to be a game, it was meant to be fun—wasn't it? Lily often laughed, giggled shrilly; wet her pants with squealing; scrambled on her hands and knees, wanting only to please her sister, who had an unpredictable temper—the more readily Lily gave in to Sharon's whims, the more likely Sharon was to relent, sometimes even to join her. For the test seemed to be the act of command and the response of obedience in themselves. Like the unpredictable God of the Hebrew Bible (as Reverend Donner called the Old Testament out of deference, he said, for his brethren the Jewish people), the scourge of Judah and Jerusalem and the sinful cities of the plains, little Rose of Sharon needed to know she was master.

There were times in fact when Sharon had taken the lead. Boldly and recklessly scrambling up onto the steep roof of the church, for instance, and commanding Lily to follow; making her way across a rock dam in the creek, to the opposite shore; venturing out onto the frozen creek in winter; crawling on hands and knees through a tunnel of wild rosebushes alive and buzzing with honeybees. *You have to follow me. Lily. I command you.* And Lily followed, or tried to. She'd been like one entranced, hypnotized. Frightened to obey, yet more frightened not to obey. She remembered one time when they were a little older, perhaps nine, in the presence of other children, country neighbors, and in a clearing on the creek bank, at the bottom of the cemetery, Sharon had lighted a small brush fire and intoned over it "magic" words—ZEKIL-HOSEA-OBADIAH-HABAKKUK-ZEPHANIAH-ZECHARIAH—and commanded Lily to put her hand in the flames, and Lily had hesitated, and Sharon commanded her more forcibly, and still Lily hesitated, for she wasn't such a silly fool she didn't know what fire was, and how it hurt to be burnt; and, conscious of the other children's eyes upon her, she'd shaken her head, no. Sharon cried *You have to do what I say, slave!* and pushed Lily toward the fire, pushing her head down, her hair dangerously close to the flames, and Lily screamed and wrenched away and said *No! No I don't!* and ran back up to the house.

Lily quickly put on her robe, struggling with the sleeves as if, behind her back, a prankish child were twisting them.

She was barefoot, in the hall outside the bedroom. Shivering and clammy with perspiration and her heart still beating disconcertingly fast. *Wes, just hold me. I've had the most upsetting nightmare.*

There was Deedee's room: thank God no light shone beneath the door. Sometimes Deedee stayed up late, studying, or reading, or writing in her journal; experimenting with her computer. She wasn't Wes's child biologically but she often seemed his child temperamentally: restless, twitchy in her sleep. As an infant she'd had bouts of severe colic and as a toddler she'd been high-strung, a dynamo of energy and impatience with fixed routines, bed-, bath-, nap-, mealtimes. Her cries had been lusty, ear-shattering and protracted. Yet she'd been a happy child, anyway. Husky, bold, inquisitive. Until the age of twelve or thirteen when she'd begun to change, her personality becoming more tentative, uncertain. Entering ninth grade had been sobering for Deedee; entering high school this past fall had been traumatic. All of life that had meaning was a popularity contest which only a very few pretty, self-assured "popular" girls could win. And only boys were to judge.

It angered Lily, as it angered the mothers of other teenaged girls of her acquaintance. What can you do, it's adolescence! Adolescence in America!

Deedee was Wes's adopted daughter; it was difficult to know if he loved her "as if she were his own" for how could Lily judge? She'd entered Wes's life as a twenty-two-year-old "unwed mother" with an eighteen-month daughter; a young woman with a confused and never very explicable past, who'd moved away from overly protective, God-besotted parents in the remote countryside south of Yewville. Lily sometimes thought, I am a figure in a fairy tale whose origins and whose ending I don't know.

Lily, promise! Never never go back on your word.

Someday, she would. But not yet.

Downstairs, Lily made her way to Wes's office on the far side of the house. By night, the house seemed unfamiliar; it might have been a stranger's house; and she an intruder. She stubbed her toe against something sharp-edged. "Oh—!"

The house was a woodframe and brick colonial originally built in 1919 and several times remodeled; the first house in which Lily had lived as an adult, and as Wesley Merrick's wife. When she'd moved away from Shaheen, where her parents had assumed she'd remain, as the mother of Deirdre, she'd lived in a small apartment in downtown Yewville, and worked at a succession of modestly paying part-time jobs, and taken courses at Yewville Community College. She'd met Wes Merrick almost immediately and had been astonished by his interest in her, his kindness and generosity. Yet somehow Lily had had faith that things would turn out well for her; if she didn't believe passionately in Jesus Christ as her parents had taught her to believe, she did seem to believe in a benign providence.

When Lily had been introduced to Wes, by a woman in an office in which she'd worked as a part-time secretary, he'd been presented to her as a quiet, difficult-to-know man; never married, an ex-Marine who'd had trouble readjusting to civilian life after being discharged from the service; though born and raised in Yewville, something of a mystery. He was thirty-one at the time, nine years older than Lily, but he'd looked older; not a handsome man, yet, to Lily's eye, an attractive man; with a slightly coarse, creased skin, thick dark hair sharply receding at his temples, broad sloping shoulders. He was a self-employed carpenter and builder: his forearms were dense and wiry with muscle. His eyes were of the color of stone and appeared lash-less, stark with melancholy knowledge. *What I've seen, I've seen. What I know, I know. Just don't ask.* Yet Wesley Merrick wasn't cynical, didn't seem pessimistic. If he liked you, and he'd liked Lily Donner from the start, he trusted you. If not, not. No way he could be coaxed into smiling if he didn't want to smile; he shook hands sometimes in silence, which made other men, accustomed to the exchange of glib, meaningless but assuaging banalities, uncomfortable. Lily noted Wes's habit of frowning at individuals as they spoke as if trying to decode what they were saying beneath their chatter, and this made people yet more uncomfortable. A woman who'd gone out with Wes a few times before giving up on him had warned Lily that he didn't care to be questioned about his Vietnam years, which set well with Lily, who didn't care to be questioned about Deedee and her own past.

When people inquired about Deedee, hoping to pry out of Lily one or another illuminating detail, Lily would feel her face burn, not exactly unpleasantly, and say quietly that her daugh-ter's father was not involved in their lives, by choice. Implying that the choice wasn't hers, of course; still less was it Deedee's; but they would make the best of it, here in Yewville in a "new" life.

Wes had been charmed by Deedee, as by Deedee's spunky young mother. It must have surprised and impressed him that Lily was so cheerful, so optimistic and outgoing; no moping about, no reproachful remarks about men. Why, Lily seemed to like men as—people. She'd never been a girl to arouse violent romantic passion in boys and had thus been spared emotional turmoil herself. (That province belonged to Sharon.) But she'd had a few friends who were boys in high school, and she related to men in a frank, sisterly fashion. When she took time to style her hair and wear makeup, she could be "pretty"; when she smiled, she was "prettier" still; but "prettiness" seemed hardly the point of Lily Donner, as you knew within a few minutes of meeting her. Wes had said afterward that Lily had been the only woman he'd met in years who seemed to know who she was. "You don't just invent yourself for any guy who comes along." Lily was flattered but thought, *Invent? I wouldn't know how.*

Wes had a small office downtown and an office in the house, in a long narrow first-floor room formerly a sunporch. There he sat, past 2 A.M., at his aluminum desk, illuminated as if on a screen by a single lamp. Lily was going to call out to him but hesitated. *No. You might regret it.* He was frowning at a computer screen, and at a swath of papers and documents spread across his desktop. His stiff, thinning steely-brown hair was disheveled as if he'd been running his hands through it, his jaws were unshaven, stubbled; he looked older than forty-five, clearly tired, in an irritable mood. Wes was a physically direct, blunt man who loved to work with "materials"—with his hands; who disliked the financial side of his business, the continuous and relentless task of trying to extract money from clients who owed him so that he could pay his own creditors on time. (This side of his life Wes rarely discussed with Lily, who wished she might be of more help to him.) Yet he was ambitious, as a contractor; he specialized in the restoration and renovation of old, solidly built family houses like the one they owned, not because there was money in such work (the money was in new "luxury" houses on two-acre lots in the suburban countryside) but because it was work he could respect, work with a purpose.

Lily saw then, suddenly, with a stab of disappointment and hurt, that Wes was smoking. He picked up a cigarette burning in an ashtray and inhaled with a savage sort of intensity. A pocket calculator in one hand, the cigarette in the other. *He hasn't quit after all. Or he's begun again.* In fact, Wes had quit smoking a dozen times since Lily knew him: quit, and began again; and again quit, and began again; he hated the habit but couldn't seem to overcome it. He'd smoked heavily in Vietnam, he said, and had "done some drugs," too. He was a man who disapproved of weakness in himself and others but particularly in himself; he smoked when he was angry with himself, and he was angry with himself when he smoked. But only last week he'd declared to Lily and Deedee that, this time, it was permanent. He hadn't touched a cigarette in nineteen days, twelve hours.

So sheepish, so boyish and proud, Lily and Deedee had laughed and broken into spontaneous applause.

And now. *Not only smoking: drinking. Look!* Lily saw to her dismay that Wes was lifting a glass to his mouth even as he continued to stare at the papers on his desk. Whiskey? Somehow, Lily doubted it was a soda drink or fruit juice. Wes was a man who enjoyed drinking, beer, ale, wine, hard liquor, he'd acknowledged a drinking problem before their marriage but so far as Lily knew he had no problem now, he drank only moderately she was sure. *Yes but can you be sure? Do you really know that man, at all?* She was frightened, suddenly; she shrank back into the shadows, and did not dare call attention to herself. How angry Wes would be, to discover her spying on him. He had his pride, his sense of privacy. Though Lily would never have admonished him for smoking—and drinking—he would not have accepted her silence, either.

You're alone, you see? Like me.

Slave!

Lily stumbled away from Wes's office, not knowing where to go except back upstairs. What a poor, misguided idea it had been, to rush downstairs with her fear carried like precious crystal to present to Wes, her protector. What a fool she was. She groped her way half-blind through the downstairs, unsteady as if she'd been struck a blow to the head.

The wind, the wind! Roaring overhead like a freight train with endless rattling cars. And in every car windows framing faces of the dead, the damned and dead! Lily was shivering, her heart pounding absurdly. She saw herself as a woman in a medieval woodcut possessed by spirits, devils; running mad tearing at her hair, her face, her clothing until there came Jesus Christ in a white robe to calmly cast out devils except Lily didn't believe in devils. She was a civilized woman, she didn't believe seriously in evil.

On her way back upstairs she realized that it was the eve of her (and her twin sister's) thirty-seventh birthday.

2

The Birthday

The door at the rear of the house opened, and closed. And there came Deedee's uplifted voice in the kitchen, "Hi, Mom."

A voice that was bright and animated and girlish. Or meant to give that impression.

It was 4:55 P.M. A darkening winter afternoon, mid-February. Deedee was just home from school, later than usual; Lily, who'd been feeling apprehensive through much of the day—not because it was her thirty-seventh birthday, she hoped—heard with relief her daughter enter the house by the rear door, stamp her boots clear of snow and ice, and enter the kitchen. In her cluttered workroom next to the kitchen, at her potter's bench where she was modeling a clay vase, her fingers quick, deft, practiced in their instinctive motions, Lily could picture Deedee, flush-faced from the cold, dismantling her clumsy bookbag which she wore strapped to her back like a beast of burden, letting it fall onto the kitchen counter. As if in the girl's familiar greeting Lily hadn't detected a subtle note of adolescent sadness, hurt, resignation, and sensed it in the hurried, graceless tread of Deedee's walk, Lily called out with equal brightness, "Hi, honey! Welcome home."

It was a familiar and reassuring exchange. Every afternoon when Deedee arrived home from school, when Lily was herself

home. An exchange that had continued for years. And would
continue for years. (Deedee was only a sophomore in high
school.)

Though long ago, in another lifetime it seemed, Lily had
driven to pick up Deedee at school every afternoon, preschool
and kindergarten; and the two of them stopped at a neighborhood dairy for their ritual of "afternoon tea."

In Deedee's young, foreshortened memory, those days
would seem very remote, indeed. "Afternoon tea" at Ewald's
Dairy—the kind of small islanded memory a mother vividly
recalls. Her own happiness as a young mother.

When Lily came into the kitchen, smiling, Deedee had already shrugged off her bulky sheepskin jacket and was peering
critically into the refrigerator. Lily caught the jacket as it was
about to slide from a chair onto the floor. "Hi, Mom, happy
birthday," Deedee said, humming to herself as she deliberated
what, if anything, to eat. Deedee wore jeans, a loose-fitting
sweater; she was a solid, compact girl, not fat, nor even plump,
but rosy-fleshed, like, Lily thought, a girl Renoir might have
painted. Deedee was a pretty girl but couldn't bear being told
so, at least not by her mother. A few weeks before, in her car,
Lily had happened to see Deedee walking near the high school,
a figure that appeared at first glance to be neither female nor
male, in jeans, boots, the bulky khaki-colored jacket; the girl
strode along with her head bowed, eyes downcast as if she were
searching the snowy sidewalk for something precious. Deedee
was resolutely alone and took no notice of a noisy group of
boys and girls crossing the street near her, as they took no notice
of her.

Lily washed her hands at the sink and resisted touching
Deedee where she stood slouched and sighing, leaning on the
refrigerator door. Lily would have liked to smooth down the
girl's disheveled ashy-blond hair that looked as if it hadn't been
combed for days, but she knew better. She said, "You've already wished me a happy birthday, honey, and I love the

card"—a large red construction-paper HAPPY BIRTHDAY MOM! in the shape of a heart, which Deedee had made in obvious haste, now prominently positioned on a windowsill. Deedee said, taking out a can of diet Coke and a container of blueberry yogurt from the refrigerator, "Well, it's a big day all day. And more to come." There was something sweetly forced about these words as if Deedee's mind were on other things and she was going through the motions of speaking to her mother.

Even as Lily herself was distracted, edgy. Not knowing why.

The ridiculous dream of the night before—she'd all but forgotten. She'd decided it had been the wind that caused it. But you can obliterate such trivial memories the way, with a few quick swipes of a kitchen sponge, you can clean a Formica-topped counter.

Lily said, lightly, since these were dull-motherly, damning and familiar words, "Now, sweetie, don't spoil your appetite, please. Your dad's taking us all out to dinner." Deedee sighed and rolled her eyes like a boy of twelve. Saying, "You kidding, Mom? Spoil *my* appetite?" She laughed as if the idea was preposterous. As if her appetite was deep and trackless as the Grand Canyon.

"Now, honey."

How a teenaged girl hurts her mother: by speaking crudely and disparagingly of herself.

Deedee was an intelligent, sharp-witted girl; prone to irony, but also childlike, hopeful and sweet; an A student, well liked by her teachers; physically mature for her age yet in crucial ways immature. Her face was round, moon-shaped as her grandmother's had been, with a small nose, rather small close-set eyes; inclined to plumpness; her pebble-blue eyes were shyly watchful, and to Lily beautiful. If only . . . Lily understood that Deedee ate compulsively to assuage her hurt feelings (mysterious hurts! high-school hurts! don't inquire into them), and her compulsive eating, her ten pounds or so of extra flesh, intensified her susceptibility to hurt. Lily touched Deedee after all,

drawing a hand along the girl's arm as Deedee, with an impatient gesture, pried open the lid of the yogurt container. Deedee
laughed and said, "Mom, your hand smells like *clay.*" Lily said,
trying not to sound concerned, "You're home from school a
little late today, aren't you? It's almost five." Deedee said,
shrugging, "There was a yearbook staff meeting and half the
kids were late and some didn't show up at all, *I* was the only
sophomore." Deedee spoke with both resentment and pride.
Lily said, "Try not to let them take advantage of you this year,
sweetie," recalling how in ninth grade, Deedee had been one
to volunteer for class committees, editing the school newspaper,
spending an entire day decorating the gym for the graduation
dance to which she hadn't gone. Defensively, Deedee said, "No
one takes advantage of me, I do what I want. Anyway, Mom,
you should talk—everybody in Yewville takes advantage of
you."

Lily considered: was it true? She could always be counted
upon to canvass for the local Red Cross chapter, and for the
wildlife sanctuary; she was a perennially elected officer in the
PTA; her numerous women friends were always calling her for
favors, and rarely had time to reciprocate. For the past six years
she'd been teaching pottery at Yewville Community College,
for a small salary, working with her students many more hours
than the course required; yet when there'd been an opening for
a permanent instructor, at a higher salary, the director of the
program, an affable longtime acquaintance of both Lily's and
Wes's, had passed over Lily to hire a man. Wes and Deedee had
been outraged on Lily's behalf but Lily insisted she didn't mind,
truly. *I love to teach, I love working with beginners but I'm just an
amateur as a teacher and a potter. Truly, I wouldn't have wanted the
extra responsibility.*

Deedee had brought the day's mail in with her, and was
sitting at the kitchen table sorting through it. This, too, was a
weekday ritual. "Doesn't look like much," Deedee said, pushing aside bills, flyers, advertisements; handing Lily several enve-

lopes which Lily opened with childlike anticipation—birthday cards, from women friends and relatives mainly.

Deedee said, "What's this? We-ird." She was squinting at a postcard.

Lily's heart leapt. Yet she asked calmly, "For me?"

"For 'Lily Donner.' Like whoever sent it doesn't know you're married, even."

Yet whoever sent it, Lily saw, knew she lived at 183 Washington Street, Yewville, New York.

Lily leaned over Deedee to examine the mysterious card with her. Neither could make out the signature which was in red ink, shaky as if it had been scrawled in a speeding vehicle or by a drunken person. Deedee said, " 'Far'—'Farrer'?—no, that's an S—'Starer'? The last name looks like 'Dwight.' "

Lily said, "I don't know any—'Starer.' I'm sure. Anyone named 'Dwight.' "

The postcard was an ordinary tourist's card, a glossy photograph of Death Valley in springtime: cactus flowers, sculpted and rippled sand dunes, a china-blue sky. No human figures in all that vastness. Deedee said, "Wow. I didn't know Death Valley was so beautiful. We should go there sometime . . . It must be for your birthday, Mom. See, this looks like 'Your Day, Lily'—then some words I can't read—'For this—these?—are the days of—regenance'— What's 'regenance'?"

Lily was staring at the red-inked message. She could not decipher a word. "—'vengeance,' " she said.

Deedee read haltingly, " 'For these are the days of vengeance, that all things which are—willed—' "

"—'written.' "

"—'all things which are written may be'—what?— 'suselled'?—is that a word?"

Lily said calmly, "—'fulfilled.' 'For these are the days of vengeance, that all things which are written may be fulfilled.' "

"Sounds like the Bible. Who's this 'Dwight,' Mom?"

The words, solemn and pitiless, had seemed to issue from

Lily's throat without her volition. As if, after all, she was but a hollow reed.

Lily said, without looking, "I can't read the signature, honey. I don't know."

"Maybe it's a joke," Deedee said suspiciously. "The postmark isn't Nevada, see? It's Missouri. Mailed two days ago."

Lily took the card from Deedee and stood staring at it, at the dreamlike lunar terrain of Death Valley which she had never seen in person. For a long moment she didn't say a word; then, since Deedee was regarding her with frank curiosity, she said, "Yes. It's a joke, probably."

Why! Why would you do such a thing.

Why, after years of not writing, not calling. Never caring how I yearn for you just to know you're alive.

Why such a thing, at such a time.

Our birthday.

Quickly Lily hid away the postcard. As if it were something illicit, a secret; not taped to a wall of her workroom with dozens of other colorful cards but hidden meanly away in a drawer in a mess of pencil sketches, soiled rags. Where no one except Lily ever looked.

She would not have mentioned it to Wes even as a curiosity except that, at dinner, in the restaurant to which Wes had taken her and Deedee to celebrate Lily's birthday, Deedee brought it up. Saying suddenly, near the end of their meal, "Dad, did Mom show you the weird postcard she got today? Sort of a birthday card, with a Bible message. From Death Valley."

Wes had been enjoying the meal, and the evening; he was in a warm, expansive mood, ready to be entertained. "Postcard? Death Valley. No-ooo." He smiled at Lily, curious. "Who do you know in Death Valley, Lily?"

Lily said, "It—wasn't from Death Valley, actually. Just a tourist card. Postmarked Missouri."

"Well, who do you know in Missouri?"

"I was trying to think. A cousin, maybe. On my mother's side of the family. The signature might have been her name . . ." Lily's voice trailed off as if the subject, of so little importance, could not possibly be of interest to Wes.

That morning, there'd been no sign of cigarettes, or drinking, in Wes's office. Well, perhaps—a faint odor of smoke. Lily had not wished to go into the room and had in fact stood only at the doorway, peering inside. *Spying on your own husband! How dare you.* She was not a woman who snooped in another's private quarters, she was not a mother who entered even her daughter's bedroom when her daughter was gone. Wes had finally come upstairs at about 3 A.M. and he'd risen again at his usual hour of 7 A.M.; he laughed at Lily's concern, saying he wasn't a man who required more than a few hours sleep. He hadn't lit a cigarette in Lily's presence for weeks and, tonight, he was drinking only white wine, like Lily.

If only Deedee didn't persist! But she had an adolescent's sly maddening instinct for pressing seemingly small matters that vexed her mother considerably, though Lily would never have let on. Deedee said, "Y'know, Mom, when I first saw that card, it's weird somehow I thought it might be from Aunt Sharon. Today being your birthday, and all."

"Well, it isn't."

Lily stared at her water glass, a crystal goblet in which ice was melting. She wondered if Wes and Deedee were thinking how odd, Lily hadn't heard from her sister on their birthday. Lily had no idea where her sister was.

Deedee was saying, "You haven't heard from Aunt Sharon in a long time, I guess?"

Lily said, calmly, "It hasn't been that long. We spoke on the phone when—" trying to name a year, a date; a plausible recollection. "Sharon was involved with a dance troupe, in Miami, remember, and they were going on tour, I think to— Houston, Los Angeles. And after that—"

Deedee was saying disapprovingly how "weird" it was she'd never seen her own aunt; her mother's twin sister; how "weird" that Wes had never met his sister-in-law. "If Aunt Sharon's pictures weren't in that album, I'd wonder if she existed," Deedee said. "That's how weird it is."

Lily said, "Deedee, I wish you'd find another word instead of 'weird.' There must be plenty in the dictionary."

Deedee said, with the most innocent sly cruelty, "Those modeling photos are from a long time ago, Aunt Sharon was so beautiful and glamorous but she'd be kind of old now, I guess. She can't still be *dancing*."

Lily laughed. "Sharon is exactly my age, as you know."

"Well."

The three of them laughed. Deedee was, as often at mealtimes, showing off partly to amuse Wes; it was playful enough, but exasperating.

If I can get through this day, help me God, I will be fine. This is a dangerous day.

Wes was saying, "If I'd known, Lily, when I first met you, that you had a twin sister, I'd possibly have been intimidated. There's something strange about falling in love with a person who's actually *two*."

I am not two! I am one.

Deedee giggled mischievously. " 'Strange'? *We-ird*."

Lily sighed, and tried to laugh; but it was painful to laugh; it sometimes happened that Wes and Deedee ganged up and teased her, and what more appropriate occasion than her birthday? She had to be a good sport. And Deedee was trying to be earnest, serious—"But, Dad, Mom and Aunt Sharon don't look like twins, judging by the photos. They aren't identical, they're only 'fraternal.' I mean 'sororal,' if that's a word."

It was a word, yes. A rarely used word. Lily had once looked it up in the dictionary, out of curiosity.

But she didn't say so, now. She said, an edge in her voice

to show she was getting annoyed, "I think it's time for dessert. This is a school night for Deedee after all."

"Oh, Mom. It's your *birthday.*"

"I've had plenty of birthdays. And I hope I'll have plenty more."

The evening had gone well. Better than Lily might have anticipated. She would have preferred to make dinner for them at home, of course; nothing made Lily happier than their domestic, cozy evenings; her most peaceful time of day. Especially if she'd been working intensely in her workroom, or at the college; if Wes didn't come home late from a work site, and wasn't distracted. Why do others make more of our birthdays than we do, ourselves? Lily wondered. Do they need to prove they love us, again and again?

She was smiling of course. She'd been smiling for hours. At the house, Wes and Deedee had given Lily their presents: a delicate heart-shaped locket on a thin gold chain, from Wes, who gave Lily jewelry every year oblivious of the fact that Lily rarely wore any jewelry apart from her wedding band and wristwatch; an immense clay pot of dusky-pink begonias for the window-bench of Lily's workroom, already crowded with plants, from Deedee. But Lily had been very pleased, and touched. She'd hugged and kissed both husband and daughter and stammered, "I—I love you!" and Wes and Deedee had been embarrassed and assured her they loved her, too.

You see how happy we are. My husband, my daughter.

It had been one of the surprises of her life, and one of the greatest blessings. How, when she and Wes had met, and had begun to see each other, he hadn't been jealous of her past; of what he would have been justified to perceive as her past. She was a young woman with an eighteen-month baby and no husband nor even the melancholy tale of a failed marriage; yet Wes had said simply *Tell me what you feel comfortable telling me, Lily. No more.* And so, hesitantly, feeling her way, for until that moment she hadn't rehearsed what she might say, how she would attempt to explain her peculiar circumstances, she said *He—Deirdre's father—isn't anyone I know—really.* Her heart had pounded with the audacity of her words, not a lie yet how far from the truth. *It was a—mistake* she said. And Wes startled her by laughing. Gently he said *Look, Deirdre isn't a mistake, is she?* and Lily said *No!* and Wes said *So you would not want him, the father, erased from your life, right?* and Lily said, contrite, *No.*

She'd known how she had loved Wes Merrick, then. A man so very different from her father; yet, like Ephraim Donner, a man of surpassing dignity, integrity.

A man with a beautiful soul.

During dessert, Lily was beginning to get drowsy. Wes and Deedee laughed, chattered. She had the idea they were oddly protective of her.

Across the crowded dining room was a frosted mirror on a wall and in this mirror the Merrick family was reflected in shimmering ghostly images. Lily had been watching half-consciously. As the wine went to her head—but she'd had only two glasses, hadn't she?—or three?—the reflections of the tall broad-shouldered man, the woman in a red dress and the teen-aged girl became more seductive. Lily could not see their features clearly but they were obviously attractive, happy people. They belonged together, they were a family.

You see?

No, no!—Lily wasn't drunk.

Maybe just slightly giddy and extravagant blinking tears from her eyes kissing Deedee goodnight at the foot of the stairs and calling out so that Wes, hanging coats in the hall closet, could hear. "This was my most wonderful birthday ever! Thank you so much, both of you."

Deedee laughed and said, "Oh, Mom. You say exactly the same thing every year."

Lily protested, "I do? I don't! Wes?"

Wes was whistling, pretending not to hear the question.

"Well," Lily declared, "if I say it, *I mean it*."

Deedee called back over her shoulder, halfway up the stairs, "And you say exactly that every year, too, Mom."

The long day was nearly over: midnight.

Like making her way across the rock dam in the creek, stepping upon the shaky rocks one by one by one. Hoping she wouldn't fall into the chill swift-flowing water.

No telephone call had come. No message on the answering service when they returned from the restaurant. *Lily? Please call me, I'm in need of hearing your voice. Miss you.*

And when Lily had called that time, several years ago on their birthday, dialing the number Sharon had left for her, the phone had rung and rung. Area code San Diego, California.

Eventually, a few days later, a man had answered. When Lily asked to speak with Sharon, the man uttered an obscenity and slammed down the phone.

Lily was lying in bed, pleasantly tired. Arms and legs outstretched as if she were falling upward through the night sky. Drifting, floating. Wide undulating planes of sleep appeared to her like a puddled meadow. Wes hadn't come to bed again, apologized and kissed her and disappeared downstairs. And Lily lay in the big bed in the shadowy bedroom of the house she loved; the first house of her adult life; recalling with the vividness of a dream, how, after her father had died and the old farmhouse in Shaheen had been cleaned out (by Lily, mainly) from attic to cellar and the property sold, one rainy March day, ten-year-old Deedee snug in the crook of her arm, she'd settled into the sofa in the recreation room to look through the battered old photograph album Emmy Donner had kept.

Deedee was curious, of an age to be avidly interested in her mother's girlhood. And, of course, she'd wanted to know about her mother's twin sister who was "Aunt Sharon"—the glamorous and mysterious stranger. Aunt Sharon who'd promised to visit at Christmas, or for her and Lily's birthday in February, or

for a week during the summer; yet somehow never came to
Yewville. At the last minute postponing her visit.

But why? Deedee wanted to know.

Professional commitments!

That was what Sharon told Lily, and that was what Lily had
to tell her family.

How fascinated Deedee was by the early baby pictures.
Dimpled baby girls, *Rose of Sharon* and *Lily of the Valley.* Newly
born, in their proud young mother's arms, like kittens whose
eyes haven't yet opened. Emmy Donner liked to tell of how
Rose of Sharon had been born first, an hour before her sister;
at six pounds, thirteen ounces she'd outweighed the other baby
girl by eleven ounces. Rose of Sharon had kicked harder from
the start and cried louder and fretted more and nursed more
hungrily at their mother's breast—*More, more, more!* For that
was Rose of Sharon's way and it seemed natural that everyone
should wish to please her.

There were the twin sisters in their look-alike polka-dot
playsuits and in their Sunday dresses handsewn by their mother.
Ashy-blond Rose of Sharon smiling happily at the camera as if
understanding already at the age of three how photogenic she
was; how beautiful in the glassy eye of the camera. And there
was Lily of the Valley whose hair was several shades darker,
shading into brown; a sweet startled-looking child whose smile
was shy and partly hidden by her hand.

Thirty years ago. And more. Deedee was staring, blinking
in wonder. She said, "Oh Mommy, I wish I had a sister, like
you did!" Lily thought sadly, I wish you did, too.

Somehow it hadn't happened. Clearly, Wes hadn't much
wanted it to happen. A part of his soul numbed by whatever
he'd seen, endured or done in Vietnam forever hidden from
Lily as the dark side of the moon is forever hidden, inaccessible.

As Lily turned the pages of the snapshot album with
Deedee, she felt a bittersweet ache of memory; and a stir of
apprehension. It had been years since she'd seen most of these

snapshots. How many times as a girl she'd paged through it, how carefully she'd maintained it as a teenager, and, after Sharon left home to become "Sherrill"—the high-fashion model—Lily had faithfully affixed snapshots and photos into place, in chronological order. She, Lily, was the keeper of the Donner family album. The one who will remember.

A snapshot of the white-painted woodframe country church, the First Church of Christ of Shaheen, and Reverend Ephraim Donner and his wife Emmy on the concrete front steps their arms around each other's waist squinting in the sun. A snapshot, not a very focused one, of the church interior; twelve-year-old Lily self-consciously seated at the aged foot-pedal organ in a stiff-starched pink Sunday dress, black patent-leather shoes and white anklet socks, and her tall lanky father beside the organ holding a hymnal aloft. Poor sweet Daddy who'd been minister of that backcountry church for thirty-one years. Smiling into the camera as if into the eye of God. *Always know you are loved, children. Always in His heart.* Here, a picture of twelve-year-old Sharon in a pink dress identical to her sister's yet somehow prettier, and her black patent-leather shoes shinier, and her white anklet socks whiter. Rose of Sharon with wavy pale-blond hair to her shoulders, widened blue eyes clear as glass and a sweet rosebud mouth pursed in the very act of singing. Like an angel she stood at the front of the church, the youngest member of the choir. Joyously they sang *Jesus loves me, this I know. For the Bible tells me so.* While at the organ, pumping away at the wheezing foot-pedals, Lily lost her place hearing her sister's uplifted soprano voice penetrating the thicker, earthbound voices of the others. The congregation loved her, the elderly women moved to tears and the men staring open-mouthed. The other members of the choir deferred to the minister's daughter Rose of Sharon as an angel possessed of a God-given talent, and did not envy her.

As Lily deferred to her sister, too. Not out of envy but out of admiration.

Though knowing a Rose of Sharon very different from the shining blond angel-child the congregation beheld.

You're my slave you have to do what I say. And never never tell.

It was a miracle, a mystery—where the Donner twins' musical talent came from. Lily could pick out tunes at the organ without having had a lesson; after a few lessons from a neighbor, she could play the instrument—adequately enough to accompany the choir. (Not that she had any real talent, of course. Not for playing a keyboard instrument!) And Sharon had a naturally sweet, thrilling soprano voice. It was thin, breathless, inclined to waver and lacked resonance—but no one in the Shaheen area would notice.

Ten-year-old Deedee was intrigued by the numerous snapshots and newspaper clippings heralding Sharon's success, at the age of thirteen, in the STARR BRIGHT PRESENTS AREA YOUTH TALENT SEARCH 1972. Here, stuffed into the album, too many for all of them to be neatly pasted in, were dozens of pictures from that time: Sharon in a blue taffeta dress and high heels, thin and elegantly graceful as a long-legged bird, poised on a brightly lighted stage singing beside a piano at which a girl, her accompanist Lily, sat unobtrusively; Sharon being presented with a first-prize silver plaque and a gift certificate by the bronze-blond amply proportioned Miss Starr Bright, a middle-aged "media personality" of glamorous pretensions; Sharon wiping tears from her eyes, smiling at flashing cameras. What excitement! To have won first prize in the annual Starr Bright talent search! Miss Starr Bright had been hostess of a Buffalo television program for children popular in western New York in the 1960's and early 1970's and each year, with much publicity, she oversaw a "talent search." The competition was limited to children between the ages of eight and fourteen; Sharon, at thirteen, had entered just in time.

She'd won the silver plaque, and a gift certificate for $200 from one of the prestige Buffalo department stores, and of course she'd won local acclaim, publicity. Deedee didn't inquire what the cash prize was, any American child in the media era understands that winning is in itself the prize. And there was pretty *Sharon Donner, daughter of Reverend and Mrs. Ephraim Donner of Shaheen, New York, first-prize winner of the Starr Bright Youth Talent Search 1972* featured on the front page of the second section of the *Buffalo Evening News* of April 18, 1972. Deedee murmured reverently, "Wow."

Lily recalled how she'd been terrified, at the piano. She'd practiced the accompaniment to "I'm Always Chasing Rainbows" a hundred times yet at the crucial moment she came close to panicking, depressing keys timidly, missing notes, striking a flat instead of a sharp, but hurtling on, scarcely daring to breathe, as her amazing sister faced the audience beyond the blinding stage lights—more than one thousand people!—and sang, sang as if her heart were in the simple, sentimental words; as if, offering herself so, no panel of judges and the heavily made-up ex-"chanteuse" Miss Starr Bright could deny her victory. *I prayed to win, and I made myself win. We both won, Lily!*

Of course, that wasn't true. Deedee would hardly have thought so, staring at the numerous pictures of Sharon, reading through a batch of yellowing news clippings.

Deedee was equally fascinated by the snapshots that followed: lovely blond Sharon as a high school cheerleader, her hair in a sleek pageboy, a slim vibrant girl in a navy blue jumper and long-sleeved white blouse, the white terrycloth letters Y H S on her chest. By this time, the sisters were bussed into Yewville with other country children to attend school, a distance of eleven miles; seeming even longer on unpaved back-country roads; yet it was a place Sharon seemed precociously to know, and to thrive in, while Lily held back self-consciously, shy and overwhelmed at first. She was hurt when their new classmates inquired were they really twins? *twins?* but understanding the skepticism. They never wore matching clothes any longer, nor would Sharon allow Lily to wear her hair in a style resembling her own. If Sharon wanted shoulder-length hair,

Lily had to keep her hair cut short; if Sharon decided she
wanted her hair trimmed, Lily would have to let hers grow.
*And don't hang around me for God's sake like some sad little puppy
dog. And if you can't find anyone decent to eat lunch with sit alone
and keep your dignity!* For Sharon hadn't time for Lily, at school.
She'd quickly become one of the popular girls at Yewville
High. Elected to the varsity cheerleaders when she was only a
sophomore. Dating the school's most popular boys—including
Mack Dwyer the senior football-basketball star whose well-to-
do father owned Dwyer's Realty. Of course the Donners would
not have approved of "dating" but Sharon—and Lily—
conspired to keep them blissfully ignorant: Sharon simply stayed
overnight at the Yewville homes of her girlfriends who were
also popular, and also "dated." Somehow Sharon managed to
win her parents' grudging permission to attend school dances,
assured that these dances were rigorously chaperoned; there
were several photos of such festive occasions, Sharon in gauzy
prom dresses with spaghetti straps, Sharon posed smiling beside
six-foot Mack Dwyer in a white dinner jacket, his arm around
her bare shoulders. Their eyes blazing up in the camera's flash.
Deedee asked, "Was he Aunt Sharon's boyfriend?" and Lily
said, hesitantly, for she recalled that Sharon's relationship with
Mack had gone mysteriously bad, and abruptly, "Not the only
one, but the main one." Strange for Lily to encounter Mack
Dwyer, now known as Michael Dwyer, in Yewville, and to
realize that he, the former high school star, was now a man in
his forties: still a "popular" personality, if shallow; his athlete's
muscle lapsed into flesh, his still-handsome face stippled with
tiny broken capillaries, the sign of a problem drinker; or one
who'd been, as Lily had heard, a problem drinker until recently.
"He's real good-looking, I guess," Deedee said, crinkling her
nose, "but I don't like him."

Most of the remaining pages of the album were given over
to Sharon's "professional" career as a model—interspersed, of
course, with family snapshots of Lily and the elder Donners and

other relatives and members of the First Church of Christ, at which Deedee scarcely glanced. Lily didn't blame the child: how ordinary, how *uninteresting* everyone else appeared, set beside glamorous "Sherrill." Sharon's modeling career began shortly after she won the Starr Bright competition: she was hired to appear in newspaper advertisements for the larger downtown Buffalo department stores, modeling "junior" clothes. Lily recalled the excitement of seeing her sister Sharon in these full-page ads in the *Buffalo Evening News*—the excitement of the telephone ringing, always ringing for Sharon. When she was seventeen, Sharon signed on with a Manhattan modeling agency; became "Sherrill"—sometimes with a last name, more often not; and, overcoming the Donners' objections, she quit high school, became a full-time model and moved to Manhattan. For the first year, things seemed to be going wonderfully well; Sharon claimed to be earning as much as $1000 a day, a figure almost unbelievable back in Shaheen. Then, suddenly, when Sharon was nineteen and on a shoot for *Vogue* in Mexico, she disappeared for four months; "drifted off" with a wealthy American man she'd met there; the agency hinted that drugs were involved; and "Sherrill" never returned to professional modeling again.

"Gee, Mom. Aunt Sharon is really *pretty*."

Deedee's words were hushed, in awe. As she contemplated the glossy glamor stills, now almost thirty years old. And the faded pages from *Vogue, Harper's Bazaar, Glamour, Mademoiselle.* Sometimes Sharon was hardly recognizable, elaborately made up, with dyed hair, or wearing a wig; a lovely slender girl's body encased in stunning, expensive, sometimes ludicrous clothes. Staring at this fairy creature, Deedee could have no idea, of course, of the heartbreak Sharon had caused in the Donner household; and of the havoc, eventually, in her confused life. Nor was Lily likely to tell Deedee.

The last photo of Sharon—"Sherrill"—had been taken sometime in 1978. A dreamy-eyed blonde with ivory skin, full sensuous mouth and size-four figure in crepey-black sexy clothes. *Look at me! Love me!*

"Is that all?" Deedee asked, disappointed.

"I'm afraid it is, honey."

There were no photos of "Sherrill" following the collapse of her modeling career. Her subsequent career as a singer-dancer, about which Lily knew very little, was not represented at all.

It had taken most of the morning to sort through the stuffed photo album and by the time Lily and Deedee had finished, Lily was feeling ill. *Why have you done such a thing, shown these pictures to Deedee? Risking so much, you must be mad.*

Long afterward, Lily was appalled at her own behavior. She couldn't comprehend it, for she might have simply hidden the album away as her mother had done, at the back of a closet, and never looked at it again.

When at last Wes came quietly to bed, after 2 A.M., Lily woke confused and asked him who'd telephoned, and Wes said no one, no one had telephoned, and Lily said, I thought I heard the phone ring, and Wes said no, sweetheart, you've been dreaming, and his weight in the bed beside her, his arm slung over her and his warm mouth in her hair were a part of the dream, the most precious part.

3

The Arrival

Here is how it happened, six weeks later on a brightly sunny
cold afternoon in March.

Deedee was leaving the high school, walking with two girlfriends, when she happened to see, idling in the crescent-shaped
asphalt drive in front of the building, a taxi: an unusual sight in
Yewville, where there was a single taxi company, and not much
demand for its services. And Deedee noticed, in the rear window of the taxi, just as the door was being pushed open, a face
that was familiar to her—as familiar somehow as her own, and
her mother's; yet a stranger's face, a face of strange, ravaged
beauty, partly obscured by oversized sunglasses with very dark
lenses. The woman removed the sunglasses as if to see Deedee
more clearly. Her eyes were artfully made up, beautiful though
ringed with shadows, fatigue. The woman's hair was pale, platinum blond, drawn back severely from her face into a chignon;
her skin was ivory-pale, with a faint sallow sickly cast, as if she
were only just recovering from an illness. Deedee might have
estimated the woman was in her late twenties or early thirties,
for any age beyond twenty is mysterious and "old" to a fifteen-
year-old. Yet the woman was striking, stylish: her mouth was
beige-pink, to mimic a "natural" look though it was anything
but natural; she wore a cruel-looking silver ear clamp on her
left ear, of the kind outlawed at Yewville High School, along

with nose rings and more than three ear studs; and, as out of place in Yewville on an ordinary weekday afternoon as an evening gown would have been, a black satin quilted jacket with elegant boxy shoulders, black trousers with a strip of velvet at the crease, handsome black leather boots with a distinct heel.

"Geez," one of Deedee's friends whispered, "—who is *she*?"

"Not anybody's mother, from around *here*."

The woman had stepped out of the cab and was approaching Deedee and the other girls, but was looking only at Deedee; staring at Deedee with a strange, unnerving intensity. At last she said, "Deirdre—?" Her voice was hoarse, like a voice unused for a long time.

"Y-yes?"

"You know me, Deirdre—don't you?"

Deedee stared. Her face had begun to burn as if with fever. Shyly she said, "Is it—Aunt Sharon?"

The woman in black gave a little cry, a half-sob, and came quickly to embrace Deedee, who stood unresisting, astonished, too taken by surprise to return the embrace. Dazed, she smelled the woman's strong perfume, sweet like overripe peaches, and a harsher chemical scent she could not know was the odor of bleached hair.

The woman stepped back from Deedee, smiling in triumph. "Yes! 'Aunt Sharon.' " Her eyes were delicately netted in blood. There were fine, near-invisible white lines in her forehead. Now Deedee could see that the woman was older than she'd seemed—obviously, Lily's age. And how like Lily she did look, in fact, except her features were more dramatic, exaggerated; as if Lily's pleasant plain-pretty face had been sharpened, given more definition, "beautified."

"Deirdre, get into the cab with me! We'll ride to your house."

And so, like an enchanted child in a fairy tale, Deedee got into the cab with her beautiful blond aunt Sharon, forgetting even to wave goodbye to her friends, and whoever else had come along to join them on the school steps, staring after the departing yellow-checkered taxi in amazement.

No warning!
Sudden as lightning striking.
On that day, a Tuesday like any other, Lily had been out of the house for much of the morning, attending a committee meeting at the college, doing errands, shopping; contentedly driving in the bright gusty air of March that smelled still of winter though with each passing day the sun was rising more confidently in the sky, cutting a broader swath. She discovered snowdrops, those exquisite, beautiful miniature flowers, newly opened amid the nacreous strips of snow bordering her front walk. At midday, the thermometer rose well above 32° F and the icy streets turned to slush; pedestrians were bareheaded, and some were without coats; reckless boys pedaled by on bicycles, eager to hurry the season. Spring! Spring in upstate New York!

This time, Deedee came bursting into Lily's workroom, smiling as she rarely smiled. Even before Lily saw the flowers in her daughter's hand, and absorbed the fact that they were Easter lilies, she knew that something irrevocable had happened.

"Mom? These are for you."

"For me?" Lily wiped her hands on her jeans and took the flowers from Deedee. Fresh-cut waxy-white lilies, long-stemmed, fragrant. But why?

Deedee was saying, excited, "Somebody's come to see you, Mom. To see us!"

Lily looked up to see Sharon in the doorway.

Sharon—"Sherrill." Her twin sister she hadn't seen in—how many years.

And how altered! Almost, in that first astonished instant, unrecognizable.

Sharon was smiling nervously, turning a pair of dark-rimmed sunglasses in her hand. "Lily, hello."

"Oh my God! Sharon."

Afterward Lily would think how ironic, she'd had no prep-
aration after all. No premonition. At the time of their birthday
she'd been thinking obsessively of Sharon, awaiting a call, or
even a visit—but nothing. The nightmares had subsided, or
she'd grown accustomed to them; absorbed them with such
stoic determination they were forgotten by daylight. If, as it's
popularly thought, twins have the psychic power to send each
other messages, Sharon had sent her none.

The sisters stumbled together to embrace. If for a fraction
of a second each had held back stricken, shy, not knowing if the
other loved her, now they hurried together with such urgency
that Deedee, a witness, was deeply embarrassed. Her mom she
could understand getting all teary and sentimental, that was
what you'd expect from Lily, but Aunt Sharon who was so
glamorous, sophisticated! In the taxi Aunt Sharon had told
Deedee a little of her professional career in Miami and Los
Angeles and Deedee had been impressed, a bit dazzled. But
now both women were crying; crying messily, as people really
do and not as they pretend on TV or in movies. The waxy-
white lilies Lily was holding slipped from her fingers and fell
onto the floor, so Deedee, grateful for an excuse to get away,
deftly retrieved them and hurried to the kitchen for a vase: one
of Mom's slender clay vases, perfect for long-stemmed lilies.

She was thrilled, enraptured. So this was her mother's "twin
sister" Sharon! The most fantastic aunt, ever.

There were Sharon's several suitcases, an overnight bag and a
heavy, bulky leather shoulder bag, carried by the taxi driver into
the front hall. Quickly Sharon explained that she meant to stay
in a hotel, or a motel; of course Lily protested, for Sharon must
stay with them—"We have plenty of room, Sharon! I wouldn't
hear of you staying anywhere else."

Sharon said, apologetically, "I know—I should have called
before coming. But—I guess I was afraid."

"Afraid?"

"You wouldn't want me."

"Oh, Sharon!" Lily was hurt. "What a thing to say."

"I mean—your husband might not want me. You have your own life, your family—there wouldn't be room for me."

An air of childlike self-pity, so at odds with Sharon's glamor and poise! Lily seized her sister's hands—cold, thin hands—and squeezed them, protesting, "Of course there's room for you! How long can you stay?"

"Just a few days. Until Monday, I think."

"No longer? You've taken time off from work?"

"Yes, I mean no—I mean, I'm on leave. I'm a dance instructor at a school in Pasadena, but our spring session doesn't begin for—a while." Sharon spoke carefully, wetting her lips in an odd compulsive manner.

"Dance instructor! Pasadena! That sounds very interesting, Sharon, why didn't you let me know?"

"But I did, I'm sure," Sharon said, staring at Lily. "I called you, I told you. Or I sent a card."

In the kitchen, Deedee was preparing a quick tea. She saw with relief that her mom and her aunt had stopped crying, at least for now; Sharon had carefully dabbed at her eyes, preserving most of her mascara. Strange that, if you took into account Sharon's two-inch heels, she and Lily were about the same height, approximately five feet eight; Sharon naturally appeared so much taller than Lily—so much more poised, intimidating. Lily was the kind of woman you saw but didn't *see*—just sort of took for granted.

How elegantly thin Sharon was: though removing her quilted black satin jacket reluctantly, knowing Lily would be mildly shocked, disapproving of her thinness. "Oh, Sharon, are you— well? You haven't been ill, have you?" Lily asked, and Sharon said quickly, "No, no, I'm fine," sitting at the kitchen table, fumbling through her shoulder bag for something she couldn't seem to find, "—but if you had some aspirin, or painkiller—"

So Deedee went to fetch some Tylenol, and Lily offered her sister tea, coffee, fruit juice, diet soda, and Sharon took coffee, black coffee, though saying, laughingly, she wouldn't mind something a little stronger: wine, maybe? So Lily said, "Of course! What am I thinking of, this *is* a special occasion." And took a bottle of red Italian wine from a cupboard, a very good wine, so far as Lily knew, and poured Sharon and herself two quite full glasses, and Deedee said with a playful pout, "Mom, what about *me*? I'm here, too." So Deedee was given a small amount of wine, and she and her mother and her aunt raised their glasses ceremoniously, and drank. And Lily said, smiling, though with an edge to her voice, "But why did you go to Deedee's school first, Sharon? Why didn't you just come here?"

It was an odd question, Deedee thought. Or maybe it was Lily's way of asking.

Sharon said, vaguely, "I—wasn't sure what the address was."

Deedee said, "Aunt Sharon recognized me right away! Didn't you, Aunt Sharon?"

So they talked for a while of that; of the meeting at the school; Deedee in such a thrilled, extravagant manner it was clear that the story would be told, and told, and told; for it had been, after all, very like something in a movie. Lily said she'd sent Sharon snapshots of Deedee over the years, and Sharon said yes of course, but not recently—"I'd have recognized Deirdre, anyway. Anywhere. I'm sure."

Deedee said warmly, "I'd have recognized *you*, Aunt Sharon. Mom has all your photos and things in an album, I've looked through it lots of times."

"Really! How sweet."

Lily was smiling her small fixed smile. The wineglass trembled in her fingers.

Lots of times? But why?

Sharon said, as if to placate Lily without seeming to do so (for to seem to placate Lily would be to indicate that Lily re-

quired placating), "—I just wasn't absolutely sure of the address.
I didn't want to arrive at the wrong house. But I should have
telephoned first, I'm so sorry." She was fumbling again in the
shoulder bag, searching for cigarettes perhaps. The shoulder bag
was made of a beautiful soft leather, russet-red; obviously very
expensive, though much the worse for wear. Lily saw without
meaning to stare that Sharon was wearing expensive-appearing
jewelry, several rings including a large blue gem on her left
hand, a sapphire?—and a platinum wristwatch that slid about
on her thin wrist like a bracelet. Her throat was lined, more
visibly than Lily's, and so she'd tied a black-and-gold silk scarf
about it; a tiny label showed—Yves Saint Laurent. In the whorl
of one ear there gleamed a cruel-looking silver clamp and
around Sharon's neck there was a conspicuous gold chain, glittering like scales. Her platinum-blond hair had been skinned
back so starkly from her face that the shape of her skull was
evident; the hair was surprisingly thin, and did not have a
healthy lustre. Lily felt a stab of apprehension for her sister, and
for herself. *Was* Sharon ill? It would do no good to inquire
directly; if you wanted to know any fact from Sharon, you
would only learn it indirectly if at all. You would probably
never learn it from Sharon herself.

Sipping wine, Sharon explained how she'd been traveling—
traveling for weeks—and had mislaid Lily's exact address; in
fact, she'd blanked out on Lily's married name—"I mean, I
know it of course; but I know so many names, they crowd one
another out of my head." She and her dance troupe had been
touring on the West Coast, most recently in Seattle, and had
had quite a success; though, ironically, it looked as if the group
was fated to break up—"We have so many competing careers.
Our agents are at one another's throats." Still, Sharon was smiling as she spoke; baring her perfect teeth in a smile of childlike
hope, expectancy, yearning; the dazzling spotlit smile of "I'm
Always Chasing Rainbows"; a smile calculated to melt the

hardest of hearts, the most skeptical of judges. *Here I am! Don't send me away! I've come to you helpless.*

Lily had all she could do to keep from suddenly gripping her sister's hands, and hugging her again. Here was Sharon, returned to her! So unexpectedly.

Lily dreaded the moment when they would speak of their father. And of the Shaheen property. She hoped Deedee wouldn't be present, or Wes. She hoped she wouldn't break down into wracking sobs.

Lily poured Sharon a second glass of wine, for Sharon had finished her first quickly, swallowing down two of the painkiller pills; she was hoping, she said, to ward off a headache. Lily asked if Sharon would like to lie down, take a nap before dinner?—and Sharon said at once, no, she was fine; she'd flown into Buffalo the evening before, a long flight from Seattle, and had taken a Greyhound bus to Yewville today, wasn't accustomed to bus travel any longer, the sort of Americans you meet, how *real* America is from the perspective of ground travel; but she was fine, fine. " 'Starr Bright' sees America via Greyhound!" Sharon said, laughing, raising her wineglass to click against Lily's, and Lily laughed, too, but was puzzled—" 'Starr Bright'?—why do you say that?" And Sharon, searching again in her shoulder bag, ignored the question, or hadn't heard; she was saying, chiding, "Lily, you should have warned me how changed everything is! The bus trip to Yewville was like a dream, one of those nightmares where things are familiar but changed, distorted. So much of the countryside is gone, the farmland! So many new houses, shopping centers—the highway is four lanes wide—the new bridge at Edgarsville—Fairfield Park still looks the same. Yewville is a real city now, almost, isn't it?—like any other city in the U.S. The identical McDonald's, Wendy's, a Holiday Inn—gas stations, car dealers. The high school looks so different, I finally figured out it has a new facade, and an addition at the rear. And the old train depot—a restaurant! If the First Church of Christ is changed, too, or van-

ished, Lily, please don't tell me just yet, *I don't want to know.*"
Sharon was smiling at Lily and Deedee, that dazzling forced
smile; making a joke of her own agitation. "And, coming into
town, everywhere I looked I saw names I knew, on billboards,
signs—'Reigel Plumbing'—'Hendrickson's Fruit & Produce'—
'Dwyer's Fence City.' All our old classmates, grown up."

Carefully Lily said, "It isn't Michael Dwyer—Mack—who
owns Fence City, it's his brother Steve. His younger brother."

" 'Michael'—?"

"That's what he seems to be called, now. Michael. He
works for the mayor, heads one of the municipal departments.
A few years ago he ran for state senator on the Republican
ticket but lost—by a narrow margin." Lily paused, awkwardly.
She'd never known why Sharon and Mack Dwyer had broken
up and had never dared to inquire and now after more than
two decades she would not have been able to surmise, seeing
her sister's composed, slightly ironic expression. "It's Steve I
know, from PTA. Michael Dwyer I don't know at all."

Sharon said evenly, "He'd be married, of course. With a
family." When Lily vaguely nodded, Sharon said, laughing,
"Everyone is married in Yewville! Of course."

"Well, some are divorced. Among our classmates. It seems
to be going rapidly past us—life."

"Past some of us," Sharon said, sighing, "more rapidly than
others."

Now she will speak of Father's death, Lily thought.

Instead, Sharon said brightly, "But *you're* happily married,
Lily. And with a *daughter.*"

Lily laughed, embarrassed; felt her cheeks burn, not altogether pleasantly; not knowing if Sharon was patronizing her?
teasing? With such an elegant person, sincerity could seem artificial. Yet Sharon seemed sincere enough, inquiring after
Wesley, whom she'd never met, listening as Deedee proudly
explained her father's work, building houses and restoring older

houses like the one in which they lived; Sharon said, smiling at Deedee, "*You* must be proud. D'you take after your father?"

Deedee glanced at Lily, and said, shyly, as if she'd only now just recalled, "Daddy's my stepdad. Actually."

"Oh. Yes. Of course."

There was a pause. Lily felt her temples throb. Her elation at Sharon's appearance was effervescent, like gassy bubbles that, burst, released a sickish aroma. *I am in danger* Lily thought.

But Sharon was smiling, and sipping her wine—"This is delicious, Lily. May I have a little more?" And talking of Yewville, and the neighborhood in which Lily lived; and of old classmates whom she hoped to telephone, perhaps even visit; if she had time. She was going to stay for only a few days, she was en route to New York to meet with her new agent. She'd begun to search again, more purposefully, in her shoulder bag; and Lily prepared herself to object, politely but firmly, if she brought out a pack of cigarettes. *Excuse me, Sharon, do you mind not smoking in the house?* Sharon had begun smoking as a young teenager, a secret from their parents of course; a secret in which Lily had been a reluctant accomplice. In emulation of her precocious sister Lily had tried smoking, and had hated it. "Here! Lily, Deirdre—for you," Sharon said gaily, bringing out of the bag two gaily wrapped packages, gifts for Lily and Deedee.

Deedee, with girlish pleasure, opened hers: it was an exquisite necklace of emerald-green glass beads, turquoise stones and filmy speckled-golden feathers on silver links. "A Navajo keepsake," Sharon said. "Isn't it beautiful?"

"Oh *yes*."

Lily's gift was a heavy silver bracelet inset with turquoise stones. She slid it on: how inappropriate it looked on her wrist, glittering, regal. "I picked them up in Santa Fe," Sharon said, "on my way to"—laughing suddenly as if the very whimsicality of her words struck her—"wherever. *Here*."

Deedee thanked her aunt Sharon profusely, and, except for

shyness, would have hugged and kissed her. Lily thanked Sharon, and did kiss her sister's dry, heated cheek.

I should call Wes Lily thought. *To prepare him.*

Deedee stood at a wall mirror trying clumsily to fasten the necklace around her neck; the silver links, and then the feathers, caught in her thick springy hair. Sharon leapt up to help her with surprising energy. "Like this, Deirdre. Lovely!"

"Thanks, Aunt Sharon. Wow."

Deedee regarded herself with pleasure in the mirror, turning her head from side to side. The unusual necklace, silver, emerald-green, turquoise and fine, floating feathers, gave to her plain features a look of the exotic. Sharon stood close behind her, several inches taller than the girl, gazing intensely, almost greedily into the mirror. Her thin, beringed fingers rested on Deedee's shoulders. Lily expected Sharon to lower her chin to rest it playfully on Deedee's shoulder as she'd done years ago when they were girls together, with Lily.

We can't ever be lonely like other people.

We have each other.

Sharon said excitedly, "Lovely, isn't it? Lily, look: it brings out the greenish-blue in Deirdre's eyes."

Lily called Wes several times at his office, finally connected with him by way of the phone in his pickup truck as he was driving somewhere north of Yewville. The connection was poor, and Lily had to raise her voice, which was quavering with excitement, a strange wild elation. "Wes? My sister is here. My sister Sharon. She just arrived, she'll be staying a few days—" Wes said genially, as if from a long distance, "Well, honey, that's a surprise, but of course she's your sister—she's welcome." There was a pause, Lily could envision Wes creasing his forehead, rubbing fiercely at his nose. "As long as she wants to stay. Fine."

Lily felt immense relief. Lightly she said, "Wes, you don't need to say *that*," and Wes laughed, and said, "I was just hoping to impress you."

*   *   *

"Oh, Lily. It's lovely."

The lavender-and-cream guest room on the first floor, rear, had windows overlooking a side lawn of shrubs, evergreens and oaks; its own private door to the outside; a spacious closet and adjoining bathroom with gleaming fixtures and tile and a shower curtain smelling of newness. Lily realized, flushed with pleasure, helping Sharon hang some of her clothes in the closet, that she'd decorated this room with Sharon in mind. Unconsciously waiting for Sharon to come, to stay in this room.

Deedee had helped her pick out the floral cotton-and-silk bedspread in a vivid lilac print; matching pillows, curtains; the Laura Ashley wallpaper; the rich purple wall-to-wall carpeting that, though a bargain at a local rug store owned by a friend of Wes's, looked wonderfully luxuriant, expensive. Deedee had said it was a room for Princess Di.

You see, Sharon? For you.

Sharon said, her eyes widened, in a voice of utter sincerity, "Lily, how lucky you are! And how lucky I am, to be here."

Impulsively, Sharon gripped Lily's hands and squeezed them. A pang of happiness ran through Lily like an electric current. Lily recalled how, when they were girls, in high school especially when she'd feared she was losing her sister, Sharon would sometimes grip and squeeze her hands like this, in an ecstasy of emotion; confiding how someone, invariably an older boy, had spoken to her that day, or taken her for a ride in his car. How flattered Lily had been, singled out by Sharon's attention, which was like a dazzling blinding light.

Lily admitted, awkwardly, "I've been missing you so much, Sharon. I was hoping, in February—at the time of our birthday—"

Sharon was shaking wrinkles out of a glamorous silver lamé tunic, unless it was a minidress. Distracted, she said, "Oh, yes— our birthday. Actually, I was in Hawaii at the time, trying to get a little rest between engagements. I've told you about my friend James Fenke?—who owns a cable station in Pasadena?—he has a lovely house in Honolulu, on the water. A pink sandstone mansion. And such clean white *sand*."

Lily didn't believe she'd been told about James Fenke; but she murmured yes, to be agreeable.

"In Hawaii, you lose track of calendar time. Maybe there isn't even such a thing as time. So, if we had a birthday, I'm afraid I wasn't aware of it."

Lily laughed uneasily. "That's the wisest course, I'm sure."

Trying not to think *But why are you here, Sharon? Why now? After fifteen years, and more, of staying away. What motive?*

The last time Sharon had come home, to Shaheen, she'd been desperate. Suicidal. Eight months, three weeks pregnant.

As if reading Lily's mind Sharon said, in a neutral voice, "She—Deirdre—'Deedee,' you call her—is so"—her eyelids fluttered as if she were searching for the ideal, the perfect word, but could come up only with "—sweet."

"Oh yes, Deedee is. Except sometimes, on the surface, just slightly sarcastic."

"But intelligent, too. Like you. And so—grown up."

"Sometimes!"

Lily laughed. It was a mother's prerogative, to be affectionately critical of her child.

"She seems very—happy."

"Deedee is an American teenager, a sophomore in high school. She isn't happy twenty-four hours a day," Lily said reprovingly, sensibly. "But she's happy in her soul, I think. She's happy with Wes and me."

"God, yes. I can see that."

Sharon shuddered, as if the prospect of Deedee in another life had passed rapidly through her mind.

Lily was hanging up a pair of silky slacks, champagne-colored. There was a stain as of nail polish in the fabric but she hesitated to point it out to her sister. She said, instead, groping, almost shyly, "We all made the right decision."

"Yes."

"With each passing year, it seems more certain."

"Oh, yes."

"And it was—wasn't—so difficult after all. Deedee's birth certificate with my name on it—the doctor never doubted, you were me. I mean—I was you. He'd only seen us a few times, he wouldn't have guessed."

Sharon said slowly, as if the words gave her pain, "Because, yes—*we are twins.*"

"And no one had seen either of us for weeks. At the camp-grounds in the mountains. And people had thought I was living in Buffalo, going to school there—a place a girl could get 'in trouble' in." Lily paused, breathing quickly. She felt almost faint. "And Wes—has never asked questions. A girl can make a 'mistake,' plenty of guys make mistakes Wes says. I don't be-lieve I have actually lied to him, I believe that in some way he *knows*; I mean, he knows the truth of my love for Deedee. And he's a man who lives in the present, rejoices in the present. He loves Deedee as much as he would if she were his own child."

"Well," said Sharon, sniffing, "—*that,* you don't know. No one, not even the man, would know."

"*I* love her so. Oh, Sharon!"

Lily's voice was pleading. She hadn't known she would speak in such a way, blinking panicked tears from her eyes.

Quickly Sharon said, "Don't worry, Lily! I haven't come back to—interfere. You must know that."

"It's just that I love her so—and she doesn't know."

"There's no reason for her to know. Her, or anyone. You kept your promise to *me.*"

"Of course I did, Sharon."

Sharon said slowly, again as if the words gave her pain, "*You*—are *me.* You bore the baby, and the sin."

Lily laughed. "Sin?"

"In the eyes of the world, I mean. Not in ours."

"An 'unwed mother' isn't such an object of scorn any longer, or even pity. There are some—Wes included—who seem even to admire us."

"Still, there was sin. A loveless copulation, selfish drugged-out people. Deserving the worst." Sharon shuddered, as if revolted.

Lily persisted, trying to smile. "*I* don't believe in sin any longer, Sharon. I don't think I ever did, really. Even Daddy—he was no theologian, but he had a way of calculating Jesus' message so, after the crucifixion and the resurrection, it was all 'good news.' But I do believe in forgiveness."

"So do I!" Sharon said with a shrill little laugh. "I hope my own sins will be forgiven."

No maternal instinct in me she'd said fiercely, almost proudly. *No more than a bitch who devours her own pups.*

Though it didn't appear to be completely empty, Sharon was roughly zipping up the larger of her suitcases; shoving it beneath the bed before Lily could come help her with it. Her other suitcase, made of a chic dark blue weatherproof fabric, contained, like the Gucci overnight bag, mostly silken undergarments, stockings and toiletries. Something had spilled in it, cologne, hair spray, cosmetics. A sweetish-stale odor emanated from it which (Lily gathered) Sharon herself couldn't smell.

Now Sharon did search for a pack of cigarettes, in the shoulder bag. Her hand shook visibly as she placed a long filter-tip cigarette between her lips and lit it. Belatedly asking, "Do you mind, Lily? I'm kind of—anxious."

"No! Of course not."

Sharon sat heavily on the edge of the bed, and crossed her legs. Long swordlike dancer's legs. She tried to smile at Lily as if, for an alarmed moment, she'd forgotten who Lily was; why they were here together; like lovers thrown together, passionate yet exhausted. The skin beneath her eyes was discolored, crepey; very like Lily's, when she was tired. Yet the black mascara, even slightly smeared, gave her a glamorous, exotic look. The pupils of her eyes were dilated as if she were feverish, or drugged.

Lily did not want to think *Of course: she's taking something.*

Lily did not want to think *How many years has it been since my sister has not been taking something?*

Sharon spoke in a low hurried voice as if fearful they might be overheard. Her old air of secrecy, urgency. "It all seems so long ago now, doesn't it, like something in a dream! Out there in the country—another lifetime. Remember how we prayed? On the bare floorboards, the four of us? Praying. And what came of it was right, I knew in my heart." She paused, exhaling smoke. "I was so strung out on amphetamines, even the pain might've been happening to another person. It *might* have been you, Lily."

The sisters laughed together, thinly, wildly.

Lily said, "That's how it seemed to me, too. It seemed almost logical. Daddy promised that God would bless us, Jesus would watch over us. Almost, that night, I felt Him—His presence."

"I did, too. I did."

"Though I don't believe, really. I mean—"

"Oh, but we don't *know.* Don't say you don't 'believe,' Lily—when you don't *know.*"

Lily said, firmly, "The only thing that mattered was that the baby should be born, and live; and be loved."

"Yes."

"There's a sense in which a baby, human life, doesn't 'belong' to any individuals, anyway. Biological mothers, or fathers. It's life that begets life."

"God begets life."

"I didn't matter, or you. Or Daddy or Momma. Just the baby. God's will."

" 'He hath led me, and brought me into darkness, but not into the night.' "

Lily was struck by the calm, clear, bell-like voice in which Sharon spoke these words, from—was it Lamentations? She, Lily, would not have remembered.

Lily said, "It might have been me, Sharon. Holding your hands, helping you give birth—those hours. So many times afterward I'd catch myself remembering *it had been me.*"

Sharon said, "You are her mother, not I; you, Lily, her rightful mother. That was God's will, He allowed us to know."

Lily felt compelled to say, for the sake of her own integrity, "I don't believe in the supernatural, in 'divine intervention' in human affairs. And yet—"

Sharon interrupted, "You do, Lily! You do believe! As Daddy and Momma taught us! When we were girls, you believed more than I did; you cried, remember how you cried, when Momma told us about the disciples betraying Jesus? And Jesus on the cross?—remember? That doesn't change. I thought it did, I thought I'd grown away from it, but God never changes. Even when we sin, Lily, even when we are cast low as swine, into the very belly of the beast—even then God *is*. His will be done. *You know that, Lily of the Valley.*"

The sisters stared at each other. Lily was so deeply moved, she could not trust herself to speak.

The gusty March afternoon had waned abruptly to dusk. Deedee was upstairs in her room, Wes hadn't yet come home. How strange this room in which they were together, a pretty feminine lavender-and-cream bedroom cozily lit—a bedside lamp casting a warm roseate glow onto the sisters' rapt faces. Sharon was smoking her cigarette in rapid puffs as if these mouthfuls of smoke were breath itself, pure oxygen. Lily was wiping at her eyes, smiling; about to burst into tears—she was so happy.

Yes. I know.

I am Alpha and Omega, the beginning and the end. The first and the last.

It had been more than fifteen years ago, in the late summer

of 1981, that Sharon, "Sherrill," had come home to the Donners, despairing and suicidal and sick with pregnancy. She'd
been abandoned, it seemed, by her lover in Mexico. She'd lost
her employment as a high-paid fashion model. She'd refused to
have an abortion for God had allowed her to know that abortion is murder. Yet, in Shaheen, hidden away in her parents'
house, she'd raved of drowning the baby "like a kitten" if it
was born; or stabbing the baby in her womb, the baby and
herself. She'd wanted to die, she'd wanted the baby to die with
her. Unless Lily would take the child as her own.

It could not be, yet so it was. So it came to pass.

For there was the holy power residing in Ephraim Donner:
the power of Jesus Christ to heal sickness, to cast out devils. On
their knees for ten hours praying, praying. Fasting, and praying.
*O Lord have mercy. Jesus, help us. Though we walk through the valley
of the shadow of death. Thy rod and Thy staff shall comfort us.* And
so Jesus had seemed to speak to them, to suggest the wisest
course. The sins of subterfuge and deceit in the eyes of mankind
were of little consequence set beside the terrible sins of infanti-
cide, suicide. For there had been no doubt among the Donners
that Sharon was capable of acts of violence against herself and
others. Had she not in her desperation slashed at the tender skin
of her forearm with a razor, deep enough to sever an artery?
Had she not raked her nails across her face, her breasts? Had she
not swallowed pills that made her heart race and leap, cause
sweat to ooze like oil from her pores? Had she not tried to
starve herself to deny the baby growing in her womb? Had she
not pinched her milk-heavy breasts? Raving *I am filth, undeserv-
ing of life. Take my baby from me and give her to God.*

It could not be, yet it was. So it had come to pass.

Sharon said, as if she'd been unconsciously reading Lily's
thoughts, "Yes. You did that for me. You, Daddy and Momma
—saving my life, which probably wasn't worth saving, and the
baby's. And how did I repay you?"

Lily lowered her gaze as if to indicate she didn't know.

Sharon said sharply, "They didn't tell you?"

"I'm not sure."

"I stole their money, what little they had. Before I left without saying goodbye. Oh, Lily—it was only sixty-five dollars. Momma had maybe been saving it for years, in a bureau drawer. I would have stolen church funds except I couldn't get into the church office." Sharon had begun to cry almost without expression, her bluish-gray eyes glittering like glass. Yet she continued to smoke, sucking at her cigarette as if it were life to her.

Lily came near to choking, smoke stinging her eyes. "Oh, Sharon—you couldn't help yourself, you were sick. You weren't yourself, really!"

Sharon said, "That's so, Lily. It was as if *you* were somehow *me*; while I was—I don't know who. In Mexico, I was so God-damned naive! In New York I could handle the glamor, the men—the attention; at least, I thought I could, though I'd gotten started with drugs there, mainly to fight exhaustion. And starvation! But I was being exploited all along, and it became obvious on the Mexico shoot. And then—that son of a bitch who 'fell in love with me'—talked me into quitting my job, traveling with him. He was 'an independent film producer'— 'an associate of Bertolucci's'—'a friend of Dustin Hoffman's'— saying he was crazy about me, my face, my style; he wanted to marry me, finance films for me; I was going to be 'a new Grace Kelly'—he said."

Lily reached out to touch Sharon's hand, to clasp her icy fingers.

"Well. You couldn't have known."

Sharon said, with surprising fury, "It might have been so!— that's the irony. How do any movie actresses—Julia Roberts, Sharon Stone—Meryl Streep—get started, except by meeting someone who can help them? Someone with connections, with power? In fact he'd been involved in distributing a Bertolucci film in the U.S. He may even have known Dustin Hoffman.

And I did look like 'a new Grace Kelly' if I was made up in that style. *I could be made to look like anyone!*" Sharon paused, smoking, brooding. Lily saw a vein throbbing in her left temple. "If only I'd had a better agent, someone who'd protected my rights, gave a damn about my future instead of simply raking in twenty percent off the top of my earnings. Oh, Lily, I know I was naive, I was selfish, and stupid, and getting pregnant—I must have been drunk at the time, or stoned out of my head. Yet—it might have been so, everything that bastard promised. *Everything might have happened as it was promised, like a fairy tale.*"

Except, Lily thought, Deedee would not have been born.

Of course, Lily didn't say this. She was comforting her angry weeping sister as if she, and not Sharon, were the "elder." Lily of the Valley at whom no one ever glanced twice in the radiant presence of Rose of Sharon.

Sharon flinched in self-disgust, as if, another time, she'd been hearing, or sensing, Lily's thoughts. "Oh, Christ," she said, "listen to me. Always me, me, me! Blinded by vanity like that peroxide-blond 'Starr Bright' in her pancake makeup and false eyelashes and girdle! That old hag! And here I am, your sister 'Sherrill'—thirty-seven years old and ignorant as a country girl of thirteen."

"Sharon, you're too hard on yourself. You've always—"

"Does your husband know I'm here? Does he want me here?"

"Of course, Wes wants you. He's looking forward to meeting you at last."

"You called him, did you? Just now?"

"Yes."

Sharon was looking searchingly at Lily as if trying to determine what she really meant. She said, with a wan smile, "Well, I'll know within a few minutes. If he doesn't want me. And if so, I promise I'll leave, tomorrow. I would never come between you and your family, I promise."

Of course you won't, how could you?

Sharon had removed her tight-fitting leather boots, and was pacing about the room in her stocking feet, smoking, flicking ashes onto the deep-purple carpet. Unobtrusively, not wanting to seem fussy, Lily set one of her sculpted clay bowls on the bedside table, for her sister to use as an ashtray. Sharon had reverted to their previous subject and was lamenting, "Oh, Lily, how could I have stayed away, when Daddy died? And then the funeral—I was coming to the funeral, I *was* coming, but—my life became too complicated, somehow. I got sick, or—I had surgery. And it was too late."

Lily had once or twice inquired what the nature of Sharon's surgery had been, but Sharon's reply had been vague; she didn't think it prudent to inquire again. She said, consolingly, "I know, Sharon. It's all right."

"Did Daddy say anything about me—at the end?"

"Of course."

"Or had he forgotten me? Erased me from his memory?"

"You know better, Sharon. Daddy always loved you."

"But could he—forgive me? Stealing from him and Momma like that—"

"Sharon, you know what Daddy and Momma were like. They didn't need to 'forgive'—they loved you."

"But they loved you better—they must have. After what I did."

Sharon was watching Lily closely, anxiously. Lily felt her face burn with an emotion she could not have named.

Of course they loved me better, I was the daughter who loved them. I was the daughter who behaved like a daughter to them. I was the mother of their only grandchild. What could you expect, that they could love you more?

But Lily only repeated, quietly, what had been true enough: "They always loved you, Sharon. It wasn't their way to compare us."

Sharon said, aggrieved, "Oh, I loved *them*! I just didn't have a chance to show it, as you did. I went out into the world, I didn't stay close to home, like you."

Sharon paused to light another cigarette, shaking out the match and tossing it onto the bedside table—not quite into the clay bowl. Unobtrusively, Lily put the match into the bowl, and handed it to Sharon to use. She said, "You've never asked about how Daddy died. You know it was cancer of the liver? But, at the end, it wasn't so bad actually. He was semiconscious much of the time, didn't seem to be in pain; kept drugged, I suppose. Wes had arranged for him to have a private room at Yewville General and we visited him every day, I was there through much of the day, for weeks, we talked, we even sang sometimes, you know how Daddy loved those old hymns. It was like Momma was in the room with us, we talked to her, too, sometimes. Daddy was a good man, Sharon; I know people would describe him as simple, a simple unquestioning Christian; but I always thought he was a good man in his heart, naturally; like Momma, too; their religion didn't make them 'good,' they made their religion 'good.' You know, Daddy was unusual as a preacher in that he didn't give much credence to 'evil.' Never preached much about the devil or hell. I think that people like him and Momma die more easily than others—I mean, people without bitterness or fear. They live more easily. So, when you didn't come to see him, Sharon, of course Daddy was disappointed, but he didn't stop loving you. He didn't judge you at all. He always thought of Deedee as your gift to— the world. He always had more faith in us, I think, than we could have in ourselves."

Lily was speaking quickly, pleadingly; never had she spoken at such length to her sister; but Sharon, pacing about, smoking her cigarette and giving off a hectic, perfumy heat, hadn't been listening closely. Strands of dry, ashy hair had escaped from her chignon; creases bracketed her mouth. She said, "God, I despise myself for not coming back in time! And now Daddy is gone forever. And Momma. *I loved them so.*" Tears flashed in her eyes, glittering like the gold chain around her neck, and the cruel silver clamp in her ear. "It's just—my life is so complicated. Not like yours, Lily: I envy you! *I* had to take my chances when they came. You can't let personal life get in the way. It's like a—cruise ship casting off, and you're in danger of being left behind. A minute too late and you're on the dock staring after. Oh, Lily, you can't know how easy it is *not to exist.*" Sharon spoke excitedly, bitterly. Yet glancing at Lily to see how Lily was affected. She said, "Now God has run me to earth, Lily. I'm burnt out, exhausted. But God has His plans for me, He has determined not to allow me to rest but to make of 'Starr Bright' a scourge of sin, evil—emissaries of Satan. To repay Him for my wickedness when I was young."

Lily was perplexed, troubled. There was something in her sister's vehement words that struck her. "What do you mean, 'Starr Bright'? Why do you speak of her?"

Sharon frowned, and stared into a corner of the room as if into the distance.

"Did I say 'Starr Bright'? I didn't."

" 'To make of myself a scourge of sin, emissaries of Satan'—? How? I don't understand."

Sharon changed the subject abruptly. She said, smiling sadly, "I used to be so *young*, Lily! Both of us—so *young*! Remember, you played the organ, and I sang at the front of the church and everyone stared at me, I was an 'angel' in their eyes. I could see myself in your eyes—all of you. Remember—" And Sharon began suddenly to sing, turning her eyes upward in a gesture of innocence too unstudied to be mocking or ironic, these familiar words:

> "Rock of Ages, cleft for me!
> Let me hide myself in Thee!
> Let the water and the blood
> That from Thy wounded side doth flow . . ."

Her voice trailed off, husky and cracked as if it had been unused for years. Lily was shocked at her sister's coarsened voice. *Why, she can't be a singer any longer. Her voice is gone.*

Sharon said, as if reading Lily's thoughts, "Lily, I'm run to earth. That's why I've come to you. God has run me to earth." Lily stood, and gripped Sharon by the shoulders. In her stocking feet, Sharon was Lily's height exactly. Yet how frail, how defeated she looked; how tired, ravaged; hiding her face in her hands. Lily said gently, "You can stay with me, Sharon. You can rest. You do seem tired—exhausted. You're welcome here, as long as you want."

"It isn't just that," Sharon said, shivering, "—but—also—someone is after me. Stalking me."

"Someone is after you—? My God, Sharon, who?"

"He won't find me here with you, maybe. He thinks I'm a thousand miles away."

"But—who is it?"

Sharon shrugged weakly, as if it would do no good to name the man; as if his presence were ubiquitous, yet invisible. She lowered her voice. "A man. Death."

Lily said, frightened, "But—what do you mean? 'Death'?"

In a faint childlike voice Sharon said almost inaudibly, "Lily, you're all I have left in the world. Don't turn me away."

"Sharon! Of course not."

Lily embraced Sharon, hard. Her heart was pounding with certainty, elation. She held her weeping sister thinking *Yes, you're safe with me, I am strong enough, I will show you.*

4

"Starr Bright"

Not on the first evening of her visit but on the second, when she was feeling stronger, Sharon joined the Merricks for dinner.

When Lily returned home that day from a hurried afternoon of appointments, with groceries for the evening meal, there, to her surprise, was her sister in the kitchen. Smiling nervously at her, almost shyly.

As if she feared trespassing in Lily's territory, Sharon said, hesitantly, "Lily, remember that 'Mexican' chicken casserole Momma used to make? I saw you have some canned tomatoes in the cupboard, and rice, and chili powder—" Lily laughed, setting her bag of groceries on the counter. "And here's the chicken, and lots of other things. Let's get started."

It was as Lily had hoped but not as she'd expected.

My sister, visiting for a few days. Yes, we have so much to catch up on. Yes, we've always been very close.

Lily saw that, without makeup, Sharon's face was startlingly pale and sallow. But the deep shadows beneath her eyes were less conspicuous; she'd been able, she said gratefully, to sleep through much of the night—"Such wonderful quiet here!" Her eyes were quick-darting and still finely netted with blood; enormous in her thin face. She wore casual clothes: a black jersey blouse, a red silk scarf tied tightly about her hair, slacks

129

of some oddly shimmering silvery-beige fabric. In flat-heeled sandals, working in the familiar space of Lily's kitchen, Sharon looked both sophisticated and almost ordinary.

All that morning and afternoon Lily had been thinking of what Sharon had told her the previous evening. *Someone is after me. Stalking me. A man. Death.* She felt a sensation of dread, perplexity. Each time she'd tried to bring up the subject again, Sharon had managed to deflect it.

And now Deedee was with them, a cheery, enlivening presence.

Rare, Lily thought, bemused, for Deedee to be so enthusiastic about working in the kitchen, helping prepare a meal. Yet today, Deedee had volunteered to make dessert. She plied her aunt Sharon with questions—"I suppose you eat in restaurants all the time? When you're dancing?"—"Do people bother you, asking for autographs after a performance?"—"What do you think about when you dance, or is your mind filled just with the music?"

Deedee's aunt Sharon was circumspect in replying. As if, here in Yewville, her other life was distant to her, not very real.

In turn, Sharon drew Deedee out with questions about her life. Lily was surprised that Deedee answered so freely, and with such unexpected idealism. She told Sharon things she'd never told her parents: her hope of "traveling around the world someday, and keeping a photographic journal"—"making a contribution to society"—"writing poetry." It was touching to see how, in her glamorous aunt's presence, Deedee was so positive, vibrant, hopeful.

Proudly Deedee reported that her classmates had been asking about "the blond woman in the taxi who looked like a model or an actress"—but she hadn't identified Sharon except to say that Sharon was a friend of her mother's visiting for a few days. That was all.

Sharon leaned over to kiss Deedee's cheek, in gratitude. "Thank you, Deirdre. How thoughtful of you."

Sharon had made Lily, too, promise not to tell anyone she was back. In a day or two, Sharon said, she might telephone some old friends, relatives . . . or maybe not.

Of course Lily had agreed. She would have agreed to virtually anything Sharon requested, to please her, to allay her fears. Always there was something satisfying, even exciting, about a secret with someone both strong-willed and helpless-seeming like Sharon.

Even when you didn't quite know what the secret was, or might mean. What unknown obligations it might put you under.

The evening before, Sharon had been too exhausted, she'd said, even to meet Wes. She hadn't had any appetite for food but wanted only to soak in a hot bath, and go to bed early.

Well, maybe she'd have just a little to eat, if Lily didn't mind bringing her some fruit, cheese, bread. (Lily didn't of course.) And the rest of the wine they'd opened?

When Wes had come home, bringing a bouquet of long-stemmed white and red roses, he'd been surprised and disappointed to hear that his sister-in-law wasn't going to have dinner with them that night. "Is she sick?" he asked.

Lily bridled at the word "sick." It seemed somehow too blunt, vulgar; it could not suggest Sharon's fragile emotional and psychological state. "Not 'sick,' Wes," Lily said reprovingly. "Spiritually exhausted, I think."

Deedee explained that her aunt had traveled a long distance—from Seattle to Buffalo by plane, from Buffalo to Yewville by bus.

"Strange," Wes said, "she didn't call first. To let us know."

Wes was right, of course; yet Lily rather resented him passing judgment on her sister, about whom he knew nothing. That Sharon was desperate, fearing for her life—had no one to turn to, except Lily.

Run to earth. God has run me to earth.

Stalking me. A man. Death.

No, Lily wouldn't confide in Wes, about Sharon's secret. Until such time, if ever, that Sharon gave her permission. It would be their secret, among others of old.

Rose of Sharon, Lily of the Valley.

⋆ ⋆ ⋆

They were to have dinner in the dining room, by candle-light. A ceremonial occasion after all. Lily felt exhilarated as a young girl thinking *I miss a larger family, I have love enough for—more.*

When Lily introduced them, Wes and Sharon shook hands formally, rather shyly. Clearly, Wes was surprised at the woman he was meeting: judging by the glossy "Sherrill" photos he'd seen, and what he'd heard of Sharon over the years, he'd expected a glamorous, hard-edged person, and here was Sharon in her subdued, deferential, intensely feminine mode—her pale blond hair in a sleek chignon at the nape of her lovely neck, her clothes dark, sophisticated but conservative; a single gold chain glittering around her neck; small gold studs in her ears. Her face was pale, without makeup except for a light coral lipstick that gave her a youthful, vulnerable look, at least by candlelight.

His face flushed, Wes told Sharon how good it was to meet her, at last—"I've been hearing lots of things about you." And Sharon said, warmly, "And I've been hearing, from Lily and Deedee, lots of things, very nice things, about you, Wes."

A perfect answer. In Sharon's throaty, sexy voice. His name intimate as a caress: "Wes."

Sharon presented Wes with a gift, a small box wrapped in bright tinselly paper. Self-consciously Wes opened it to discover, of all things—cuff links. Lily hoped that neither Wes nor Deedee would make an awkward joke about the fact that Wes Merrick had never owned a shirt with French cuffs in his life, but Wes managed to thank Sharon sincerely enough. As if no other gift would have pleased him quite as much.

The cuff links were platinum gold with matching pearls on one side and the engraved initials *W M* on the other. Wes said, "'W M'—that's me, I guess," and Sharon said, "I hope you like them, Wes. I had them especially engraved for you."

An odd remark, Lily would recall afterward. But so many of Sharon's remarks were odd.

Lily was more troubled that the cuff links were so expensive a gift: did her sister really have that kind of money? Many of her things, Lily couldn't help but notice, were worn, frayed, even stained—though of high quality. And there was some ambiguity, about which Lily hadn't wished to question her, about exactly where Sharon was living.

Dinner went well, at least initially. The Mexican chicken was declared a great success. (Though Lily noticed that Sharon managed to eat only a portion of her serving.) Deedee took part in the adults' conversation in a manner that made Lily proud of her; and she looked transformed—her hair neatly brushed; fingernails cleaned and filed; wearing not her usual shapeless jeans, but a wool skirt and a white turtleneck sweater, and the striking Navajo necklace Sharon had given her. (Which Wes admired, too.) In emulation of Sharon's model posture, Deedee was even making an effort not to slouch as she usually did, sullenly self-conscious of her breasts; she smiled, not scowled, when Lily asked her how school had been that day. And Wes, though unaccustomed to guests at dinner, as to strangers in his household, was warm and engaged and welcoming to his mysterious sister-in-law.

Of course, Sharon was deftly flattering, subtle in her seductiveness. Lily had to admire her, though they were such very different people.

Fixing him with her somber eyes, Sharon said, "Tell me about your work, Wes. Your houses. It must be magical, building houses for people to *live in*."

Wes laughed, embarrassed. "It's magical when people pay me on time. *That* I appreciate."

Sharon said, leaning forward earnestly, "Yes, but you are doing something *real* in the world. Your work isn't just an idea—or shares in the stock market or—a performance. 'All flesh is grass, and the goodliness thereof.' But a house is real and human beings are affected by it and you are contributing to human happiness, Wes, and that's why I believe it's *magical*."

No one spoke like this in Yewville: nor in such a throaty, dramatic manner. Wes and Deedee gaped at Sharon, charmed. Lily smiled, thinking she hadn't heard Sharon speak like this since the evening of the Starr Bright Youth Talent Search 1972 when, before singing, Rose of Sharon Donner had introduced herself to the audience, utterly captivating them with her sweet Christian-girl idealism.

Wes was encouraged to talk about his work, his favorites among the area houses he'd been hired to restore; his ambitious plans for the future. Lily learned a few things she hadn't known and Deedee, eager to be included in the conversation, said, with childlike enthusiasm, "Aunt Sharon, we can take a tour of Daddy's houses while you're here. There must be twenty really nice ones in town. And some new houses, too, on the River Road."

Wes said, dryly, "The money's in new houses, I'm afraid, not restorations. And in government contracts—which are out of my league."

Sharon sympathized. It must be so unpredictable, frustrating, to be in the construction business—"You never know how the economy might change." A Miami friend of hers, she said, had made millions of dollars building condominiums in the real estate boom in the 1980's—at least $100 million—and then, virtually overnight, the condos stopped selling, there was a glut on the market and even today many buildings are partially empty. "Last I heard, he had to declare bankruptcy."

There was a moment's startled silence. Deedee shifted in her chair and murmured, "Wow! One hundred million dollars." Wes laughed wryly, pouring more wine into Sharon's and his emptied glasses. "*That's* out of Merrick, Inc.'s league, for sure."

Lily said quickly, to deflect the subject from such daunting sums of money, "I don't really understand it but, in construction and real estate, doesn't everything depend upon the interest rate? When it's low, business is good; when it's high—"

Wes said, trying to be affable and not bitter-sounding, "You're screwed."

Deedee giggled reprovingly. "Dad-*dy*."

"No other word for it: screw-*ed*."

They talked about the economy and Lily was uneasy, hearing Wes so vehement, sardonic; she hadn't known the extent of his bitterness. He was telling Sharon that the Federal Reserve sets the interest rate—"As guided by the big American moneymen. The men who don't pay a penny in taxes. It isn't God on his throne who sets the rates."

Inevitably then they spoke of real estate in the Eden Valley, and in western New York generally. The region had been in a recession for some time; many factories had been shut down in Buffalo, Tonawanda, Port Oriskany. As for farmland—

Sharon said suddenly, to Lily, "And how is—the family farm?"

Lily had never heard the property described in such a way. Never in her memory had her parents' fifteen acres of rocky, partly wooded land adjacent to Reverend Donner's church been tilled except for Mrs. Donner's small vegetable garden. Awkwardly Lily said, "Well, you know, Sharon—it's gone. Sold. After Daddy died."

"Sold?"

Sharon stared at Lily. She did not appear to be acting, but utterly sincere. In the candlelight her eyes looked enormous, black with pupil as a cat's. Lily explained that she'd told Sharon, certainly; after their mother's illness, and then their father's,

there were so many medical bills, and taxes on the property—
"We would have loved to keep it but we had no choice, really."

"Lily, it isn't *ours*? It belongs to strangers? The Donner *family farm*?"

Lily said, faltering, "Sharon, I'm sure I told you," and Wes intervened, saying, "By the time your father died he was deeply in debt, Sharon. The land in Shaheen was sold for taxes and the old houses and outbuildings razed. *I* arranged for the sale, and I believe I got a good, fair price from a local farmer."

Sharon wiped tears from her eyes. Saying, to Lily, "But— it's *gone*? The house we grew up in? I dream of it so often, it's so real to me, I can't believe this—"

Lily apologized, guiltily, "Sharon, I'm so sorry. I thought I'd notified you, all along. It's what Daddy wanted, at the end. We—Wes and I—didn't feel we had any—"

"What about the church?" Sharon asked, suddenly sarcastic as a hurt child. "Has the 'First Church of Christ of Shaheen' been sold and razed, too?"

Lily explained that their father's church had relocated to the village of Shaheen at the time of his retirement. It was in new, larger quarters—much had changed.

Sharon protested, "I've always had this dream, Lily, of coming home. It's kept me going. 'In the valley of the shadow' it's kept me going. And now you say that our home is *gone*? And Daddy's church? And Daddy himself—*gone*?"

Sharon was staring at Lily with her bright, tear-glittering eyes, and Lily was staring at Sharon guiltily. Candlelight shimmered on the sisters' taut, pale faces; the air was charged as if with static electricity. Lily murmured another time, "I'm sorry, Sharon," and Sharon said in a wounded, wondering voice, "If only you'd told me, Lily, when the sale was. And when the funeral was, for Daddy. *I would have done anything to get here, to see him one last time.*"

Wes said, delicately, that certainly Lily had informed Sharon of their father's death; as of his long illness, and their mother's.

And certainly Lily had informed her of the sale of the Shaheen property.

Sharon shook her head, as if not hearing. There was a tiny silver lighter in her hand, she lit a cigarette with shaking fingers. "How can Ephraim Donner be *dead*! He's so alive in my heart. I see his face, I hear his voice. The kind of man Jesus would have been—if Jesus had truly lived."

There was a bitterness here that alarmed Lily, frightened her. She thought *But you believe in Jesus, Sharon! Aren't you the one of us who believes?*

Sharon said, "I always thought *he* would outlive *me*. All of you in Shaheen would outlive *me*. And of course 'Deirdre' "— she turned suddenly, unexpectedly to Deedee, reaching out to seize the girl's wrist—"would outlive 'Starr Bright.' For God will use me as His wrath and His scourge, and then He will abandon me—I know. 'A sword shall pierce my soul.' "

The Merricks were amazed. Sharon released Deedee's wrist and lapsed into a brooding silence. She was smoking her ill-smelling cigarette as if it were her very breath.

Lily saw that Sharon was genuinely upset; it was obvious she was unwell, and not altogether responsible for what she said; another time she began to apologize, and Wes interrupted, annoyed now at both Lily and Sharon, "Excuse me, Sharon, but one crucial fact you should know: your father's estate, such as it was, was left to Lily."

Quickly Lily said, "Because, you see, Sharon, I was *here*— I'd been taking care of him. It hardly means that Daddy didn't love you just as much as he loved me."

Sharon was staring at Lily with her teary, glassy eyes. A look that seemed to indicate *Yes I want to believe you, yes please lie to me, how can you insult my intelligence by lying to me, you don't know me at all.* And still Wes was saying, more curtly than he probably wished to sound, he who avoided domestic confrontations however assertive he was with business associates, a man other men did not wish to cross, "As I said, Sharon, I happen to think

I got a good price for the property. Maybe you'd like to examine the paperwork?"

Sharon said, grinding out her cigarette in one of Lily's fluted floral plates, "Thank you, no. I couldn't bear it."

Through this exchange, poor Deedee had become increasingly uncomfortable. Now she said, in desperate good spirits, so that Lily's heart went out to her, "Aunt Sharon, why don't we drive out to Shaheen, too? Along the River Road? Now that it's almost spring, the roads won't be so bad. I used to love going out into the country when I was a little girl."

Quietly Sharon said, with a glance at Lily sharply reproachful as a flick of a whip, "That's a kind, generous idea, Deirdre. But I doubt I'll be in Yewville long enough."

Lily silently protested *But you only just arrived yesterday, you can't be thinking of leaving already!*

Suddenly, then, interrupting their meal, there was a knocking at the back door.

"Who—is that? Don't let him in—"

It was probably just one of Wes's workmen, dropping by the house instead of calling as they often did, but Sharon reacted violently, almost dropping her wineglass, cowering in her chair like a frightened child. Lily explained the circumstances; no reason to be alarmed; they could hear Wes open the door, speak with someone named Eddy; but still Sharon was trembling, and then rueful, defensive. When Wes returned to the table, apologizing for the interruption, Sharon remarked if this were Los Angeles or Miami he wouldn't be so trusting about someone knocking at his door after dark, and Wes said, genially, "But this isn't Los Angeles or Miami, it's Yewville."

Lily felt a stab of pity for her sister. Neither Wes nor Deedee knew what she knew: that Sharon believed herself pursued—"stalked." She tried to imagine what it would be like, to be so panicked at the sound of someone knocking at the door; to be always so vigilant, nervously alert.

Someone is after me. A man. Death.

Lily contemplated Sharon, wondering if her story was true. Obviously, her emotion, her panic were genuine; the evening before, when Lily had held Sharon in her arms, comforting her, there was no doubt in her mind that something had happened to Sharon, to rouse her to such terror. But since she'd been a child Sharon had always exaggerated fears; embellished incidents to make her life more intriguing. Sometimes Lily thought it was unconscious, sometimes it seemed fully conscious. Sharon's clouded blue eyes demanding *Believe me! or I'll know you don't love me.*

Though there had been times, in high school for instance, when Lily had suspected that Sharon hadn't confided in her; hadn't told all there might have been to tell. Hiding away in a locked bathroom crying, and, in the night, prowling the house in secret . . . Something had happened between Sharon and her boyfriend Mack Dwyer, and out of hurt pride, or shame, Sharon had told no one about it. Not even her twin sister.

It was just "nerves," Sharon said, the way she'd reacted to the knocking at the back door; truly, she was fine. She insisted upon helping Lily and Deedee clear the table for coffee and dessert, but she was unsteady on her feet and, in the kitchen, had to lean against a counter until a wave of dizziness passed. Lily wanted to say *Why didn't you eat more, and drink less?* Lily was annoyed, too, when Sharon declined the cherry cobbler Deedee had prepared for them, saying with a shudder she'd as soon eat broken glass as so many calories. Lily saw the look on Deedee's face: it would seem to her, and perhaps it had been intended to be, an allusion to her weight.

And wasn't there a not-so-subtle dig here, too, in Lily's side? *How can you, this girl's mother, allow her to be even a few pounds overweight? I would never allow it.*

Back in the dining room, Wes asked Sharon when she was scheduled to begin teaching in Pasadena. She looked at him so blankly he corrected himself—"Or is it Seattle? The dance school Lily mentioned."

Sharon said slowly, "I might not, after all. Might not go back. I'm on my way to—Manhattan. An old friend. We've both had heartbreak."

Deedee glanced at Lily, perplexed. Earlier that evening as the three of them had worked in the kitchen, quite enjoying themselves, Sharon had impulsively invited Deedee to fly out and stay with her when she got settled "on the West Coast."

Deedee said, uncertainly, "I guess you travel a lot, Aunt Sharon?" and Sharon said, "As long as I don't mind being manipulated by agents demanding fifteen percent of my income, I travel constantly." Wes asked, "When can we see you and your dance troupe perform, Sharon?" and again Sharon stared at him blankly, and Lily quickly intervened, "Sharon's dance troupe is disbanding, unfortunately." Sharon said, shrugging, "Disband*ed,* to be precise. Which is just as well. I'm ready to move on. The so-called glamor professions use women like Kleenex, then toss them aside. Exactly like Kleenex." She paused, reaching for another cigarette. "I knew Margaux Hemingway. We weren't close but we'd worked together on several shoots. She couldn't deal with it—the glamor, the excitement, and men— and what comes after. *I* survived because—I wasn't quite as successful." Her voice trailed off as she smiled mysteriously, recalling memories best unspoken.

Deedee, who'd read about Margaux Hemingway in *People* and had seen some morbid film clips on TV, asked Sharon what the former model and actress had been like, and Sharon said that Margaux had had her weaknesses like everyone else but lacked the strengths others had. Deedee asked, "*Was* it suicide, how she died?" and Sharon said bitterly, "It's always suicide, Deirdre," and Wes said, an edge of annoyance to his voice as before, as if he wanted to protect his daughter from such cynicism, "What do you mean by that, Sharon?" and Sharon said, "If they don't commit the act themselves, they drive you to it," and Wes said, "Who?" and Sharon said, almost spitting out the words, yet with satisfaction, grim pleasure, "Pigs and fornicators. Emissaries of Satan. 'He hath led me in dark places, as they that be dead of old.' "

The Merricks regarded Sharon with perplexity—was she joking? Or was she, uttering these strange, archaic words, deadly serious? Lily could not recognize the Bible verse, assumed it must be the Old Testament. There was a pale glisten to Sharon's skin and her beautiful dissatisfied mouth twisted downward in derision.

Lily thought to turn the conversation to another, more positive direction. "You'll love teaching, Sharon. Working with others is so rewarding! I was shy at first, but I've come to love my night class at the community college."

Deedee said, "Mom's students love her, too. They keep signing up for the course semester after semester, even the ones who can't 'pot' worth a darn."

Coolly Sharon said, "But my teaching will be different from yours, Lily. The Pasadena School of Dance is a professional school. We only accept talented students, only about fifty percent of our applicants; not just anyone, like a community college."

Lily might have been expected to feel insulted by this offhand remark, but instead she found herself laughing. How like Rose of Sharon, who'd pretended to be Lily's older sister in high school, insisting upon differentiating between them. Lily said agreeably, "No, my students aren't greatly talented as potters but they *try*. And I'm no genius, myself."

Deedee objected, "Mom, you're *good*. Mom made this vase here, Aunt Sharon, it's cool, isn't it?"

It was a slender, tubular ceramic vase of the color and sheen of mother-of-pearl, placed on the center of the dining-room table, containing the beautiful white and red roses.

Sharon touched the vase with her forefinger, almost in doubt.

"It's very—professional."

"But to achieve this single vase," Lily said, "I had to make, and discard, probably two dozen. *That* isn't very professional."

Through the meal, Lily had been noticing how her husband and her daughter were gazing at her sister. With what intense, unwavering interest. Had either ever looked at her in quite that way? Even when Wes's love for her had been new, even when Deedee had been a baby? Lily was sure she wasn't jealous. Never could she be jealous of her twin sister. For what was Sharon but *a blond Lily, a far more beautiful and mysterious Lily?*

They talked of classes; of Deedee's high school, which had been, of course, Lily's and Sharon's high school, twenty years before; of teachers who'd retired, or died; of names, nicknames—"I wish I wasn't called 'Deedee,' " Deedee said suddenly, to her parents' surprise. "I hate that silly name."

Lily said, hurt, "But, Deedee—it's a sweet name—"

"It is not, Mom. It's a silly name."

Wes said, "Since when?"

"I don't know since when. Since always."

There was an awkward silence. Sharon said, carefully, "But the name 'Deirdre' is beautiful, I think. If I had a daughter—I'd like to have named her 'Deirdre.' "

Deedee frowned. "You think so, Aunt Sharon? 'Deirdre'? Isn't it kind of weird?"

"Certainly not. It's Irish, it's like poetry. 'Deir-dre.' Yes, it's beautiful."

This seemed to have settled the issue with Deedee, at least for the moment. Lily felt dazed, tricked; as if, under cover of caressing her, Sharon had pinched her, hard. *If I had a daughter. I'd like to have named her "Deirdre."*

In fact, Lily, her mother, and her father had named the baby Deirdre, after a distant relative of Lily's mother. Sharon who was "Sherrill" had had no interest in naming the baby, had never responded to news of the baby's name at all.

As if sensing the drift of Lily's thoughts, seeing the vexed expression on her face, Sharon said, reaching over to take Lily's hand and squeeze it, "Lily, I can't tell you how happy I am to be here. Thank you, all of you—for your hospitality. It's as if I was dead and now—I am alive."

Though she was looking very tired; there was a feverish edge to her voice. When Lily protested that she was exaggerating, she said, "No, it's true. I've been tormented, and put to the test; I've been made to pass through 'the valley of the shadow'; but I think I've come out on the other side now. Somehow you, Lily, here in Yewville, kept me alive. All these years. Even when I seemed to have lost you."

"Lost me? What do you mean?"

"Or maybe *you* lost *me*. Temporarily."

Wes said, "Sharon, you know you're welcome to stay with us as long as you like. If you need a quiet place to rest, to relax—"

Sharon laughed sharply, but her manner was flirtatious. "Is that a gentlemanly way of telling me I look tired, Wes? *Sick?*"

"Of course not. But—"

"But I am, of course—a little tired. I've been working hard. I've been run to earth."

"Well, we have plenty of room," Wes said, gesturing expansively. His cheeks were flushed from the wine, the good food, the intense conversation, so unlike the Merricks' usual dinners at home. "As Lily has told you, I'm sure."

Lily was still smarting, her heart pounding uncomfortably in her chest. *If I had a daughter. I'd like to have named her "Deirdre."* She wasn't quite sure what Wes and Sharon were talking about, and why Deedee was looking on with a wide, hopeful smile, the feathery-glinting Navajo necklace around her throat.

Lily had put on the Navajo bracelet, but it weighed so heavily on her wrist, and hadn't seemed quite appropriate for the occasion, so she'd removed it again. To wear another time, perhaps teaching her potting class. Her students, most of them adult women, would notice and admire it at once.

This? A present from my sister.
Oh, yes. I have a sister. I haven't mentioned her?
A twin. But not identical.

Dinner was over, it was nearly nine o'clock. Yet no one seemed eager to leave the table. As if the Merricks' strange, mysterious visitor, that fever-glow to her face and eyes, held them captives; willing captives. Sharon had been answering questions of Deedee's about her modeling career, about "Sherrill"; now suddenly she smiled, and said, "Oh, Lily—remember 'Starr Bright'? *She* started it all."

How odd, that Sharon had spoken that name several times since her arrival in Yewville. That transparently phony, showbiz name. Lily would not have wished to confess how she'd come to dislike the woman who called herself "Starr Bright," finally. That vain, self-promoting and bossy Buffalo TV personality who'd been fired from her job for driving while intoxicated, filed a lawsuit against the television station which she'd eventually lost, and ended her days, as Sharon probably didn't know, in a Buffalo detox center where she'd died of cirrhosis of the liver at the age of fifty-seven.

Her real name had been "Stella Breznick." She'd never married, had no children.

Lily said of course she remembered "Starr Bright"—how could she forget the woman who after all had changed their lives? But Deedee insisted upon knowing more about Starr Bright; and Wes, though he'd grown up in Yewville, claimed to know nothing at all about her; so Sharon spoke animatedly, amusingly—"A busty blond Liz Taylor was what she tried to be, but she never got beyond *The Starr Bright Hour* on Saturday mornings, for children. Remember, Lily, how we'd write for tickets, weeks ahead of time? The tickets were free to children, but you had to reserve them. It was a long drive for us, thirty miles from Shaheen, and the studio audience had to be seated an hour before the show began. Daddy drove us a few times, and once or twice Momma, and what a treat it was! Except, having to get there so damned early, still you had to wait in line—"

With a startling vehemence Lily said, "Yes, and once inside the studio you'd wait, and wait—"

"—and the younger children would get restless, have to be taken to the bathroom—"

"—and everyone was so excited, but time seemed to stop—"

"—just waiting, and waiting—"

"—and finally Bessie the Cow would come out on stage, and we'd all scream—"

"—and the Ducklings and Goslings chorus, they were actual children, in costume—"

"—and Louie the Lion—"

"But still you'd be waiting, and waiting—"

"—because the show didn't actually begin until Starr Bright appeared, it was part-taped, and part-live—"

"—and always they'd say 'just a few more minutes, boys and girls'—"

"—'Starr Bright will be with you soon'—"

Sharon jumped to her feet, and pulled Lily from the table to join her, and the two women began singing, in mock child-voices, arms around each other's waist, the simple nursery-rhyme tune, the theme song of *The Starr Bright Hour,* which Lily would have sworn she hadn't known, had long forgotten.

> "Starr Bright will be with you soon!
> Starr Bright will be with you soon!
> Starr Bright, Starr Bright!
> Starr Bright will be with you soon!"

Lily was laughing giddily, seeing in Wes's and Deedee's faces a single expression of amazement, that she, Lily, wife and mother, was behaving in such a way. *Well, then, you don't know me, do you! No more than you know my sister Rose of Sharon do you know me, Lily of the Valley.* But abruptly then her laughter stopped, she felt weak, sickened; frightened; the way Wes and Deedee were staring, as if they scarcely recognized her, trying to smile, to see the joke. It came to Lily in a wave of panic that something terrible would happen, she was powerless to prevent it.

Once Lily went silent, Sharon too ceased her abrasive, jeering song. Her arm around Lily's waist that had been so tight slipped weakly away. She seemed suddenly faint, light-headed; leaning against the back of a chair; Wes leapt up to help her, but Lily was already gripping her sister's thin shoulders, gently yet firmly. "Sharon? What's wrong?" Lily asked anxiously. Sharon touched her fingers to her forehead, her eyelids fluttered. She whispered, "No—nothing. Just tired." But she was more than tired, clearly: the blood had drained from her face, leaving her haggard, aged. Strands of acrid-smelling hair had escaped from her chignon and her breath smelled of wine and cigarettes.

Wes suggested they drive Sharon to the Yewville General emergency room but Sharon, trembling, pressed into Lily's arms pleading No! no! she was only tired, exhausted, she'd had too much to drink and wanted only to go to bed. Lily helped her walk cautiously from the dining room to the guest room at the rear of the house; Wes and Deedee followed uncertainly, not knowing what to do. "Don't let them look at me, stare at me," Sharon begged, clutching at Lily like a child, "—don't let them touch me, Lily! I'm so afraid." Lily assured her sister that no one would touch her except Lily herself, if that was what she wanted.

Long ago, when they were girls in Shaheen, sharing a single bedroom in which there were twin beds—how vividly it was returning to Lily, in fleeting patches of memory—she'd sometimes helped Sharon lie down on her bed and try to relax after one of her emotional outbursts (temper tantrums, "nerve-attacks" as their mother called them); their relationship at such times was that of nurse-patient; play of a kind, yet serious play. How startling that strong-willed Rose of Sharon, the master, should be so dependent upon Lily of the Valley, her slave; what pleasure to suddenly reverse their roles. Lily had not known whether even at such times Sharon remained in control; or whether somehow, as if by magic, she, Lily, had seized control.

More briskly than she meant, Lily told Wes and Deedee that everything was under control, and closed the door behind Sharon and herself. She helped Sharon lie down, removed her absurd high-heeled shoes, loosened her clothes. The gold chain lay glaring against Sharon's just slightly lined throat and though it could have weighed virtually nothing, Lily didn't like the look of it, and undid the clasp and removed it. Sharon was moaning how dizzy she was, how the room was spinning. Lily went into the adjoining bathroom to soak a washcloth in cold water, and brought it back to press against Sharon's feverish face. Sharon was trembling almost convulsively. Her teeth chattered. Feebly she clutched at Lily's hand. "Oh, Lily, forgive me, I'm so—afraid! 'Starr Bright' has done things and things have been done to her and—I will have to be punished." Lily asked, "Shall I call a doctor, Sharon? And make an appointment for the morning?" She meant to be practical, to hide her anxiety; she'd been good at playing nurse, quietly assuming her temporary control. Sharon pleaded, "No! No doctor! No one must know I'm here, Lily, you promised."

Lily said, stroking her sister's thin, frantic hands, "Yes, of course I promised! You're safe with me, Sharon."

In this way Lily Merrick's ceremonial dinner welcoming her lost sister Sharon back home was ended.

★   ★   ★

This talk of Starr Bright what was it but raving drunken nonsense.

After so many years. Lily refused to think of it, erasing her thoughts one by one like spraying a grimy window with cleanser and briskly wiping it clean.

And what did Wes know of Sharon. To speak of Sharon as he did.

Might Sharon have a drug problem? a drinking problem? mental problem? Shouldn't she see a doctor?

No, Wes knew nothing. A man could know nothing.

But she loved him. Wanted to be fair to him. Conceded yes her sister surely had problems, emotional problems after the way she'd been exploited. Psychological problems, yes possibly. And she'd drunk too much wine at dinner out of nervousness, excitement. Why had he kept filling her glass? You can hardly blame her for that.

Wes, in bed beside Lily. Saying softly Look I don't blame her, honey, I'm just concerned. For her, and for you.

Waiting for him to fall asleep. His prickling thoughts to shift from her.

Downstairs, was Sharon asleep? Or, like Lily, anxious, awake?

Run to earth.

God's wrath, and God's scourge.

In the guest-room bathroom Lily had seen: jars and tubes of cosmetics, lipsticks, a container of "ivory" face powder spilled as if with a shaky hand.

On Sharon's bedside table, face down, Lily had seen: a book with a cheap soft cover, fake gilt letters HOLY BIBLE.

STARR BRIGHT WILL BE WITH YOU SOON. STARR BRIGHT WILL BE WITH YOU SOON. STARR BRIGHT WILL BE WITH YOU SOON!

Beside the sleeping lightly snoring man who was her husband Lily lay part awake part dreaming in dread and anticipation.

YEWVILLE RESIDENT FOUND DEAD IN CAR
POLICE INVESTIGATE APPARENT SUICIDE

YEWVILLE, N.Y. (April 4) Stanley Reigel, 39, of 542 Brisbane Street, South Yewville, was found dead early Tuesday morning in his car parked in an empty lot of the Buffalo & Chautauqua Railroad yard.

Mr. Reigel, owner of Reigel Plumbing, was said by his wife Constance to have failed to come home after working late at his office Monday evening. He had informed her he would not be home for dinner because of "emergency bookkeeping matters" and when he failed to return home by 11 P.M. Mrs. Reigel made several calls to his office as well as to friends and acquaintances. At approximately midnight Mrs. Reigel and 16-year-old Benjamin, the couple's son, drove to Reigel Plumbing on Huron Road to find no one there.

At 6:45 A.M. Tuesday morning, Mr. Reigel's 1996 Ford Cutlass was discovered by Leo Mark, security guard for the Buffalo & Chautauqua Railroad, in a secluded area of the railroad yard. Mr. Reigel's body was in the backseat.

A preliminary examination determined that death appeared to have been caused by severe slashings of Mr. Reigel's wrists and forearms. An alleged "suicide document" is in the custody of Yewville police.

There are no indications of robbery.

Relatives of Mr. Reigel claim that he had no reason to take his own life. Eden County coroner Bill Early will be conducting an autopsy today. Anyone with information to aid in the police investigation is requested to call (716) 687-9592.

1

The Broken Bowl

N ow the house at 183 Washington Street seemed, in Lily's eyes, to glow with a secret interior light. When she drove home and turned her car in the driveway she felt her pulse quicken.

She'd long been accustomed, during the day, to returning to an empty, rather lonely house. Wes was at work, Deedee at school. But now Sharon was visiting: Lily had only to enter the kitchen breathless and call out, "Sharon? I'm home."

Yes we've always been close. My twin sister Sharon and me.

Even with thousands of miles separating us. Even those years she was lost to me.

It was the second week of Sharon's visit. Time had passed with magical swiftness.

Lily had pleaded with Sharon not to continue on to New York just yet. Not in her shaky condition. Not with her migraine headaches, nausea and depressed appetite. It was obvious she needed rest and calm; she needed to gain at least fifteen pounds; to regain her old vigor and spirit. (Of the person who was "stalking" her—whatever danger he represented—Sharon declined to speak any further.) Apologetically she said, "Oh, Lily, I don't want to presume upon your hospitality—yours, and Wes's. Are you sure he doesn't mind if I stay a little longer?'' and Lily said adamantly, squeezing her sister's hand, "Of course Wes doesn't mind! Hasn't he told you so, himself?''

Though Wes, being Wes, a naturally reticent if strong-willed man, was difficult to read. Having a stranger in his household clearly made him uneasy and self-conscious; equally clearly, he liked Sharon, whom he saw for only a small period of time each day, in the evening, and whom by accident he called "Sherrill" more than once—to his acute embarrassment. Sharon laughed nervously but assured him she didn't mind— "There are people who know me only as 'Sherrill' and not all of these people have been cruel to me. In fact, some have been kind.''

Though he didn't tell her so himself—he left such issues to Lily, of course—Wes persisted in thinking that Sharon should see a doctor. Or a therapist of some sort. He'd had some experience with alcoholism—drug addiction—in Vietnam and elsewhere—and he knew the symptoms, he said.

Lily and Sharon quarreled—almost—about whether Lily should arrange for Sharon to be examined by a doctor. "You seem to be running a chronic fever," Lily scolded, "and I hear you coughing in the mornings. You might have a respiratory ailment that could be cured with antibiotics.'' Sharon said, with a little-girl air of pleading, "Lily, it's just these damned cigarettes. I'm trying to *quit,* I promise.'' Lily said, "But you scarcely eat. You say you're not hungry," and Sharon said, backing off, "No doctors! I can't bear being poked, prodded, pierced by any man, M.D. or otherwise—I'm terrified of needles.'' Lily said, "What about a woman doctor, then? I've heard of a new woman gynecologist who's said to be wonderful, very gentle. I would switch to her myself except I feel loyal to—'' and Sharon said, sharply, "Damn it, Lily, *no.* It isn't like when we were girls, I'm not your slave now to be *commanded.*''

Lily stared at Sharon. She was seated at her potter's wheel, in her workroom—Sharon in a chenille robe, barefoot, her damp hair wrapped in a towel, had come in to watch her work—but her hands and feet had ceased their motion. Her heart beat steadily, calmly.

"What? What did you say?"

Sharon said peevishly, "I'm not your slave, 'Lily of the Valley,' you're not my master, to tell me what's good for me—to command me at your whim."

But you commanded me. You were Rose of Sharon my master, I was Lily of the Valley your slave.

Sharon fumbled in the pocket of the robe, drawing out a pack of cigarettes. She was trembling but defiant; on the verge of an emotional outburst; it would be dangerous to push her, to upset her any further. So Lily bit her lip and suppressed her words and after a tense moment Sharon came to take her hand, her hand that was damp with clay, and, in an impulsive childlike gesture, in that way that endeared her to all the Merricks, she raised it to press against her own cheek—which was indeed hot, feverish. "Lily, don't be angry! Everyone can't be strong, like you."

One evening Wes returned home with a mysterious purchase, showered and came downstairs to dinner wearing a new shirt—a white cotton dress shirt with French cuffs. And the platinum-gold and pearl cuff links engraved "W M" Sharon had given him.

Lily laughed, and kissed him on the cheek. "Honey, what a surprise! You look so handsome."

Sharon was delighted, too. And Deedee, who said teasingly, "Wow. Daddy is becoming *style-conscious.*"

Wes, blushing, admired the cuff links, holding out his wrists so that they glinted in the cheery bright light of the kitchen. He complained of spending ten minutes getting the damned things through the slits in the cuffs—"But it's worth it, I suppose."

Lily was surprised, well Lily had always been surprised, by her sister's unpredictable behavior. Her unpredictable nature.

You would expect the convalescing "Sherrill" to be self-pitying and self-absorbed and oblivious of the tasks of running a household, such mundane chores as cleaning up after meals, running and emptying the dishwasher, keeping the downstairs rooms clear of accumulating debris like newspapers, spot vacuuming—but there was Sharon, sometimes wearing dark glasses, her hair hidden by a scarf, her face quite pale and resolute, throwing herself into housework; nerved-up, breathless, embarrassed if Lily or Wes should discover her, for instance, vacuuming the living-room rug, or, so strangely, as Lily discovered her one afternoon, on her hands and knees in the kitchen, scrubbing the floor with a hand sponge (when of course Lily had a sponge mop, clearly visible in the kitchen closet)—"I hope you won't mind, Lily, I just thought I'd help you out a little."

Lily was amazed. For Sharon had also scrubbed the sinks and the counters and the stove top and the oven with steel wool; she had sponged the interior of the refrigerator; loaded and unloaded the dishwasher; trimmed Lily's raggedy spider plants hanging above the windowsills. She wore Lily's loose floppy yellow rubber gloves but even so her carefully manicured nails had been cracked and broken. Her skin was sallow, even sickly, but glowing with satisfaction, pride. Lily thought *But my kitchen wasn't dirty!* She said, "Sharon, thank you. But—should you be exhausting yourself? I thought you were going to relax today."

"Oh, no, I'm a dancer—I mean, I was. I need to *move*. I need to know I'm *alive*. And I don't want to be a burden on you and Wes, *please*." This, from Sharon who as a girl had hated all household tasks, had performed them hastily and carelessly, with a look of being tortured; who, as an eighteen-year-old model, living in Manhattan in an apartment with maid service, had boasted to her sister back home in Shaheen that she never made her bed, never troubled to hang a towel evenly, or to pick up a plate after herself. *Heaven!* she'd laughingly described it.

Lily said, not knowing what she meant exactly, "But, Sharon—are you sure?"

Sharon laughed and said, "Sure about what? That I don't want to be a burden on the Merricks, or that I'm alive?"

A vague thought troubled Lily, a ridiculous thought never to be shared with another living being: that Sharon's eagerness to please was a mimicry, almost a parody of—well, Lily herself. Lily Merrick at the community college volunteering for committees which other, more seasoned and better-paid (male) faculty members avoided; Lily Merrick at PTA meetings, faithfully attending for a decade, resolutely smiling, good-natured, dependable; Lily Merrick who could be relied upon when others were too busy with their more important lives. Wes remarked of Sharon, after she'd volunteered to help him with his home office-work (Wes declined, of course: he didn't want anyone in his desk or files), "Your sister really isn't anything like I'd expected, you know? I'm wondering if you hadn't misrepresented her a bit, I don't mean consciously, but—unconsciously." Lily smarted, thinking *But you haven't met "Sherrill" yet! Wait till you meet her.* She said, "Well, but Sharon is older now, Wes. And she wants to make a good impression on you."

When Lily was home, in her workroom, Sharon frequently drifted in; wanting to watch Lily sculpting her pots; hoping she wasn't intruding. (Of course she was, to a degree; for Lily required solitude to do her best work.) Lily assured her sister she was welcome so long as she didn't smoke, though, invariably, after perhaps twenty minutes, out would come the pack of cigarettes from a pocket, and the little silver lighter with its mysterious engraved initials—not "S.D." but "P.B.," Lily had noticed. Lily would say, reluctantly, for she hated to be a scold, "Sharon, can you open a window, at least?" and Sharon would say, startled, as if, staring at Lily's swift-moving hands, she had no idea she'd lit a cigarette and sucked in and exhaled a luxuriant cloud of bluish-toxic smoke, "Oh—what? God, I'm sorry" hurrying to a window to open it, the damned cigarette gripped between her teeth.

No wonder you cough, no wonder you're sick, why are you poisoning yourself?

Like her admiration for Lily's married, maternal life generally, Sharon's admiration for Lily's work was enthusiastic, and seemed to be genuine. As she wandered about the workroom she frequently touched things—pots, vases, bowls. Some of these objects hadn't quite turned out as Lily had wished and a few were frankly misshapen, but Sharon had a kind word for all, as if she distrusted her judgment about such things or, more probably, felt that Lily, always the less secure of the two sisters, required indiscriminate encouragement. "Of course you're attractive, for God's sake," Sharon used to say, when they were in high school, "—we're *twins*, don't forget." It was meant to be a playful exaggeration of Sharon's own vanity, but clearly she was serious too. One day in Lily's workroom Sharon lifted Lily's most recent finished work, a heavy, glazed, earthen-hued bowl of about eight inches in diameter and five inches deep, a bowl Lily was hopeful about showing to a local gallery owner; Sharon turned it in her hands, a cigarette awkwardly burning between two fingers, as if it were a puzzle, and Lily at her potter's wheel, but no longer working, stared at her thinking *Don't drop it, please!* Sharon said, "Now, this is really beautiful, Lily. I hope you get a good price for it—one hundred dollars at least." Lily, who'd been hoping so, too, said, "Well. We'll see." Still Sharon turned it in her hands, peering at it, at eye level. Lily felt perspiration break out in tiny pinpoints all over her body. Sharon was saying that Lily's "talent for art" hadn't shown itself when they were girls, had it? and Lily pointed out that in their high school art class she'd done a number of charcoal drawings and watercolors and clay sculptures that their teacher had liked very much; she'd done illustrations for the school newspaper; she'd won a class day prize as "most promising artist"—but, still, Sharon shook her head, mystified. Lily knew that Sharon was recalling how their teacher had asked her to pose for the charcoal life-drawing sessons; how tranquil and aloof she'd seemed, and how beautiful she'd been, seated there on a stool at the front of the room, their teacher Mr. Hanson sketching her, himself. Twenty-five students, girls and boys of widely varying ability, staring at her, trying to capture her face, hair, shoulders in mere charcoal, on thick white paper. Sharon said, "I guess I don't remember. Are you *sure?*"

At last setting the bowl back down, carefully, onto a table. So Lily sighed with relief, thinking herself a bit ridiculous.

Lily offered to teach Sharon how to pot, but Sharon quickly demurred, saying you had to be "centered," didn't you, to be a potter?—"And I'm anything but." Lily said, "But maybe it would help you. It's calming, it's a meditation." Sharon laughed nervously, and prowled about the workroom, murmuring, "I read the Bible, and I pray. *That's* my 'meditation.' " It was a brightly glaring April day; not warm, but blindingly sunny; fearing migraine, Sharon wore smoke-tinted glasses even in the house, yet still flinched away from the windows. Her hair was skinned back behind her ears and in the unsparing light she looked both her age and exotic, with a model's gaunt hauteur. Lily stared thinking how strange, her sister's beauty was returning as if indeed she'd been convalescing in Yewville, absorbing nourishment and strength. Biding her time before moving on.

And where would she go, when she left Lily? Was there really anyone awaiting her in Manhattan?

In a corner of the comfortably cluttered room was a large cork bulletin board to which Lily had tacked all sorts of things—snapshots of Wes, Deedee, and friends; snapshots of pottery she'd given away or sold; a calendar; schedules relating to her teaching; postcards. One of the numerous postcards was of Death Valley; the colorful glossy photo of Death Valley in springtime, brilliant pink cactus flowers, eerily sculpted sand dunes, a sky so brightly blue it looked artificial. Lily saw that

Sharon was staring at this postcard; she'd gone very still, the cigarette burning in her fingers. After a moment, aware that Lily was watching her, Sharon said, "So many postards!—you have a lot of friends, Lily." Lily said, "I just haven't taken any cards down. They go back for years." Sharon said, "This one of Death Valley—it's very striking," and Lily said, frowning, "Which card is that?—I don't remember. It's years old, I think," and Sharon said, "I've been in Death Valley, in winter, that's the only time to drive in the desert. I'd been in Las Vegas with—a friend. A long time ago." Sharon's face was hidden from Lily, whose heart had begun to beat rapidly. Lily said, as if just recalling, "I couldn't read the handwriting on that card very well but I think it's from a cousin of ours—Louise Widener?— she moved to Ohio, I think, when we were in high school." Sharon marveled, "Are you still in contact with Louise?" and Lily said, "Well, apparently!" And laughed.

Sharon laughed, too. And began at once to cough—an ugly hacking sound. She backed away from the bulletin board and turned blindly and, still coughing, collided with the table upon which the glazed earthen-hued bowl had been placed; and before Lily could leap up to steady it, the bowl toppled to the floor—toppled, and shattered into pieces.

For these are the days of vengeance, that all things that are written may be fulfilled.

Lily hadn't needed to reread the Death Valley postcard, that drunken-scrawled red message. She knew it vividly, by heart.

"Oh, my God! Oh, Lily! I'm so *sorry.*"

Of course, Sharon was appalled, crestfallen at the accident.

There was no doubt in either sister's mind—it had been an accident.

Sharon pleaded with Lily please forgive me! dropping to her knees to gather up the broken pieces even as, fighting back tears, her heart pounding in fury, Lily assured her it was nothing, not important, only a bowl—"Please! Never mind."

But asking Sharon to go away for a while, to leave her alone to sweep up the broken pieces by herself.

Guiltily Sharon pleaded, "Oh, but Lily—"

Lily could not trust herself to look at her sister. Sharon had removed her tinted glasses in a dramatic gesture to stare at Lily in dismay; she was visibly trembling, as if frightened.

Lily whispered, through gritted teeth, "Sharon, *please.*"

★　　★　　★

Like Lily, Sharon was revulsed by stories of violent crime and tragedy and so she declined to watch TV news with the Merricks, nor did she apparently watch much TV at all. (There was a small set in her room but she'd mentioned to Lily she had yet to turn it on—"I don't want to contaminate my thoughts if I can help it.") For the first several days of her visit she'd avidly read the *Yewville Journal* in the kitchen, with Lily, particularly seeking out names of old friends and classmates; then, abruptly, in her impetuous way, losing interest.

Which was just as well, as Lily remarked to Wes. For the story of Stanley Reigel might have upset her.

It had been the Tuesday, April 4 issue of the *Journal* that carried the front-page news, complete with photograph and inch-high headline, of Reigel's death. Seeing the dead man's picture, reading of the "alleged suicide," Wes had been shocked; he'd known Stanley Reigel for years though they'd never been friends. And Lily was acquainted with Connie Reigel from PTA.

Naturally there was a good deal of flurried attention paid to the case by the local media, since such news—violent, mysterious death of any kind—was a rarity in Yewville.

Subsequent issues of the *Journal* and news reports on local television mainly repeated the original story, however; the basic

facts remained unchanged. The county coroner ruled that Reigel's death was indeed suicide and that he'd been heavily drinking for hours before he died. Mrs. Reigel was unavailable for
comment but relatives and friends of the dead man reiterated
that he had no reason to take his own life; a friend, Michael
Dwyer, an aide of the Yewville mayor, was quoted in the *Journal*
saying that Reigel might have been having business troubles but
there was nothing crucial that he knew of, and that he "just
wasn't the type to commit suicide."

Wes had heard from mutual acquaintances that Stanley Reigel had in fact been having financial problems; drinking problems; and marital problems. He'd been separated from his wife
intermittently for the past several years. Until recently, he'd
been attending AA meetings but had begun drinking again.
He'd been found dead in his car with a torn-out page from a
Bible with verses marked in red ink folded inside his shirt—this
was what police were calling a "suicide document."

A page torn from a Bible! How strange.

Lily and Wes took care to speak about Reigel's death in
lowered voices, not wanting Deedee, in an adjoining room at
the time, to overhear. Wes had had disagreements with Reigel
over the quality of his work and his billing practices, and hadn't
approved of Reigel's private life (Reigel was often seen in the
company of women, in local taverns) but he was reluctant to
speak ill of the dead. "Suicide is a terrible thing. For the survi-
vors especially."

Hesitantly Lily said, "But everyone claims Stanley wasn't
the type—"

Wes said bluntly, "Under the circumstances, everyone is the
'type.' "

It was that remote, eclipsed side of Wes Merrick speaking,
that Lily feared. The Vietnam veteran, a battered survivor of
alcohol, drugs, wartime horror—Lily dared not imagine.

Seeing the look in Lily's face, Wes immediately softened,
taking her hand—poor sweet Lily, so easily upset!—and assur-

ing her with a smile that of course *he* wasn't the type; not so
long as he had her and Deedee. Lily kissed him, as if this was a
truly placating remark, and pressed her cheek against his shoulder. She supposed that, in any number of Yewville households,
in the privacy of their bedrooms, worried women were extract-
ing from their husbands such assurances as she'd indirectly extracted from hers. For of all violence suicide is the most
terrifying, as it is the most mysterious.

It occurred to Lily that Sharon probably knew nothing
about the death and would not know unless someone told her,
since she'd stopped reading the newspaper and never watched
TV and, if she went for brief walks, wouldn't be speaking with
anyone likely to inform her; Lily would caution Deedee not to
bring up the subject. "In her state of nerves, anything can upset
her," Lily said. "She'd gone out with Stanley Reigel, I believe.
Just for a while, when we were all in high school."

★   ★   ★

There came Sharon somber and shyly repentant to the door
of Lily's workroom. Asking forgiveness another time; berating
herself for her clumsiness. "—I started to cough, got faint-
headed—so dizzy I almost blacked out—lost my balance and
next thing I knew—"

Lily interrupted the flow of rapid, anxious words with a
touch to her sister's wrist. "Sharon, it's all right. It was an accident. I've broken plenty of bowls." Adding, not quite truth-
fully, "Bowls as nice as that one."

"But it was beautiful, it was special—wasn't it?"

Lily hesitated. "I can make another."

"Will you allow me to pay you for it, at least?"

"What? Of course not!"

"Suppose I'd bought it? And took it away with me? It was
worth at least—five hundred dollars."

"Sharon, don't be silly."

"Then I'll know you aren't angry, Lily."

In a gesture Lily couldn't help but see as theatrical, but riveting, there stood Sharon in Lily's workroom drawing out bills from a wallet (sleek alligator hide, expensive, a large flat wallet of the kind a man might carry); as Lily stared in astonishment, Sharon drew out bill after bill—$50, $100 bills.

Lily was shocked. "What on earth are you doing, Sharon? What can you be *thinking*? Stop."

"But I want to repay you, Lily, however I can. Not just for the bowl I was so damned clumsy I broke but for—everything. My visit here. My being so welcome here."

"Sharon, you're our guest. I haven't seen you in years. I won't hear of it."

Stubbornly Sharon said, "But I do owe you money, Lily, don't I? You're just too generous to mention it. I borrowed money five or six years ago when I was down on my luck—in Houston, I think—I don't remember how much but I remember you came through for me." Sharon breathlessly pushed the bills at Lily, who was too surprised to know how to respond. "I have money, Lily—I'm not poor—men have paid what they owed me—some of them, at least. Just the groceries for my visit—won't you let me contribute something?"

"Sharon, you're our guest. This isn't right."

Lily had forgotten the money she'd lent Sharon; for it had been a secret from Wes, and being a secret from Wes had gradually faded out of Lily's consciousness.

"Can I give it to Deedee, then?"

"To—Deedee?"

"Or—isn't that a good idea?"

"I don't think that's a good idea."

Since their initial conversation about Deedee, Lily and Sharon hadn't spoken of Deedee in that way again; it was as if, altogether naturally, Sharon were truly the girl's aunt. This, too, Lily had nearly pushed out of consciousness as she'd been feeling, since Sharon's arrival, a sense of pride, elation, privilege in being a mother, and not a childless woman like her sister.

Sharon said, impatiently, "Then let me give something to you and Wes, for household expenses. Here."

Lily, embarrassed, refused to touch the money. But Sharon left it on Lily's cluttered workbench, a heap of crisp new bills—$2300.

2

The Secret Journey

Always unpredictable! Sharon had decided, she informed Lily, not to call her old friends and classmates, even their Shaheen relatives, just yet.

"All I really treasure of the past, Lily, is you."

She'd been looking through the old scrapbooks their mother had kept. Laughing, and crying; absorbed for hours; then bursting into Lily's workroom with a childish complaint— "The last part is so *messy*! Everything's out of *order*! So much is *missing*!"

As if Lily were curator of "Sherrill's" career.

As the days passed, however, Sharon grew restless; needed to get out-of-doors, to exercise her long lovely dancer's legs. Walking, even in the freezing mist, in the wind, in harsh sunlight, wearing her darkest-tinted glasses and a scarf tied tight around her head.

She'd discovered a frayed old coat of Lily's in the hall closet, a khaki-colored trench coat with a hood. It was a coat Lily would have sworn she'd tossed out years ago. Of course, Sharon could wear it all she wished. As well as Lily's boots.

"Where do you walk, Sharon? I'd love to join you."

Quickly Sharon said, "Oh, no. People would see you, Lily, and recognize you, and next thing you know they'd recognize *me*. And I'm not ready for that yet."

Though, now it was April and the days warmer, the wind likely to be from the south and not the chill Canadian north, Sharon was looking stronger, healthier. Of course she was still thin—far too thin, by Lily's standards—but some of the color had returned to her cheeks and her eyes were less blood-veined and there was an air almost of jauntiness about her, a smile playing at her lips.

Lily was disappointed, but supposed she saw Sharon's point. "Well. Someday soon, I hope. Before . . ." Lily's voice trailed off, she might have been about to say *Before you leave us*. Or *Before it's too late*.

Sometimes by day, sometimes by night.

Slipping from the side door of the house, her private door.

Restless and excited and purposeful in her sister's khaki-colored coat worn with the hood. Even on overcast days wearing her dark-tinted glasses. Even, sometimes, at night.

Reasoning *If they are hunting "Starr Bright" they will not recognize me.*

Or, veins thrumming with one of her sparely administered speed capsules, of which she had perhaps thirty left hidden in the lining of her suitcase, *If I am "Starr Bright" I am invisible!*

In the frayed glamorless coat that was Lily Merrick's yet would not have been identified even as Lily Merrick's for it was one of how many hundreds, thousands of such coats in Yewville. In the black rubberized boots, she winced and laughed to see on her feet. So ugly! No style at all! Yet dear Lily her sister, almost-twin-sister, had chosen them of her own free will.

The first of her walks she'd undertaken shyly, when she'd only just arrived at her sister's. Not yet trusting her strength. Her brain dazzled by weeks of flight, body exhausted. When she'd been so jumpy the sound of a ringing telephone at the Merricks' or a knock at the door or simply Wes's footsteps (unconsciously heavy, urgent-sounding on the stairs to the second floor of the house) could throw her into a panic. But quickly she grew more confident, bolder. She slipped from the house and cut through the rear yard, through a gate in the wooden fence and into the alley behind; a narrow unpaved old-fashioned lane where trash cans were neatly kept and where some homeowners had garages, converted stables. This residential neighborhood had been semi-country not many decades ago. At East Avenue, she might cross to follow the alley to the end of the next long block; at Hawley Street she might cross to follow the alley to the end of that long block, where the houses and yards were smaller, though still neatly kept. Occasionally a cat would peer at her from atop a fence, or raise its tail to approach her, mewing questioningly in that way of an animal saying *Do I know you?* and Sharon would pause to pet it if allowed. Occasionally a dog would bark at her, friendly or otherwise, and she'd hurry on by. She might follow the alley to its end in a field below the Yewville Water Refinement Plant and above Route 209, a two-lane state highway of gas stations, fast-food restaurants and video stores and strip malls that had been rapidly thrown up in the 1980's. So far! The ordinary little alley that passed behind 183 Washington Street! Who would ever have guessed she, Sharon, presumed to be unwell, physically and emotionally a cripple, could have hiked so far, so quickly?

And so she might turn back, return home.

Or she might not.

A more circuitous route was also through the alley (for she would not have wished to be seen leaving the Merricks' house by the front, onto Washington Street) in the opposite direction, to Bank Street; across then to All Saints churchyard where, following graveled paths into the interior of the old cemetery, she might have been mistaken for a mourner—hooded head bowed in submission before weather-pocked crosses, wide-winged apocalyptic angels. (One afternoon discovering engraved on a black marble marker of 1859 *He hath led me, and brought me into darkness, but not into the night.*) At the rear of the cemetery was a secret way out through a partly collapsed stone wall, a quick glance behind her to see if anyone was watching *But no: God has rendered me invisible in His mercy* and she stepped through!

And followed then gropingly a rough-trodden path through underbrush and scrub trees that led gradually downhill, running parallel with East Avenue but hidden from view even in leafless late winter. Crossing then the raised meridian of the Buffalo & Chautauqua Railroad track. *And again no one to see! And no locomotive rushing at her.* Entering then breathless a jungle-like area of dumped debris, abandoned stained and torn mattresses and smashed lamps, ravaged furniture as in a vengeful holocaust of domestic bliss; a sight that left her panting with excitement as if such must be a sign sent to her, for her eyes only, from above. Crossing then an edge of the railroad yard where on the night of April 3 a pig would die bleeding to death behind boxcars derelict and lonely-seeming on rusted tracks. And so out to Depot Street, shabby row houses and vacant buildings, and beyond then a short block to State Road, Route 11, where there were no sidewalks, open areas of thawing mud bravely traversed in Lily's sturdy boots. Here too were gas stations, motels, X-rated videos and branch banks, a 7-Eleven store open twenty-four hours a day, the Circle Beer-Liquor-Wine and the Eight-Ball Lounge and Artie's Tavern. Also an upholsterer's shop, a dry cleaner's, Suzi's Chinese Take-Out, Rita's Beauty Salon. In the near but hazy distance, across four lanes of rushing traffic, was a new Ford dealership all gleaming vehicles and flapping flags, and, only just visible from the 7-Eleven, a high-rise Ramada Inn lifting from a landscape gouged out as if giant children had dug and maimed it with picks. Fifteen years ago all this had been open fields, farmland. Wild!

All flesh is grass, and all the goodliness thereof is as the flower of the field.

Where she'd seen, by the sheerest chance, unless of course it was a sign of God, a pickup truck bearing the broad white letters DWYER'S FENCE CITY hurtling by.

In disguise then as a plain, dumpy middle-aged woman with

a sallow skin and no makeup, slumped shoulders in a shapeless
trench coat, in mud-splattered and comically ugly rubberized
boots, she purchased a carton of filter-tip cigarettes in the 7-
Eleven; and a can of ice-cold Diet Pepsi, laced with caffeine,
which she drank where she stood, thirsty as a dog. If the clerk
was busy with other customers she paused to glance quickly
through tabloid papers in search of news—"STAR" KILLER
STRIKES AGAIN IN SAN DIEGO?—L.A. COP PSYCHIC UNEARTHS
"STAR" VICTIMS BURIAL GROUND. She smiled to read of new
outrageous and unsolved cases of murder and mutilation and
bloody graffiti thousands of miles away. She smiled to think
how "Starr Brights's" power would outlive even her who had
brought it into being.

On April 4, April 5 and April 7 purchasing copies of the
Yewville Journal since she no longer read it at home.

"*I* knew that guy. You'd see him around."

The 7-Eleven clerk, a stocky young man with slick quills of
hair, a scruffy beard and a harsh asthmatic breath craned his
neck to see what his customer was reading so intently between
swallows of Diet Pepsi.

"Really?"

"Yeah. Reigel. Plumbing guy. He'd come in here for cigarettes—Camels. And next door." Next door was the beer-
liquor-wine store. "He'd hang out at Artie's over there."

"He killed himself, they're saying. You believe that?"

Surprisingly, the clerk shrugged. Sharon regarded him slant-
wise through her dark-tinted glasses. "Sure. There's lots of people kill themselves, these days." He spoke sadly, as if recalling
names, faces. "Somehow it's easier now."

"It's a sin, no matter what."

Sharon left the 7-Eleven as if she'd been obscurely insulted.

Across the way was Artie's—pink neon sign HAPPY
HOUR HAPPY HOUR winking in the window. So inviting! She
was dying for a drink. But a lone woman in such a place, packed
at this time of day with men on their way home from work,

truckers stopping for supper, even a plain, dumpy middle-aged woman with a sallow skin and no makeup, might attract undesired attention.

She wasn't prepared for any pig's company. Hadn't her protection with her. Not so soon after S.R.

Sharon entered the Circle Beer-Liquor-Wine to purchase a single half-bottle of wine. Chardonnay like the kind her brother-in-law had served at that first dinner they'd all had together—the Merricks making her feel so *welcome*. So *wanted*.

God, I love them all.

God, thank you for bringing me to safe harbor!

It was a thunderous late afternoon. Fluorescent lights illuminated ten-foot shelves, row upon row of gleaming bottles. All the customers except Sharon in her disguise were male; no one gave her more than a cursory glance; pigs' eyes sliding off her, a woman of no evident sex. *I am invisible, like God!*

Sharon located the wine she wanted. Her nerves were taut as piano wire, mouth watering for a drink. *Certainly I am not an alcoholic* she was explaining to her sister Lily, whose only fault was she pried into Sharon's life, forever *thinking thinking thinking* about Sharon and several times bringing up "Starr Bright"— why, exactly? *Alcoholism is genetic. No one in the Donner family was alcoholic. Momma and Daddy never drank for God's sake! So don't you look at me accusing me!* Lily's only fault was trying to tell Sharon what to do. Issuing commandments like when they'd been girls. When they were girls no longer.

Still, Sharon adored Lily. Lily, and Wes, and Deedee. What a happy family. What a good, decent, generous family. And what Wes and Deedee would never know, could never hurt them. Wild!

Sharon was about to bring the wine to the cashier's counter at the front of the store when she heard a familiar voice, and saw a tall, burly, graying-haired man in a light jacket pushing six-packs of beer along the counter—her brother-in-law Wes.

Wes Merrick, here!

Sharon held back, partly hidden by a display of discount wines. Thinking what a coincidence it was, she'd been thinking of the man and he'd appeared. She'd been thinking of him innocently and he'd appeared causing her heart to race as in the long-ago days when she'd see Mack Dwyer at school and feel an actual stab to the heart loving him so until he'd betrayed her.

Sharon could overhear Wes talking with the cashier whose name he knew, did she hear the name "Reigel"—"poor bastard"—"terrible thing"—couldn't be certain. In the weirdly convex mirror above the cashier's register was Wes Merrick's handsome ruddy face distorted yet to Sharon's eyes instantly recognizable.

Her brother-in-law Wes, in neutral territory.

Never glimpsed the man before outside the house on Washington Street—Lily's house.

Suppose they'd met by accident? The first day Sharon had come to Yewville. In fact she'd had a drink at a place next to the Greyhound station downtown before getting into a taxi. Suppose Wes had dropped in. An accidental meeting. It might have happened—why not?

Big-boned, clumsy-gentle. A fleshy mouth for eager damp kissing. A strong-willed man who would not be pushed beyond a point but until that point he's putty in your hands.

And how big a penis, blood-engorged to its full size, only Lily would know; and, being Lily, wouldn't ever tell.

It was unfair, Lily had always had all the luck. Not many boyfriends in high school but the few she'd had had respected her. Not crazy about her maybe, for how could any guy be crazy about Lily, but nice to her and decent as the guys tended to be to one another if they were friends; but rarely to girls; and never to Sharon. Who was the beautiful one of the Donner sisters, so unfair!

Not that Sharon had been seriously jealous of Lily. She'd had all the guys she wanted. Except they treated her like shit. Mack Dwyer who was the first she'd allowed to . . . touch her.

That way. Mack she'd loved like crazy and would have died for and he'd gotten bored with her and treated her like shit saying *If you don't like it, leave me alone* but she was so weak, desperate in love and he'd passed her on to his buddies and even then . . . for a while . . . well, what could she do, she was just a kid. Stan Reigel had been one of them.

Well. *He'd* died. Twenty-two years afterward but that began to even things up, almost.

Yes, Lily had had all the luck without seeming to realize it. And still did.

"Mr. and Mrs. Wesley Merrick"—so most of the mail came, delivered to 183 Washington Street. Lily of the Valley, a married woman! A woman with a daughter! Who'd even come to resemble her, and Wes.

For unto every one that hath shall be given, and he shall have abundance: but from him that hath not shall be taken away even that which he hath.

Never had Sharon understood these harsh words of Jesus Christ, and she did not understand them now.

Wes had his wallet out, was handing the clerk bills. Sharon bit her lower lip smiling like a mischievous child thinking why not step out, declare herself *H'lo Wes! Can I ride back to the house with you, I've been getting some fresh air and exercise* and Wes would blink at her amazed *Jesus, Sharon—is that you?* And laughing she'd snatch off the dark glasses so he could get a good look liking it meeting her like this in neutral territory. And Lily who was "Mrs. Merrick" nowhere near. Wes would say *How about a drink, Sharon, at Artie's before we drive back* and Sharon would say, touching his wrist, *Hell, no, Wes, I have a better idea, let's get a bottle right here and we can park somewhere private and secluded— how'd you like that?*

Sure, he'd like that.

He was a man, any man's a pig in his innermost heart.

Instead, Sharon waited until Wes was safely gone from the store before coming forward.

Never, God help me! Never.

Never to Lily her own sister she adored. Lily of the Valley who was all that remained of the old, lost world of Shaheen.

That could not be part of God's plan for her—could it?

She was sickened thinking of it. Icy-cold in her bowels.

"Starr Bright" and—Wes?

Never had God suggested such. He had guided her across thousands of miles seeking sanctuary here. Where she might heal herself in Lily.

God, You would not be so cruel.

She would read the Bible that night until dawn seeking a sign, if any sign be offered.

3

Bleeding a Pig

T here had been no plan, of that she would swear.

One day run to earth by her enemies and confronted with her crimes and made to plead guilty as "Starr Bright" butcherer of pigs and duly sentenced to death by the State of Nevada by lethal injection to which she would acquiesce as a lover the most passionate and voluptuous of her lovers she would so swear. No plan, no thought of vengeance bringing her east to home.

I don't want to kill. Not the most filthy of pigs deserving to die. I am Rose of Sharon, I am not one who kills.

That was so! God help her.

It was a safe harbor with her sister Lily she had wished. Only that. Lily whom she loved solely of the earth's inhabitants. Lily of the Valley who was her almost-twin and wiser than she in many respects. Lily she adored. Whose husband she would never *she would never!* seduce and bring to harm.

Wes who had opened his household to her though guessing (ah, she knew!) her sluttish past. Yet magnanimous, kindly. Like Christ extolling *Judge not, and ye shall not be judged; condemn not, and ye shall not be condemned.*

Though he look upon her with lust in his heart, knowing not it was lust for her he felt, she would never bring the man to harm.

173

Lily, I promise!

Certain too that there had been no wish of vengeance bringing her home to set "Starr Bright" upon those who had used her cruelly more than twenty years ago. Destroying her innocent girlhood with their grunting pig-lust.

Statutory rape, it had been. For Sharon had been only fifteen years old, her high school lovers had been seventeen and eighteen.

Mark Dwyer, Stan Reigel, Budd Petco—and others, their names faded as their faces. She would have supposed they might still be living in Yewville; but truly had not thought of them, not once, set upon her long pilgrimage home.

How "Starr Bright" eluded the police of several states alerted for a young glamorous beauty who did not exist.

How "Starr Bright" wiped away all fingerprints, all traces of her being in the wake of carnage. In Malibu shrewdly leaving behind twisted in the dead man's fingers three strands of hair taken from beauty salon debris in a Dumpster behind a strip mall. In Malibu as subsequently in Yewville leaving in the wake of carnage a single page torn from the Bible.

Yet not the Bible lying on her bedside table, which she believed Lily had seen. But the second of her Bibles, hidden in the lining of a suitcase. For the one Holy Book was her own, the other to be desecrated in the service of the Lord.

No. She'd had no thought of Dwyer, Reigel . . . the others. There had been no motive except wishing to be healed, bringing her home.

The ugly memory of the swimming pool at the park and the jeering boys *Hey Blondie Blue-Eyes! Don't be scared!* was fresher. Billy Ray Cobb had paid richly for that memory.

For where one pig could not be touched in vengeance, another might take his place; in butchery, one pig is identical with any other.

For truly she believed *God will not allow us to commit any act that is evil. That is not ordained by His wrath.*

In Yewville, she would consecrate herself to good.

In Yewville, she would emulate her sister Lily.

Truly she'd vowed. In her innermost heart. On her knees scrubbing the kitchen floor. Scouring the sinks, the grease-splattered interior of the oven. Speedy from a pill she'd swallowed one day when all the Merricks were gone and she was blissfully alone in the house kneeling panting in each corner of each downstairs room to swab it clean with wetted paper towels. And along the baseboards, crawling on hands and knees which was the only way to clean the room absolutely. In such a way erasing sin from the world. Never doubt, it can be accomplished!

Carefully rinsing each plate and each fork, spoon, knife in hot water before placing it in the dishwasher. Setting the kitchen cupboards in order—canned goods neatly aligned on the shelves, boxes in regimented rows. In the recreation room, dusting and polishing and taking up Deedee's tossed-down things to fold and set aside. Stacking magazines and papers as they accumulated. Cleaning with Windex the TV screen which she never watched.

So Lily laughed uneasily, saying *Sharon, we don't live in a church!*

Yet of course they did, not knowing.

Lily laughed saying *Sharon, you never used to be like this when we were girls.*

Sharon smiled in silence. Thinking *How many ways I didn't use to be when we were girls, Lily will never know.*

★   ★   ★

And then one day. Fourth day of her visit. Restless, and suddenly bored. Alone in the house. An actual house! Not a condo, and not rented. Lily had been begging her to see a doctor, *let me make an appointment please Sharon, get a blood test at least;* did Lily, did Wes, worry she was infected with AIDS?

That was an insult if so. Never would God infect "Starr Bright."

Lily was out, Deedee was at school, Wes was at work.

There came "Sherrill" boldly to a mirror, trying on her wigs and examining herself critically. Only two wigs remained, curly strawberry blond and shoulder-length silky jet-black like Cleopatra. The others, utilized by "Starr Bright," had of course been carefully destroyed: burnt.

No evidence. No trace.

Restless in the strawberry-blond wig. And naked. Boldly prowling the house upstairs and down, in high-heeled shoes. (What if: a delivery man rings the doorbell, peers through a window, sees her, wild! Mistaking her for respectable Mrs. Merrick, wild!) She appeared floating as a ghost—a beautiful, naked ghost—in a mirror of the master bedroom upstairs; Wes would be lying, buck naked, giant erection flopping on his belly, on the bed. She used the adjoining bathroom which Lily had decorated in a fussy-pretty Laura Ashley style. "Sherrill's" naked buttocks on the powder-blue plastic toilet seat. Where Lily sat her bare ass. And Wes.

Used wads of faintly scented blue toilet paper to dry herself, fastidiously wetted from a faucet. Never, in "Sherrill's" romantic experience, do you know that within the next hour some ardent lover isn't going to want to kiss you *there*.

A vicious lover of hers, years ago hallucinating on peyote, Deedee's father possibly, now dead, once screamed at her *Wash yourself! Between the legs! I can smell you across the room!*

Wanting to die of shame, slash her breast, cunt and wrists and *die*.

She'd tried. And no luck.

In Deedee's room she stood naked in high heels posed in a mirror. Ghost-body. One of the pigs had actually killed her and she was a ghost prowling a house in which she didn't belong. In which others were happy. Unknowing of their good luck, and happy. And that was unjust.

It *was* unjust, God must understand. Lily had all the luck.

Deedee's room was a dull-girl's room you could see. And Deedee for all her sweetness and admiration of Aunt Sharon was a dull girl. Wasn't beautiful, and would never be. Her features were only so-so. And that pudgy chin, nose. Baby-fat. At least fifteen pounds overweight. Why didn't Lily make the girl diet? Sharon had to laugh: Deedee more resembled Lily than she did her real mother, and more resembled Wes than she did the very man, that bastard, who'd fathered her. In a careless squirty-spasm in a Mexican hotel.

At least, Sharon thought she recalled Deedee's father. Though possibly she was mistaken.

In those days she'd been a careless girl. When you looked like her, you could be careless. Traveling with whoever was most crazy for her, could spend the most money.

Downstairs, Sharon prowled through Wes's office. Any secrets here? All men have secrets though possibly not at home. Not where someone might snoop. She drew her fingertips across the edge of Wes's desk, patted the seat of his well-worn swivel chair. He was a hefty, heavy man; with the look of an athlete beginning to go to fat; must weigh two hundred twenty pounds at least. Lily's husband! You'd have thought Lily Donner would have ended up with someone meeker, less manly. Sharon methodically looked through Wes's files and desk drawers where, she knew, Lily would never venture; discovering, in the lower left-hand drawer beneath a folder of tax forms a pack of Camels, two-thirds full. *And Lily was so proud her husband no longer smoked!* Sharon laughed. "Love you, big guy." She took one of the cigarettes to smoke in solitude, later, in her room. The cigarette was harsher than her own brand, lacking a filter-tip. The taste of Wes Merrick on her lips, tongue.

She'd found his name in the telephone directory—*Dwyer, Michael*.

On an impulse dialing the number but got only an answering machine. And a nasally woman's voice on the tape. Mrs. Dwyer? Furious, she laced her fingers over the phone receiver and grunted *You tell that fucker husband of yours to keep his filthy hands to himself fuck him and fuck you!* And slammed down the receiver. Panting.

"Oh my God, did I do *that*?"

Shaking, she'd been so excited. Hadn't known. A tight, keen sensation between the legs she hadn't felt in quite a while.

Wondering at the look on the woman's face. Serves her right, married to *him*.

Big Mack Dwyer. She'd wanted to die for. Almost did.

A sword shall pierce through thine soul.

Better luck with Reigel Plumbing. Just dialed the number, no secretary or answering machine, a man answered on the second ring. And "Starr Bright" begins cooing, as only she knows how. *Hello! is this Stan? Stan Reigel is it?* and he says *yes* and she says *Hey you'll never guess who this is back in town on a visit* and he says *who?* and she says *C'mon hon: guess!* and there's a pause like the guy is blown out of his skull and in a lowered voice at last he says *Cindy?* and "Starr Bright" moans like she's hurt and mock-growls *Who the hell's Cindy? Better guess again!* And so it goes, back and forth for a while, "Starr Bright" is funny and easy going never in the slightest reproachful just out for a good time and sounding as if she's had a few drinks already this early in the afternoon finally cooing *Stan, honey, if you have a few minutes one night this week we could meet like old times and you'll remember me, fast.*

That easy. You'd never think so, but "Starr Bright" knows men.

So it had not been intended, had it? It had simply happened.

I accept my fate. I bow my head to Your will.

He'd picked her up at 10:30 P.M. of April 3, on Bank Street near Washington, where she waited sheltered in a darkened doorway of All Saints Church. There was a light drizzly rain, but freezing. And "Starr Bright" in miniskirt, high heels and silky textured black stockings.

And the sexy black lace gloves. A real turn-on, she knew from past experience.

Sliding into Reigel's 1996 Ford Cutlass. Perfumy, breathy. Long silky dancer's legs and tiny velveteen skirt, the curly strawberry-blond wig and makeup so professional it masked completely her washed-out skin. And glossy crimson lips pursed for kissing.

He'd whistled *Jez-us! Do I know you?*

Maybe not yet "Starr Bright" murmured giving the guy a peck-kiss *but you will, Stan-ley.*

His breath smelled already of whiskey. Good sign.

Stan Reigel she hadn't seen in twenty years. Thickset, balding, forty years old with a boy's pug face. (Would she have recognized him? Was this actually *him*? Good question.) He was asking nervously how's about a drink at the Eight-Ball or Artie's and she laughed, laying a black-lace-gloved hand on his wrist *Hell, no, Stan, I have a better idea, let's get a bottle and we can park somewhere private and secluded and get reacquainted—how'd you like that?*

Stan liked that just fine.

Stan blinked dazed not believing his good luck.

Stan read *Playboy* probably. Back in high school, he'd groaned with the other guys over the luscious centerfold girl-bunnies.

And so in the Buffalo & Chautauqua Railroad yard where twenty-two years ago in the back of Mack Dwyer's camper guys had fucked Sharon Donner. Taking turns, drunk and giggling. She'd been drunk, too, and giggling feebly warding off their hands or trying to. Maybe she'd said no, maybe she hadn't.

When he began to fight her it was too late. She'd slashed as deep and unerring as "Starr Bright's" strength would take her.

Once they'd climbed laughing together into the backseat of the Ford Cutlass and eagerly he'd removed his coat, his shirt-sleeves rolled up and trousers loosened. *Now d'you remember me, Stan?*

He'd been too surprised to scream. At first.

D'you remember me—now?

Now?

NOW?

She'd used a straight razor. She'd practiced the technique.

It was all "Starr Bright"—as when the lights came up blinding and she swiveled into her routine.

They would discover a tissue-papery page neatly torn from a Bible, the Book of St. John, 8. In red ink shaky block letters a self-hating drunk like S.R. might laboriously print SORRY FORGIVE ME. S. There was an urgent, loopy circle in red ink around verse 34: *Jesus answered them, Verily, verily, I say unto you. Whosoever committeth sin is the servant of sin.*

Tucked into the blood-soaked shirt against a dead man's heart.

"Alleged suicide"—she'd laugh over that, later.

Thinking how, in the Southwest and California, where "Starr Bright" had achieved renown, local cops wouldn't have come to such a conclusion.

At midnight telephoning Reigel's home number from a pay phone outside a gas station. Only two blocks from the darkened car where the pig was only just bleeding to death. But "Starr Bright" was flying high, "Starr Bright" was one to take risks. Wild! Dialing the pig's number and when a woman answered on the first ring she begged in a stricken little-girl voice *C'n I speak to Stan?—oh please!* and the woman asked *Who is this? What's wrong?* and the little-girl voice was wailing *Please please let me speak to Stan, I know he's there* and the woman demanded to know who this was and the little-girl voice interrupted *Mrs. Reigel he doesn't love you he loves me he's told me hundreds of times he can't stand you it's me he loves please tell him I'm sorry, I'm so sorry, I was wrong, I want to see him again, it's O.K. about what happened I forgive him*—and she's crying, sobbing as if her heart's broken, just a drunk hysterical young girl maybe fifteen years old young enough to be the pig-bastard's daughter.

4

The Happy Family

I am not what I appear to be in your eyes.
In all the world only one person knows my heart: my twin.

✳   ✳   ✳

"That's quite nice, Janet—only just a little more on this side—yes, perfect."

"Becky, terrific! Didn't I tell you, last week?"

"Now don't be impatient, Anita: it's coming along nicely. It *is*."

Smiling, though she was rather tired this Thursday evening, Lily moved among her students in her pottery class at Yewville Community College. It happened that all her students this semester were women, eleven women ranging in age from twenty-six-year-old Becky, who was eight months pregnant, to seventy-nine-year-old Madeleine, who'd been a widow, as she'd briskly informed them on the first day of class, for a quarter-century; ranging in ability from Laurie, who'd taken art courses at the college for years, moving from instructor to instructor like clockwork, yet reluctant, as she grimly said, to "set out on her own," to poor Anita, who was no more than Lily's age but behaved like a woman of sixty, melancholy, long-faced, always breaking things, whose frequent unconscious sighs of *Oh! my goodness!* made them all laugh good-naturedly.

Lily loved teaching. She surprised herself by liking her students more or less equally, talented or otherwise. A class was like a family, really. If someone was lagging behind, you helped her (or him: sometimes, Lily had male students) catch up; if someone was in a bad mood, you teased her out of it. Lily had been teaching for only five years, and not each semester, but already she'd accumulated in the Yewville area dozens of former students who kept in contact with her; sent her snapshots of their new work, plus pictures of children and grandchildren. *A network of women. Sisters.* Wes was happy that Lily was happy with her teaching, as he often said; but he disapproved that she was willing to teach for such a relatively low salary compared to other, male teachers at the college. It was an old issue between them.

You undervalue yourself, Lily. Consistently!

Well, at least I am consistent.

Lily didn't want to think about it. Already the spring term was half over, and she hadn't heard from the department head whether she would even be hired for the following fall semester, though contracts had gone out to other part-time teachers weeks ago.

Moving from student to student this evening, overseeing their diligent if frequently erratic work, the fashioning of generic pots, vases, bowls, "decorative objects for the home"— Lily felt strangely disoriented. As if she were in the wrong place, as in a dream. As if she should be elsewhere—but where? (At home?) She recalled her sister's tactless words: *But my teaching will be different from yours. The Pasadena School of Dance is a professional school.* Sharon had been rudely dismissive of Lily's work; but as so often with Sharon, accurate. Lily's students were not professionally committed to the art—or even the craft—of pottery, any more than Lily herself was. Most of them were middle-class housewives looking for something to do. Only one of

them had the imagination of an artist—but she was fatally lacking the courage and self-confidence; a part of her wanted only
to remain an amateur forever, basking in the praise of community college instructors. These were women, very nice women,
who yearned to "express" themselves—to a degree. Like Lily
herself. They were fond of Lily as an instructor and as a person
and wrote admiring letters to her and about her, to the college
administration. A network of women, former students of Lily
Merrick. *They are your sisters, too. Can't you draw happiness from
them?*

No, Lily thought sadly. I have only one sister.

Lily heard someone laugh. Startled, she woke from her reverie at the front of the room to discover the entire class smiling
at her. "Must be contagious," Anita said wryly, "you're sighing,
too, Lily!"

★   ★   ★

Lily was troubled about Sharon.

Obsessed with Sharon.

Wondering *Is she in danger, really? Who is after her?*
Has she brought my family into danger, too?

It was April 11. The length of the evenings and the inter-
mittent warmth of sun-filled days seemed abrupt, disorienting.
Some days—like this very day—were intoxicating with smells
of moist earth, newly revived vegetation. In other years Lily
couldn't wait for spring, this year she'd told Wes half seriously
she wasn't quite ready for it.

Already, Sharon had been staying with the Merricks for two
weeks and Lily had yet to suggest to Wes that Sharon was in
some sort of danger, or believed she was. She couldn't violate
her sister's confidence! And when she brought up the subject
to Sharon, Sharon became flurried, agitated—"Oh, Lily! I can't
deal with that now. I'm fighting a migraine, *please don't spoil this
entire day for me.*"

So that, if Lily pursued the issue, she would be persecuting and harassing her sister, too.

The two-week period had been, for Lily, both dizzyingly fast and mysteriously slow; as if Sharon had been with them, in the downstairs guest room, for six months. The household was wholly altered by her presence. (And her absence: if Sharon was out on one of her lengthy walks, the question was when would she return? Rarely did she tell anyone she was slipping away from the house, still less where she was going, and for how long. Deedee reported having sighted Aunt Sharon in All Saints cemetery "as if she's praying or something"; Wes, driving on Hawley Street, was certain he'd seen her walking briskly along the back alley, in Lily's old trench coat and boots.) She'd changed remarkably since her arrival, when she'd been so exhausted and ill; now, her old vitality was returning, as if with spring, and her old restlessness, that air of stopped-up electric energy that had always made her attractive even to those others (girls, primarily) who'd disliked and feared her. *Can't resist me, don't even try!* she seemed to proclaim, baring her teeth in a beautiful gloating smile.

Now Sharon had more energy, ironically she hadn't nearly as much time for housecleaning of the fanatic, fastidious sort she'd done earlier. Carelessly, she tossed still-damp towels into the laundry chute, and required fresh towels daily; she changed the sheets on her bed several times a week, adding considerably to the volume of laundry Lily had to do. (Which most of the time Sharon was quite content to allow Lily to do, unassisted.) After dinner she drifted away as if oblivious of Lily and Deedee cleaning up in the kitchen, or, more frequently, she lingered over coffee with Wes, smoking a cigarette and querying him about his business, or the economy, or politics; to Lily's annoyance, Wes seemed suddenly to have all the time in the world for idle conversation, where once he'd rushed his meals, needing to return to work, if he'd come home to eat at all. But Sharon remained diligent about helping Lily prepare dinner, for it was a time when the sisters could be together, engaged in a practical, pleasant task. Also, as Sharon nervously joked one day, "You know, Lily, I like to see exactly what I'm *eating*. What it actually *is*. I've been poisoned by bad food too many times."

"Seriously? *Poisoned?*" Lily smiled quizzically.

But Sharon shrugged mysteriously. *For me to know* she'd tease when they were girls *and for you to find out*.

Though Sharon still declined to watch TV in the evening with whoever might be watching in the recreation room ("I just don't want to be upset by something I might see—a news bulletin maybe"), Lily had the idea that she turned on the set in her room occasionally. (Not that Lily was eavesdropping on her sister. But she heard faint voices in the room now and then when she passed by in the hall.) And Sharon was using the telephone, Lily knew. Who are you calling? Lily inquired, thinking Sharon would say the names of girlhood friends or relatives, but Sharon replied vaguely, airily, "Oh, no one special—just business, Lily. My professional life is damned *complicated*."

Once she said rather sharply, "No, Lily. I am not calling any old boyfriends. I am not calling Mack Dwyer, *trust me*."

Another time, when Lily brought up the subject of their parents' graves in the Shaheen cemetery, asking if Sharon would like to visit them, Sharon said quickly, "I just can't be morbid-minded, Lily. Not at this time. I'm fighting for my life, fighting to *breathe*—can't you sympathize?"

Sharon began to leave the house more frequently on long rest-less walks, but she never invited Lily to accompany her. She was still fearful, she said, of being recognized.

"We'd look like sisters, side by side. In the open air."

Lily wanted to protest: Sharon so disguised herself in smoke-tinted glasses, her hair in a tight, thick twist entirely hidden by a scarf, her mouth a slash of crimson in a chalky face, how could anyone have identified her as Lily's sister?

She doesn't want me with her, Lily thought, hurt. *She's bored in my company already.*

It happened then that Sharon began to borrow Lily's car. Just for brief drives, she promised. Just to "get some air." Lily must have looked doubtful or reluctant at first, for Sharon said, with sisterly defensiveness, "Look, Lily, I have a valid driver's license from California, for God's sake." Lily murmured, "Yes, of course. I mean—I suppose." "Oh, you! Ridiculous!" Sharon snorted, and marched off to her room to locate the license, which was hidden away somewhere amid her things; Lily trailed after her guiltily assuring her there was no problem, no need to show her the license, of course she could borrow Lily's car.

Sharon said, huffily, "I'll bring it back in exactly the condition it's in, Lily. I *promise.*"

Watching Sharon drive her car, a no-frills economy Toyota, out of the drive and onto Washington Street and away, with a sudden spurt of speed, Lily thought how, as girls, Sharon had learned to drive long before she had. At first, Sharon had stealthily practiced on their father's old Nash, on a nearby country lane; in time, as a precocious twelve- and thirteen-year-old, she'd been instructed by older neighbor boys who were pleased to oblige her. (Lily watched, from the sidelines.) As soon as she turned sixteen, Sharon acquired her driver's license; at that age Lily was only just starting driver's education at the high school, one of the shyer, less confident students. Lily hadn't applied for her license until she was nineteen, by which time her sister was the high-fashion model "Sherrill" long departed from Shaheen and Yewville, living in Manhattan and boasting of driving a Mercedes coupe—"A gift from an admirer."

True to her promise, Sharon didn't cause injury to Lily's car. But she upset Lily, and Wes, by turning up unexpectedly at the high school to whisk Deedee off shopping at the North Yewville Mall, only just opened. There, Aunt Sharon and her adoring niece whom she pointedly called "Deirdre" visited only the most stylish stores, buying clothes, shoes, makeup for the girl. In all, Sharon must have spent $300, and paid in cash. Gap jacket and pants, Benetton sweaters, Polo jeans and bleached shirts, lace-up shoe-boots so clunky and ugly in Lily's eyes she had to know they were teenage high fashion. Deedee was euphoric of course, the happiest Lily had seen her daughter in years, but Lily was discomforted. "But Sharon, can you really afford all these things?" Lily asked, as if the mere outlay of cash were the issue. "What a question!" Sharon retorted, as if her very honor were at stake. "I'm not a housewife on a budget, Lily, dear—I'm a career woman with my own income." Wes too was uneasy when Deedee, startlingly made-up in bright lipstick, eye shadow and eyeliner, modeled her "spring outfit" for him—snug pants, loose-fitting shirt and safari jacket; he told Deedee curtly that she looked "like something on MTV"—the channel of all channels Wes hated. In private, he warned Lily that he didn't want the shopping excursion repeated. "She's your sister. *You* make it clear."

One of the items of clothing Sharon bought for Deedee was a Gipsy Horse minidress of crushed purple velvet—size 8. Deedee's size was 12. "Deirdre and I decided she needs some incentive," Sharon said. Lily asked, " 'Incentive' for what?" and Sharon said, "To lose a few pounds, Lily. Obviously." Deedee, who was listening in, said, "Oh, God, more than a few!" sighing and pinching at her waistline, and her young, shapely breasts. "I'm *gross*."

Lily realized her daughter had already begun to cut back on food—no rich desserts, smaller second helpings at meals.

That evening Lily came to speak with Deedee in her room, gently scolding her for saying such things about herself. "Deedee, you're a lovely girl. Don't you know that?"

Deedee, sprawled across her bed, applying Revlon purple-plum fingernail polish to her nails, another gift of Sharon's, snorted and rolled her eyes. "Oh, Mom. You don't need to lie to make me feel good."

"Lie?" Lily was hurt.

Deedee said, sighing, as if it fell upon her shoulders to utter the most obvious, banal insight, one known to everyone except her dense mother, "Well, Mom, you never exactly tell the truth—do you? Not like Aunt Sharon. She just looked at me, and smiled, and said, 'Deirdre, you're fat.' I respect her for that."

I am not what I seem to be in your eyes.
When you learn, will you forgive me!

Lily's pottery class began more or less at 7 P.M. and was supposed to end at 10 P.M.; but her students lingered, of course. As usual, it was past 10:30 P.M. when Lily arrived home.

She was thinking about her sister Sharon, and she was thinking about her daughter Deedee.

I am not what I seem. Forgive me!

Someday, perhaps soon, she would have to tell Deedee that she was adopted; it was all the fashion now, such painful disclosures. But Lily's parents had believed that a child was far better off not knowing; and in Lily's case, when Sharon so adamantly insisted upon giving her baby to Lily, only under the condition that no one outside the family ever know the truth—what choice had Lily? Fifteen years later, it seemed to her that her promise, made as much to her mother and father as to Sharon, still held; she could not see, morally, that a vow of such a kind would not be binding through life.

Lily wondered: would it be enough to tell Deedee that she was adopted, and not to tell who her mother was? (Lily hadn't any idea who Deedee's father was, and had been given to believe by remarks of Sharon's that Sharon didn't precisely know, either.) Deedee would want to see adoption papers; and there were none.

But to tell Deedee who her mother was, and to incur Sharon's wrath—that was impossible.

Mom, you never exactly tell the truth, do you?

It was a simple, uncanny insight. In her innocence Deedee had spoken more truly than she knew.

Yet how could Lily say *I am not your mother, I am your aunt. Your glamorous aunt Sharon—is your mother.*

No, it wasn't possible! Even in her imagination Lily couldn't shape such painful words.

She would lose Deedee. She might lose Wes, as well.

Lily felt a wave of dizziness sweep over her, as if the very axis of her life were shifting. She had to grip the steering wheel of her car tight to maintain control.

But even before Sharon had arrived, with the explosive emotional force, in Lily's settled life, of a meteor, Lily had had a premonition of change. Some strange, frightening alteration as of the very molecules of her soul. Those dreams of last autumn and winter. Such disturbing, mysterious dreams. *You're my slave you have to do what I say. And never never tell.*

As if the cruel child Rose of Sharon had reentered Lily's life, commanding her to—what? What course of action, against her will?

And now Sharon was returned to Yewville, and Lily was the imposter.

Yet: was there a secret pleasure in all this?

A secret pleasure in the very fact of living a *secret*? As Deedee would say, with typical adolescent bluntness, a *lie*?

Turning into the driveway of her home, Lily felt, as always, her heart leap at the sight of the house; the downstairs windows, warmly lighted. There was a faint, chill fog, oddly stale-smelling, wafting across the lawn. How Lily loved her house, her home! It seemed to her a miracle that she, of all people, lived here.

Lily parked the Toyota in front of the garage, and hurried along the walk to the back door, and glanced into the lighted window of the recreation room to see a sight that stopped her

in her tracks: there were Wes and Sharon on the sofa watching
TV, each with a can of Wes's favorite beer in hand, and, on the
floor between them, Deedee, hugging her knees to her chest.
Reflections and shadows from the animated TV screen played
across their rapt, smiling faces. Sharon was wearing a soft-
looking pale yellow sweater Lily hadn't seen before, and her
blond hair was newly shampooed and brushed, fluffed out
about her face; she looked ten years younger than her age, startlingly beautiful. And there was Wes, ruddy-faced, grinning at
the TV—Wes, who rarely had time to watch even news programs. And Deedee laughing. *A happy American family.*

Lily hurried inside, almost stumbling on the steps.

"I'm home!"

No one answered. No one heard. The TV must have been
on too loud.

5

In Lily's Toyota

*H*e hath led me in dark places, as they that be dead of old.

Driving slowly past the brick-Georgian house at 99 Parkway Lane. In the borrowed car driving slowly and thoughtfully and with no bitterness in her heart. For now "Starr Bright" was master, and would exact her vengeance methodically, without haste.

Not here, and not now. Another time. Soon.

Taking note that the house was of a style hardly distinguishable from its neighbors. Large, obviously expensive, a family home, six bedrooms at least. In "prestigious" Country Club Estates, where all the houses were new, large, made of brick: family homes. America is families, American homes are family homes. You observe them from the outside exclusively, at a distance. You would not be welcome inside.

In the directory she'd located him with no difficulty. A business phone and downtown Yewville address, and a home phone and address here at 99 Parkway Drive. *Dwyer, Michael D.* Lily had remarked she didn't think he was called "Mack" any longer but Lily would be mistaken. Mack's old friends, his high school buddies, certainly called him "Mack." An old girlfriend could only call him "Mack."

Remember me, Mack? No?

Sure you do.

Noting that the back lawn of the Dwyer home opened out onto the golf course of the Yewville Country Club, in mid-April puddled with sheets of glittering water amid the emerging green bright as artificial grass. Did Mack play golf now, like his father? The Dwyers' lawn, the lot, must have been two acres at least, larger than the Merricks' in an older residential neighborhood of the city but, being more recently developed, had fewer tall trees. There were open spaces between houses in Country Club Estates. You could not approach such houses from the street, or from the rear, without being exposed. But "Starr Bright" would never seek such entry.

And there appeared a great wonder in heaven; a woman clothed with the sun; and the moon under her feet, and upon her head a crown of twelve stars.

Not here, and not now. Another time. Soon.

It was a windy, chilly April day dazzling with sunshine. Shutting her eyes feeling the sun's warmth on her face she understood that it was the identical sun, the identical warmth, that had nourished her months ago in—had it been Nevada?—silently departing the room of the Paradise Motel splattered with a pig's blood yet "Starr Bright" herself spotless, untouched. *In His sign. In His terrible justice and mercy.* She had driven across the desert embraced by the emerging dawn, she had not been afraid, not even when a Nevada highway patrol car passed her, for His blessing was upon her, she could not be touched by mere humankind.

And so it had been, and so it would be. In all these months not once had she been in danger of being *seen, known, named.*

Driving now, in no haste, for never did "Starr Bright" act in haste, north to Route 209, which partly circled the city. She'd disliked Lily's little economy Toyota at first, it so lacked heft, dignity; but now she was getting the feel of it, the tight handling of the steering wheel, the low ceiling and cramped interior. Of course, "Starr Bright" was accustomed to luxury cars but this would do, in Yewville, for her purposes. And she was wearing, not Lily's old trench coat, but a newer coat of her sister's, a red plaid car coat with wooden buttons—a suburban-mother car coat! She loved it, such American anonymity. *I could be one of them—a mother. A housewife.* On her head was a tight-fitting beige knit cloche hat she'd bought at the mall the other day while Deirdre was trying on clothes and beneath the hat, hardly visible, silky jet-black hair, an attractive fringe of it across her forehead. And the smoky-black sunglasses of course. Without these, the sunlight would have pierced her eyes like ice picks.

Could have been a wife to him. And Deirdre our daughter.

Not fat "Deedee"!—but a lovely slim girl of whom "Starr Bright" could be proud.

But she would not remain in Yewville much longer. Following her date in a few days with Mack Dwyer she would depart.

Yet in no haste. Invisible.

She parked the Toyota at the rear of a strip mall on 209, behind Qwik-Photo. Approaching the rear entrance to the shop but instead quickly and deftly and without being seen searching through a large cardboard trash box out of which she selected a dozen prints apparently discarded for imperfections. And afterward parked elsewhere on 209 she sorted through the prints and tossed away all but one: a poorly focused snapshot of a girl of about twenty with a pretty, sullen mouth, lank dirt-colored hair, and eyes that stared as if about to burst from their sockets. *You don't know me Mrs. Dwyer but I know you. He loves me NOT YOU.*

Though undecided: if she should mail this snapshot and message to Mrs. Dwyer just before her date with Mack, or if she should mail it just after. Either way, the woman, the widow, would receive it the following day.

6

Lovesick

You're fat. But you needn't be. Exert your will! Be beautiful.

Lovesick Deedee drifted downstairs in the waning afternoon light to the rear of the house in the hope that her aunt Sharon's door might be open, or ajar; or her glamorous aunt might be in the kitchen preparing a cup of coffee and seeing Deedee would smile, hands on her hips. *Well, Deirdre! Hel-lo.*

Since the shopping trip, since Aunt Sharon had been the kindest to her that anyone in her lifetime had ever been, there was a special understanding between them. Deedee woke in the night startled and suffused with a sense of anticipation, keen almost as dread. *I love you, Aunt Sharon! Don't ever ever go away. Or—take me with you. Please.*

No luck this afternoon. The door of her aunt's room wasn't open, nor even ajar.

"Aunt Sharon?" Deedee knocked shyly on the door.

Her heart was beating quickly, her palms had broken out in perspiration. She had so much to tell her aunt: that morning she'd weighed herself naked on her scales, and her weight was just under one hundred twenty-eight pounds—a pound and a half down from the previous morning, and almost seven pounds down from her original, disgusting weight of one hundred thirty-five. But, after gym class, after having eaten nothing all day except a cup of watery plain yogurt and a half-apple at noon, she'd weighed herself again and her weight was one hundred twenty-six pounds and five ounces. *Fantastic.*

And she was feeling good. She was feeling great. Not light-headed or dizzy but like her head was filled with helium-happy thoughts. *Fantastic!*

Aunt Sharon had predicted she could be wearing the purple crushed-velvet dress by May first if she truly wanted to; if her will was "concentrated" sufficiently. And so it would seem to be. *And so it would be.*

Upstairs Deedee's geometry homework awaited and a chapter to read in her history text and as usual there were damn old boring old household chores Mom was expecting her to do. But Deedee drew a deep breath and knocked again on her aunt's door, calling gently, "Aunt Sharon? It's me." Hearing then, or imagining she heard, a voice say *Come in!*

So she pushed open the door, which was unlocked. But the lavender-and-cream room, which smelled of perfume, cigarette smoke and something acrid and ashy, was empty. "Aunt Sharon? It's Deedee—I mean, Deirdre." She listened: running water? The shower in the adjoining bathroom? More than once, after showering, Aunt Sharon had allowed Deedee to perch on the edge of her bed and observe as she applied makeup to her face, or brushed and artfully styled her beautiful, shimmering pale-blond hair. (Aunt Sharon believed in being impeccably groomed for their evening meal.) Best of all, Deedee's aunt might offer to apply makeup to her face, too; or briskly brush and style her dense, springy hair, which was several shades darker than her aunt's. Once, Deedee had said, seeing her aunt and herself side by side in the bureau mirror, "We look alike, sort of, Aunt Sharon—don't we? A little?" The older woman had stared at her for a blank moment, meeting Deedee's hopeful eyes in the mirror, and Deedee was mortified thinking *Oh God! I've insulted her* but her aunt murmured something vague and pleasant that sounded like *That's sweet, Deirdre* and the painful moment passed.

Later, they'd shared one of Aunt Sharon's cigarettes. Deedee had choked a bit, coughed, her eyes spilling tears, and her aunt had laughed at her and tenderly touched the tip of a forefinger to her nose.

Exactly like me, Deirdre, at your age.

Sharing a forbidden cigarette, and sharing other confidences, was part of the special, secret understanding between Deedee and Aunt Sharon. And so when Mom asked, casually, in that way of hers that thinly masked hurt, *What do you and my sister find to talk about so much?* Deedee had shrugged and said, evasively, *Oh, Mom. Nothing.*

The guest bedroom, always so neatly maintained by Lily, and rarely disturbed, had become, by this time, wholly Aunt Sharon's room. Her fascinating things were spread out everywhere: clothing, lingerie, cosmetics, glittering bottles and jars and tubes. The closet was filled with more clothes, at which Deedee had been allowed to look, with her aunt overseeing to explain where she'd purchased what, for what occasion, and who had accompanied her, and what had happened; a sexy black silk Pierre Cardin pants suit, for instance, had been her outfit for an Academy Award ceremony in Hollywood she'd attended two years ago with Jack Nicholson and mutual friends. (Eagerly Deedee inquired what was Jack Nicholson like, and Aunt Sharon said, with a fastidious wrinkling of her nose, as if she both disapproved and was impressed by the man, *Exactly what you'd expect.* Deedee hadn't quite known what this meant but she'd giggled excitedly just the same.) There were wigs in the closet, too, "play-wigs" as Aunt Sharon called them. Rarely worn.

It was surprising that some of Aunt Sharon's jewelry, including the gold chain, lay atop the bureau, in plain view. Deedee went to examine the chain, which looked so beautiful around her aunt's neck, and which she so frequently wore. Then it was in Deedee's hands, lifted to her neck; Deedee noted its weight—of course, it was solid gold. Peering into the mirror, admiring the rich golden glow against her flushed skin, Deedee felt a thrill of—what? Never would she be beautiful like her aunt; but the possession of such a striking piece of jewelry would grant her a mysterious power.

"Deirdre! What are you doing?"

There stood Aunt Sharon behind her, staring. She must have slipped silently into the room; Deedee had not heard any sound, nor seen any movement through the mirror. Her aunt's normally smiling face was taut and waxy-pale and her eyes were narrowed almost to slits. And how harsh her usually welcoming voice.

Deedee began to stammer guiltily, "Oh, gosh! I'm sorry, Aunt Sharon, I—I was just looking at—this." In her fright she'd dropped the gold chain onto the bureau as if it were on fire.

Aunt Sharon was clearly angry, breathing quickly, but she maintained a cool poise. "It isn't good manners, miss, to enter another person's room uninvited. I'd have thought your mother would have taught you that."

Deedee saw that her aunt had just strode in from outdoors; she was carrying a tote bag, her hair was windblown and she'd just removed her dark-tinted glasses. Lily had taken the car for afternoon errands and Aunt Sharon might have supposed herself alone in the house.

Deedee was terribly embarrassed, her face flushed red as if she'd been slapped. "I'm so sorry, Aunt Sharon—I thought I heard you say come in. I knocked, and—I thought you might be in your bathroom. I—guess I don't know what came over me." And that was true enough.

Thank God, Aunt Sharon decided to forgive her. Deedee's repentance was so genuine.

"Well! You're here now. Good to see you, Deirdre."

Aunt Sharon dropped the tote bag onto the bed, went to shut the door to the hall, and, to Deedee's immense relief, managed a smile—almost, a smile of spontaneous welcome. Sitting on the edge of the bed, whose lavender-and-cream floral-print

Laura Ashley comforter had the look of having been pulled up
hastily over rumpled bedsheets, Deedee's aunt lit a cigarette;
exhaled slowly, her eyes shut; recalled Deedee's presence and
offered her a "drag"—which, under the circumstances, Deedee
could hardly decline. Like an obedient child she took the cigarette from her aunt's just perceptibly trembling fingers (but
how glamorous the nails: inch-long, maroon-polished and
gleaming like lacquer), inhaled, choked, but managed, thank
God, not to cough.

"And how've you been, sweetie? What's new?"

Deedee, grateful as a puppy for having been forgiven for
her trespass, feeling the need to be praised and comforted, told
her aunt, in some detail, of that day's weight loss—"I couldn't
believe it, Aunt Sharon, what the scales said! It was so—
fantastic."

Aunt Sharon murmured, "Hmmm!" as Deedee elaborated
even further; she smoked her cigarette, glancing about the
room. With a part of her mind Deedee understood that her
aunt was distracted, still rather upset. *Please don't think I came in
here deliberately! Please don't think I would spy on you! Steal from
you! I love you.* Deedee complained that it was hard to diet when
Mom was always vigilant at mealtimes—"It's like she wants me
to stay *fat.* Her and Dad both. They say," Deedee continued,
with an air of adolescent outrage, "—they like me *just the way I
am.* Gross!"

But Aunt Sharon wasn't listening, perhaps; she startled
Deedee by rising suddenly from the bed in a lithe, springlike
motion at odds with her seemingly indolent manner; as if, like a
cat, she'd sighted something moving outside the window—but,
standing at the window, peering out, apparently she saw nothing. (The window, like others in the room, overlooked only an
expanse of lawn, trees and shrubs and a glimpse of a neighboring house.) "Is something wrong?" Deedee asked, alarmed; but
again, her aunt didn't seem to hear.

"Deirdre—has anyone unusual come to this house lately?"

"What? Who? I guess—gosh, no—I don't think so."

"Has anyone been making inquiries about me?"

"N-no, Aunt Sharon. Not that I know of."

"You're sure, Deirdre?"

Deedee nodded solemnly. She was sure.

In fact, it was so disappointing!—the girls who'd been curious about the glamorous blond woman in the taxi who'd called out "Deirdre" only twelve days ago seemed to have forgotten totally about her; and in fact forgotten within a day or two. Deedee had given brief, evasive replies to their questions, to discourage them from asking; yet she hadn't wanted the girls to *forget*.

Several of Deedee's closer friends had remarked upon her new clothes from the mall, and her experiments with makeup; to Deedee's delight, they'd noticed she was losing weight. They told her she was looking "great"—"terrific"—"really cool"— but Deedee hadn't been able to inform them proudly that it was the influence of her aunt—Aunt "Sherrill"—who'd been a top New York fashion model now with a West Coast modern dance troupe.

Her aunt who'd all but promised that she, Deedee, could come visit her in Pasadena this summer— *Stay as long as you like!*

"Your mother hasn't mentioned anyone making inquiries, either?—so far as you know?"

"I guess not."

" 'Guess'—or *know*?"

"I think I—*know*."

Aunt Sharon, still visibly trembling as if, in fact, she'd seen something outside the window, decided to believe Deedee. In any case she shrugged, returned to the bed to sit heavily, smoking her cigarette and gazing at Deedee with eyes that were just slightly shadowed, and blood-veined; the lids, glimmering with silver-green eye shadow, were puffy as if she'd had a sleepless night or was running a fever. She wore elegantly fashioned white linen slacks, the cuffs of which were grimy; and a black sequined sweater with a stretched neckline, and canvas sneakers of the kind sold at Kmart, badly worn. Her glossy maroon lipstick was partly eaten away and her face was still tight-looking, pinched. Deedee was thinking *I will die if you stop liking me! If you stop trusting me!* She heard herself say how sad and lonely she felt at school sometimes, how bad she felt, that was why she ate more than she should, hiding away chips and candy in her room to eat while she did homework and sometimes in the middle of the night—"I just get so mad and so *hungry*."

Something in Deedee's whining, desperate tone roused her aunt to attention. The glassy eyes focused on her, suddenly sharp. "What's that? What's going on at school? Why are you unhappy at school?"

Deedee squirmed in embarrassment. It was an exaggeration to claim she was *unhappy*, exactly, only just not—*happy*. "Oh, I don't know, Aunt Sharon," Deedee said, gulping for breath, "—it's just the atmosphere, you know. I mean—the other kids—" *Don't pay enough attention to me.* "—sometimes they're cruel."

"Is a boy giving you trouble, Deirdre? Boys?"

Quickly Deedee shook her head, no. "Not exactly—"

Aunt Sharon said vehemently, "Deirdre, at your age boys are frankly pigs. You would not believe how filthy-minded a teenaged boy can be." She shook her head in disgust and wonderment. "Ordinary, 'normal' boys. The male sex in adolescence."

Deedee said uncertainly, "I—guess I don't know any guys that well, Aunt Sharon. The guys on the newspaper are sort of—quiet, nice—"

"They're different from us. Absolutely. With them, everything is sex, sex, sex. Sex, and hurting. To them, sex *is* hurting. All males are rapists only just looking for the opportunity."

Deedee swallowed hard. Her aunt's voice was so authoritative, so certain. The very word "rapist" was embarrassing: she'd never heard it uttered in such an intimate, face-to-face way by any adult.

"If a man—any man—any male of any age—could rape a woman, and kill her in that way, with his penis, hammering—hammering—hammering until she was dead—if he could do that, Deirdre, and get away with it, his identity unknown—he would. Are you aware of that?"

Deedee shook her head mutely, shocked.

"It's a fact of life, Deirdre. But a fact girls like you, good sweet middle-class girls, are protected from—that's to say, kept in willful ignorance. Until one day you find out—if you're un-lucky—and after that, forever, you *know*."

Deedee could think of nothing to say except a muffled "Gosh."

Aunt Sharon continued, passionately, "That's why you must never trust them, Deirdre. Boys and men. You're young, and inexperienced, and your mother shields you—'protects' you. As she was protected, and as I was. We were led to believe that mankind is good—our father preached the gospel of Jesus Christ abiding in the heart of men and women—and we all know that Jesus is *good*—and so we weren't protected, and we came to harm. I mean—might have come to harm." Aunt Sharon paused, breathing quickly. She might have noticed the stunned, glazed expression in her niece's eyes for she relented, softening her tone. "Of course, not all men are wicked. Not all men are pigs. There are good men, too—like your grandfather Donner in fact, and like your—father, Wes Merrick—*he's* a good man, I'm sure. Though in Vietnam he was a soldier—a young man, male—" Her voice trailed off as if she'd thought better of what she was saying, and began again from another angle. "This diet of yours, Deirdre. Keep on with it! Already you look better, *I* can see the difference. And as you become more attractive to boys, remember: no trust. *You* control *them*—or stay away from them entirely."

Deedee, squirming, murmured a vague "O.K."

"You must carry yourself through life with dignity and courage, Deirdre! A woman walks on a high wire and men watch hoping for her to fall. Even good men—sometimes. They love helpless, hurt women! They call them 'good' women; they marry them. Independent women—women who walk alone—women like me—they call 'bad.' " Aunt Sharon laughed, as if she'd never heard anything so amusing. Her head fell back, the tendons in her throat were tautly exposed, her laughter was hoarse, a spasm rocking her body. Deedee grinned, and tried to laugh with her, yet somehow could not. She had the idea that her aunt was speaking with genial contempt of her mother.

Mysteriously Aunt Sharon said, "And if a brave woman defends herself—against male lust, cruelty—rape—they may charge her with being a criminal. They may *try*."

How strangely she was looking at Deedee. How almost—hungrily.

Still talking in this way, Aunt Sharon went into her bathroom; her manner was feverish, euphoric; it reminded Deedee of nothing so much as the way in which some of the girls at school laughed and shrieked together sometimes in the girls' locker room, or, more boldly, in the corridors between classes, when passing boys might overhear. Always, until now, Deedee had yearned to be a part of such strident hilarity.

Aunt Sharon opened and slammed the medicine-cabinet door, ran water into a glass, reappeared in the doorway, swaying, and swallowing down a pill, then another—"To ward off migraine." It occurred to Deedee only now that her aunt had been drinking; she must have gone out, for a drink, on foot. Deedee wished keenly that they might speak of other things but her aunt was squatting now beside the bed, rifling through her canvas suitcase. Deedee caught sight of, surprisingly, newspaper pages there, some of them tabloid size, with red banner headlines; it was one of these she selected, hesitantly at first, then handing it to Deedee with a flourish to read.

"Deirdre! Tell me what you think."

The paper was the *Inquirer,* the issue dated December of the previous year; the headline was SIX "STAR" MURDERS UNSOLVED, FEMALE SERIAL KILLER SOUGHT; the lurid, exclamatory feature, written in primer sentences, focused upon the butchery-murders of six men, whose pictures were shown, along with a graphic photo of a Las Vegas motel room splattered in blood and covered with cryptic star or pentagon symbols and the foot-high words DIE PIG FILTH   DIE SATAN. Deedee's aunt was staring at her so avidly, it was hard for her to read; she kept losing her concentration; felt hairs stirring at the nape of her neck. Aunt Sharon was saying excitedly, "A Hollywood friend of mine—a close friend of Jack Nicholson's in fact—plans on doing a movie about this 'Star killer' if he can get financial backing. He'd like 'Sherrill' for the role. What d'you think, sweetie? Cool, eh?"

The other afternoon at the mall, Deedee had exclaimed "cool!" so frequently that her aunt had teased her about it. Now Deedee could only smile wanly. "I saw this on TV—I think. A while back. It's, well—" Deedee swallowed hard. The faces of the murdered men gazed out so *unknowing*; most of them *smiling*. One of them, "Herman LaPointe of Phoenix, Arizona," bore an unsettling resemblance to Wes Merrick. "—kind of sick, I guess. I mean—isn't it?"

There was a moment's pause. Then Aunt Sharon said, with an air of reproach, "It would be a fantastic role for my first film, Deirdre. It would be a true challenge and the results would receive a lot of nationwide attention—I'm sure."

Deedee laughed uneasily. "One of those movies Mom would never see." Then, she remembered: "Or you, either, Aunt Sharon. You hate that kind of 'exploitation'—you said."

"As an actress, I'd take any role that was a challenge," Aunt Sharon said coolly. "And so would you, Deirdre. If you were a professional."

"Like being a photographer, like in wartime—yes, I guess so."

But Deedee didn't sound very convincing. Her aunt took the *Inquirer* feature back from her, to return to the suitcase. Deedee saw that it had been folded, unfolded and again folded many times, with care.

The atmosphere between Deedee and her aunt had shifted. Deedee understood that something was wrong, she'd given the wrong, disappointing answer. Everything had gone wrong since she'd pushed open that door and come inside here uninvited!

Aunt Sharon sighed, and stretched; lit another cigarette, and clicked her little silver lighter shut decisively; cocked her head at Deedee, and said, with a droll smile, "Of course, I should expect nothing. These film deals have a way of dissolving into thin air—'Sherrill' knows." She spoke now with resignation where a minute before she'd been euphoric.

Deedee said, with forced enthusiasm, "You'd be great in movies, Aunt Sharon. Maybe—I could come watch, when it was being made?"

At the bureau, Aunt Sharon impulsively lifted the gold chain that Deedee had been so reckless in admiring, and held it out invitingly to the girl. She said, "I'm sorry I overreacted, Deirdre. My nerves! Your mother knows, my life is complicated in ways hers isn't; it's hard for me to adjust to Yewville, where basically nothing happens."

Deedee had a flash of a man's picture in the *Yewville Journal*—Stanley Reigel. His son Ben was a junior at the high school. But she wasn't going to contradict her aunt.

The older woman beckoned her, smiling; obediently Deedee went to her, and allowed herself to be positioned in front of the mirror, her aunt close behind her, raising the gold chain to her neck. How beautiful it was, glittering like a golden snake's scales! "You like this, Deirdre, do you?—you have excellent taste. So simple, classical—pure gold. A man gave this to me, in Las Vegas, ten years ago on my birthday. He was crazy to marry me—I loved him—almost loved him—but I had to break his heart." She laughed, sadly. "Here. Take it. It's yours now."

Quickly Deedee said, "Oh, no, Aunt Sharon—I can't."

"Why not?"

"Thanks, but I just *can't*."

Not knowing why, Deedee tasted panic; felt desperate to escape; the cold touch of the metal against her throat, her aunt pressing close against her from behind, her aunt's warm, somewhat stale breath that smelled of cigarettes and wine—no, she couldn't bear it.

"Mom says I shouldn't take any more presents from you, Aunt Sharon," Deedee said, for this was true enough. "She says—and Dad, too—you're too generous with me."

"Too generous!" Aunt Sharon stared.

"After all those other nice things you bought me—" Deedee said awkwardly, easing away.

"But this is special, Deirdre," Aunt Sharon said, again lifting the gold chain. Her smooth forehead was knit in perplexity. "This has a sentimental value. If—"

There! Deedee heard her mother's car pull up the drive, and a moment later the car door slam. What relief she felt—it was hard to disguise it.

Deedee mumbled, "Mom's home," and headed for the door, and her aunt grabbed her arm, gripping her almost painfully, and said, "Deirdre, you won't tell your parents about"— she hesitated, glancing toward the suitcase on the floor—"my movie plans, will you? That's our secret."

"I sure won't, Aunt Sharon!"

Seeming to know it would be the last of their secrets.

7

The Good Sister

It was not so easy to speak with Mr. Dwyer of the mayor's office as it had been to speak with Mr. Reigel of Reigel Plumbing but she had no doubt she would speak with the man soon, and so proceeded with her plan. En route to Rita's Beauty Salon to acquire strands of a stranger's hair she had a sudden attack of dizziness, had to pull Lily's Toyota to the side of the road. Oh God if a cop came by! asked to see her license!—a California license expired some time ago and maybe not exactly hers but one she'd borrowed from a friend or had been given. And she had no weapon to protect herself, none on her person. But recovered then after a few minutes for God had after all entered into a pact with her, a covenant. Completed the errand as planned, the hair in a plastic bag, so thirsty and her head pounding she stopped for a drink, just one, at the Ramada Inn at this hour of midafternoon when no man would approach her, and no man did. And on Bank Street at All Saints Church she marveled to see in the churchyard amid the grave markers "Starr Bright" resplendent in white her head lifted in pride and her blond hair afire and upon it a crown of twelve stars: how they blazed, blinded!

For my kingdom is not of this world.

Yet another day also in the Merricks' neighborhood ascending the long Hawley Street hill sighting a sturdy ugly-gray car approaching. Male driver in dark-tinted glasses and male companion glancing at her through the windshield of the Toyota impassive and unreadable. And she was alert but not panicked driving on impassive herself.

Plainclothes detectives. Unmarked police car.

Trying to recall if she'd seen this car before. Cruising Washington Street, slowing in front of the Merricks' house. The unmarked cars were heavily reinforced, bulletproof. You could tell, if you knew what to look for. And the pig-look, unmistakable.

Yes but coming down from a drug high you're gonna be paranoid so factor that in always.

A guy had instructed her and she knew the wisdom of such advice. Yet: wondering if really she'd killed that one in Vegas, the one who'd been a cop, completely killed him draining the last drop of pig-blood from his veins. Deputy sheriff not of Nevada but some midwestern state. His name forgotten. *Had to break his heart!* For it was possible he'd lived.

Possible they'd all entered into a conspiracy. Police of how many states, counties. In which case the news released by Yewville police of Stanley Reigel's "suicide" was in fact a conspiracy to deceive.

Possibly they knew "Starr Bright" was here in Yewville, New York.

Known but not acknowledged.

So she drove, calmly, at twenty-five miles an hour which was the speed limit, past Washington Street. Would not return to the house for another hour minimum.

Though knowing of course they'd have the Toyota's license number in their computer. Obviously they knew to whom it belonged and the place of residence. And maybe—it made her crazy to think of this so really she shouldn't—like bringing a

lighted match too close to her own hair—or singeing her eyelashes as once for some funky reason she'd done—just maybe
they'd been questioning Lily. *Who is your sister? How long has she
been residing with you?* But Lily of the Valley would never betray
Rose of Sharon—never. *My slave. I command you. We can't ever
be lonely like other people. I love you.* So she understood that Lily
would never tell; not under torture, would Lily tell; but the
man, the husband, his name temporarily blurred, the man who
was Lily's husband—*he could not be trusted.*

Wes was his name: "Wes Merrick."

Casting his lustful gaze upon her, slow stunned smile of a
guy feeling blood seeping into his cock, dreamy-eyed watching
TV and their arms accidentally brushing together, the hairs stirring on Sharon's arm and she'd been ready for him, giving off
every signal she was ready for him, sharing a final can of beer
joking and kidding around and the girl, the sad plain fat girl,
what was her name, Lily's daughter, poor Lily's responsibility—
the girl grinning up at them like she's giving them permission
to fuck right there on the sofa.

Why not? He was hot for it, and so was she.

Except: Lily'd come home.

Poor sweet stupid Lily of the Valley blundering in un-
wanted. Knowing what was what but, like Lily, pretending she
did not.

Pretending not to know *If you died Lily your precious husband
would want to marry me, just maybe I'd take the big guy up on it.*

But then inside the house suddenly she had one of her dizzy
spells and began shaking and her teeth chattering like she was
freezing and fuck it Lily was there, Lily was a witness and
grabbed her to keep her from fainting crying *Oh Sharon!* so she
felt her sister's concern for her, and her love. And Lily was the
stronger insisting Sharon must see a doctor next morning, no
more procrastinating. So in that moment of weakness she gave
in.

For "Starr Bright" was brave as an upright flame fearing no earthly hurt. While "Sharon Donner" was a coward deserving the worst that might befall her.

Next morning of course she was fine. Changed her mind and called the doctor's office to cancel. And when Lily came to her room to get her she informed Lily she was fully recovered, she was fine and didn't need any doctor poking her with needles. So she wasn't going.

And Lily was almost speechless. Stammering, "Sharon, you p-promised! Damn you, you promised!" And Sharon laughed seeing her good-girl sister mad as hell, spots of color coming up in her cheeks. And Lily demanded, "Just what are you laughing at, Sharon?" and Sharon winked at her saying, "You."

Which really set Lily off.

Lily said, sputtering, "You promised! You promised, Sharon!"—as if they were girls of ten. "A blood test, at least, Sharon—obviously you're not well."

And Sharon said carelessly, stretching and yawning, so what if she was a little anemic, she was taking iron tablets. She didn't have leukemia for God's sake. She didn't have AIDS.

The look in Lily's face.

"Nerves. That's all."

Extending her slender beringed hands, beautifully manicured nails. Yes her hands trembled a little but so what? It was morning.

Lily said self-righteously, "Sharon, you don't *eat*. You push food around on your plate—you drink and you smoke your filthy cigarettes but you don't *eat*. You're too *thin*." And Sharon retorted, "Yes? There's plenty of people—some of them right in this house—who think I look just fine at this weight. Ask them." And Lily said, the words spilling from her pent-up and painful, "And you're a bad influence on Deedee, she's starving herself, I'm afraid she'll become anorexic. Like *you*." So they quarreled. First time in how many years. Sharon would've predicted she'd be cool, bemused, as "Starr Bright" looking calmly on, but there she was going hot in the face like her sister, heart pounding as if she'd snorted a line of coke. Cursing and pacing the room kicking at the bed, at a pillow on the floor, at her suitcase saying it was Lily who made her nervous, made her hands shake for Christ's sake always watching her! spying on her! just like when they were girls and Lily pretended to worry Sharon might get "in trouble" when she was simply jealous, pure and simple. Because she hadn't any boyfriends of her own. Saying, "I refuse to be dissected for your pity, 'Lily of the Valley.' You have no command over me now, I'm not your fucking slave. Nor am I a junkie—so fuck *that*." And Lily stared at her dazed. As if not knowing what *junkie* meant. As if never hearing the word *fuck* hurtled at her like a glob of spit.

"And if you hadn't sold the family farm, I'd have a place to live," Sharon said furiously. "I'd have a chance to get well. I wouldn't be dependent upon your precious *charity*. You and your precious *Wes*."

Lily protested, "Sharon, that isn't fair. It wasn't my decision to sell the farm, it had to be sold. I've tried to explain—"

"*You* want to believe I'm sick because it makes you so fucking *normal*. All our lives it's been *good* Lily and *bad* Sharon— right? You get off on that, right?"

Lily stepped back, as if Sharon's wild-waving hands frightened her. "Sharon, please. You can't believe that."

"If you want me to leave, Lily, just tell me. If you can't stand the sight of me!" Sharon's voice rose to a thin childlike soprano, blindly she would have rushed from the room but Lily caught her in her arms. The sisters struggled together, panting. "Stop, stop, just stop, Sharon just stop," Lily murmured, as she'd done when they were girls, and Sharon said, blinking back tears, "You don't really want me here, admit it, you don't have room for me in your life," and Lily murmured, "Sharon, stop, you know better," and Sharon said bitterly, "I don't know better! I don't belong here with you and your family I'm— trash," and Lily murmured as before to comfort her, to quiet her, and Sharon said, "I've fucked men for money, Lily. I've done terrible things. God has used me but God abhors me. God will cast me from Him. Lily, you don't know!" and Lily murmured, "Yes. I know you, I know your heart," and Sharon said, "You don't. You don't know me or my heart, you don't want to know," and Lily said, "Sharon, of course I know, you're my sister, I love you," and Sharon said, pushing at her, not hard enough to break Lily's embrace but pushing, nudging, as a fretting child might push against her mother's confining protecting arms, "How can you love me if you don't know me! You don't know my heart, Lily—you don't know 'Starr Bright,'" and Lily said, "I don't know 'Starr Bright' but I know *you*," and Sharon was crying, Sharon was crying in anguished furious sobs, and Lily said, maddening Lily as if no opposition in Sharon could dissuade her nor even discourage her from her path of righteousness, "Now let me drive you to Dr. Krauss, all right?" and Sharon lost control finally and screamed, "No, it is not all right!" and pushed Lily away, halfway across the room.

Thinking *Will I have to kill you, too, to be free of you?*

The sisters stared at each other. Their faces were damp with perspiration and their eyes dilated. In the kitchen Lily had turned on a radio, the local Yewville station was playing morning music, and now came a brisk cheery advertisement for a local car dealer, voices self-assured and optimistic and maddening too to "Starr Bright" who of all things despised hypocrisy. Saying, as if it were a curse, to Lily, " 'So then because thou art lukewarm, and neither hot nor cold, I will spew thee out of my mouth.' " Yet even now Lily stood her ground; did not retreat; fueled by the terrible strength of righteousness; the stubbornness of blind, ignorant love; saying gently, as if "Starr Bright" of all persons could be thus manipulated, "Sharon, I know you've been hurt. I know men have hurt you. I want to help you, you've come to me so that I can help you, only please let me!" And Sharon turned away cursing, and squatted beside the canvas suitcase, and removed from its lining a leather belt, a man's belt with a brass buckle, laughing, "Yes! I've been hurt! Hurt like hell, by men, yes!" rising to the rhythm of her harsh, panted words, draping the belt loosely about her hips, a belt twice the size of Sharon's slender waist; as Lily stared uncomprehending, poor Lily blinded by love as by an actual scrim before her eyes, and Sharon began to move her hips suggestively, lewdly, "Starr Bright" easing into her dance, grinning at her sister who continued to stare at her incredulously; her sister Lily who was the audience that "Starr Bright" had long sought, performing merely to men.

Lily said, "Who—was it? How did he hurt you?"

Sharon stroked the leather belt, looped her fingers sensuously about the oversized brass buckle slipping to her navel, laughed, mock-moaned and moved her hips and pelvis laughing at her sister's expression as she chanted to the beat, beat, beat of the dance—"Name's gone. *He's* gone. All of them gone. Ashes to ashes!"

8

Making a Date

She had faith, she'd never doubted. And at last connecting over the phone. In a soft sibilant voice of no reproach, still less accusation, saying, "Sure you remember me, Mack— 'S.'" And the man who'd been Mack Dwyer repeated, quizzically, "'S'—?" and she said, "—who was so crazy for you, she's never forgotten you," and Mack Dwyer said, "—What? *Who?*" and she said, "It *was* a long time ago . . . Mack," and Mack Dwyer said, uneasily, trying to laugh, "Nobody much calls me 'Mack' now," and she said, gently, still with no air of reproach or insinuation, "In my thoughts you're always 'Mack,' that's how I remember you," and Dwyer said, "Look, who is this, please?" and she said, "We were crazy for each other, couldn't keep our hands off each other. You were my first, Mack. Which is why I will never forget." And the man who'd been Mack Dwyer laughed again, uneasily, yet with an undercurrent of excitement, as if this were a game and he was late to catch on, saying, "Your voice does sound familiar . . ." and she said, "*Your* voice sounds familiar, Mack. Like yesterday," and Dwyer said, "But why wouldn't you give my secretary your name? Why is it a secret?" and she said, "Yes, I'd like to keep it a secret. If we get together. Maybe you would, too," and Dwyer said, his voice lowered, quickened, "But—who are you?" and she said, "Your little blond girl 'S'—from the country. The minister's daughter. Remember?" and there was a blank stunned moment, she believed she could hear an intake of breath and see the impact in the man's eyes, that astonished look of Mack's when, abruptly, more abruptly than he wished, he came, sometimes on her belly, or her thighs, or even her panties so she'd have to wash them out in secret not wanting her mother or Lily to know; and he murmured, "My God, is it—Sharon? Sharon—" fumbling her last name, and she didn't help him out but said, "Might be it is," and Dwyer said, "But where are you?" and she said, "Right here in Yewville, Mack," and he said, "You went away?—you were a model in New York?—a famous model, people said. And now—?" and she said, for this was the truth, "Now I'm back in Yewville visiting, just a few days; seeing just a few, very special people; people I'd once—loved."

9

The Kiss

*A*nd in those days shall men seek death, and shall not find it; and
shall desire to die, and death shall flee from them.

How could she sleep! Exhausted and her eyeballs seared in
their sockets as if she'd been staring into the sun but how could
she sleep! Nor even force herself to undress and lie down. Not
in that bed, in those smothering bedclothes. Not in that room
where the ceiling and walls pressed inward. Ridiculous floral
curtains, floral-wallpapered walls—she wanted to scream with
laughter. *As if you know me! As if any of you could know "Starr
Bright."*

Every pig she'd bled to death, he'd been Mack Dwyer.
Strange she had never comprehended that until now.

They'd made a date. The following evening. A weekday—a
Thursday. Yes certainly he'd keep it secret. The date, and her
name.

Except: how could she sleep between now and then?

Except: she couldn't risk one of her sleeping tablets, painkil-
lers—couldn't risk drinking. For one drink is never enough.

Except: she was feeling sexy, hungry for—who?

Mack Dwyer. The first. *Which is why I will never forget.*

Impatiently she stripped. Let her clothes fall underfoot. The
room was airless, smelling of her own heated body. Yet she was

too shrewd to open a window even a crack—didn't trust what might be out there.

What right had Lily to embrace her. Making such a claim. *Love. I love you. My sister.*

How she'd resented it. Lily was the stronger, always the stronger. No one had understood except Sharon. Not even Lily herself.

"Only 'Starr Bright' can match you, Lily."

That terrible strength of righteousness.

It was midnight, and then it was 1 A.M. and she could not sleep, and would not. Trying to calculate how many hours intervened between this moment of yearning and paralysis and 6 P.M. of the following day, when they would meet. In a motel room, off Route 209. Which Mack Dwyer would arrange. In secret.

There was bathwater running, pouring from the faucets. Almost-scalding water. Steam rising to calm her frantic thoughts. Except as she lay in the water naked, pale, forced to see how her breasts had shrunken and were almost flaccid, floating limply in the water, her mind leapt ahead to the motel room, and what would happen there.

Or had it happened already? Many times.

This will be the last. The last pig bled. God will release me— won't He?

She dared not inquire of God Himself. As she dared not gaze into the fiery sun for fear of going blind.

How quickly, she wondered, could she master him? She would not be using a straight razor this time, to be left with the dead man, as she'd done with Stanley Reigel and one or two others. She would use her own knife, for there was no possibility of "suicide"—this time. All that was required was leverage, and surprise; the man would be taken by surprise; naked, probably; and "Starr Bright" was practiced with naked men; once embarked upon a course of action, she would not be dissuaded; the first splash of bright arterial blood—

"Now you remember me?—yes?"

The nape of her neck against the cool porcelain rim of the tub. By degrees she was becoming calmer. Maybe she would have a drink—to help her sleep. But only one. To help her sleep. For she must not fail, and would not fail. For if she failed, "Starr Bright" would be apprehended; "Starr Bright" would be run to earth; "Starr Bright" would be exposed to staring, avid eyes; "Starr Bright" would bring shame and confusion upon Lily and her family. But she would not fail, for God would guide her hand. *For I have the keys of hell and of death.*

It was 1:35 A.M. She'd drifted into a dream, and was wakened suddenly. Hearing the door of her room being opened—so slowly! (Though knowing the door could not be opened, she'd locked it from inside.) And at once she was roused, vigilant. Sitting up in the now-tepid water, listening closely. It might be Lily—returned to seek her sister's forgiveness. It might be—Lily's husband?—whose name she'd forgotten in her distraction.

Yes, Wes. Maybe—Wes. She'd forgotten entirely about Wes!

*   *   *

By this time it was almost 2 A.M. But she dressed hurriedly, excitedly. Seeming to know he would be there, waiting.

In his office in the converted sunporch. Lily was always worrying her husband slept so poorly. Distracted by finances, Lily said. Didn't trust his bookkeeper, Lily said. People owe him money, Lily said. He tries to shield us.

Sharon bit her lower lip to keep from laughing, a good strong belly laugh. Knowing why Wes Merrick lingered in his office late at night; why he took his time going upstairs to bed with Lily.

"You know, too, Lily. Only you won't admit it."

It was an eye-catching, sexy outfit, but also easy to pull on

over her head, a clinging red-jersey sheath she'd acquired in
Palm Springs. The hem skimmed her knees, showing her long
dancer's legs. No underwear. No stockings. Damp tendrils of
hair clung to her forehead but she brushed, brushed, brushed
her hair until much of it was dry, and fluffed out about her face.
That schoolgirl look! Cheerleader look! "Guys love it." Hadn't
time to apply makeup carefully for that would require forty
minutes and he might give up waiting for her and go upstairs
to bed, so quickly she rubbed foundation on her face, which
was still, she believed, peering at herself in the steamy bathroom
mirror, a girl's unlined face if not seen in too revealing a light;
and subtle spots of rouge on her cheeks; and glossy maroon
lipstick making of her mouth a lovely open wound to be kissed,
sucked, bitten, possessed.

She forced her bare feet into high-heeled shoes. Grunting
with the effort. In a zippered compartment of the canvas suitcase was a blue-sequined purse and inside the purse "Starr
Bright's" knife and these items she would take with her. For
safekeeping or for protection—she could not have said, for she
wasn't thinking clearly.

Long ago "Starr Bright"—the TV hostess, blond, busty,
makeup like a thick crust over her tired-looking face—had told
thirteen-year-old Sharon Donner and the others backstage *Once
you get out there in the lights, kids—just trust your instinct. Don't
think!*

It was the very best advice. It was the heart of show business.

She made her way through the darkened downstairs rooms
and saw, unsurprised, that the light was on in Wes's office, and
the door partly ajar. He'd been waiting for her!—but neither of
them would acknowledge it, she supposed.

There was Wes oblivious of her, at his desk. Frowning at a
computer screen, exhaling a cloud of bluish smoke. His thinning hair was disheveled as if he'd been running his hands
through it and there were sharp creases in his cheeks like razor

cuts. He wore those prissy reading glasses. His shirt was rumpled, opened at the throat, the sleeves carelessly rolled up to show thick, wiry hairs on his forearms. At his elbow, amid papers, was a tumbler of—what? Looked like whiskey or bourbon.

"Wes! Surprise."

The way he turned startled at her low, throaty voice, blinking foolishly, you'd have thought he hadn't been expecting her after all or possibly he'd given up hoping.

"Jesus. Sharon."

Stepping forward into the light she was enjoying the slow shock of the man's eyes taking her in, the clinging jersey dress, nipples poking against the fabric like buttons, and her long bare dancer's legs and the warm glow of her skin and the sexy high-heeled shoes that made her stumble just a little, laughing. "I didn't expect you'd be up, Wes," she said, reaching over to take his burning cigarette from an ashtray and lift it to her lips, which felt greedy, "—this hour of the night." He was staring at her, a faint smile stretching his mouth as if for a moment he couldn't think who she was, what good luck this was for him. But she felt a stab of disappointment—her brother-in-law was so *middle-aged*.

Waiting for you to come to me but you're too God-damned good for that so I'm coming to you.

He was saying, frowning, "Sharon, why are you dressed like that? You're not going out, are you?" Staring at her the way he'd stared at Deedee in her new clothes, perplexed and annoyed as by a riddle. And she said, "Hell, I couldn't sleep, my nerves!"—holding out a hand for him to see, trembling slightly, the cigarette in her fingers. "It's too damned quiet around here. Washington Street." She laughed, and Wes laughed, nervously. Not knowing why.

If he'd been waiting for her why was he wearing those ridiculous reading glasses. Bifocal lenses. That old-man look that was an insult to the glamor of "Starr Bright." Like some pig not taking time to wash, smelling of underarms and crotch. Cock tasting of piss. *Pigs.*

She was furious suddenly. But continued to smile the dazzling "Starr Bright" smile. Hugging her sequined purse against her breasts.

She told him yes she intended to go out, for a walk, a walk and a drink. She couldn't sleep she said it was so quiet her thoughts were like voices. And he said it was too late to go out, almost 2 A.M. and places would be closed. And she said she'd take a walk, then; would he like to join her? And he said, "You're not serious, huh?" And she said, flirting, but annoyed, "I'm not? Sure I am. Try me." And he said, "Lily told me you canceled the doctor's appointment, why?" And she said, angry suddenly, "Why? Whose business is it, *why?*"

Thought you weren't a fucking hypocrite, big guy.

Thought you weren't like all the rest.

They were talking, and they were almost arguing. So Wes went to shut the door. In case, far away upstairs, someone should be wakened, and hear voices.

He said, "I don't think you should be walking anywhere, Sharon, at this time of night." Looking at her, the spectacle of her, as if to say *And looking like you do.* And she laughed taking another drag on his cigarette. Saying, "What sexist crap. It's an insult. A man can walk at night anywhere he fucking wants, a woman's a prisoner? Fuck that." And again the man blinked at her dumbly as if he'd never heard such words before on a woman's lips.

She was hot in the face, incensed. She remembered the secret knife in her purse and dared him to put his hands on her. Telling "Starr Bright" what to do!

He was playing daddy saying how he and Lily were "both concerned" about her and that pissed her off, too, a husband-and-wife team shaking their heads over her. So she laughed, and shrugged, saying Christ she could take care of herself, she'd been taking care of herself since the age of eighteen when her

God-fearing Christian family had washed their hands of her—
"Cast me off as a polluted sinner. A *fashion model*." But she
didn't hold any grudge, you could see. She'd made her way
alone. Modeling, and dancing; and dance instructor; and she'd
be beginning her film career soon. So she didn't need anyone's
help thank you nor anyone's charity.

It was like a TV speech. A close-up. She felt great, she felt
in supreme control. "You know me, Wes—'Sherrill.' No last
name. I've learned to take care of myself because there's never
been anyone else."

Wes shook his head, laughed, leaning a haunch on the edge
of his desk, a big-boned man going soft in the gut, but there
was a certain bruised tenderness in his face, and the silvery-
glinting stubble on his chin, and the graying wiry hairs on his
forearms and at his throat—she felt a stab of desire, a scalding
little needle at the pit of her belly. Every thought of Mack
Dwyer had by this time evaporated.

Taking that hot soaking bath had been a great idea. She was
softened up, moistened. This guy was sharp enough to get the
signals, he'd had a lot of experience she was sure.

But surprising her saying, "Frankly, Sharon, I don't know
the first thing about you. When I think I do, I learn I'm
wrong." He paused, eyeing her belligerently. "Because most of
what you've been telling us is bullshit, isn't it?"

Sharon stared at him not certain she'd heard correctly.

"What? Why—do you say that?"

"Isn't it?"

"I—I don't understand. What do you mean?"

It was like he'd slapped her in the face. Definitely she felt a
sexual attraction for him, for his very belligerence; a sweet not-
so-gentle throb in the groin. Laying a hand on his bristly forearm as if to both placate him and entice him. "Wes, I'm *hurt*.
I'm—*insulted*. I just don't—"

"This teaching job of yours? At the 'Pasadena School of
Dance'?"

"Yes, I—" She shook her head, confused. "No, wait. I've maybe decided not—"

"Well, there isn't any 'Pasadena School of Dance.' I checked."

Quickly she improvised, "Starr Bright" glib and inspired and daring him not to believe, "Oh, right! I guess it goes by another name—the school. And it isn't in Pasadena actually but in another town, for prestige purposes they align themselves with Pasadena—you know." She paused, breathing quickly. The fucker was letting her stammer and falter until her words gave out.

Wes said, "And this 'dance troupe' you've been traveling with—"

"I told you, we're disbanded. It's *over.*"

"And just why exactly did you come here, to visit Lily?"

"Do I need a reason? Lily is my sister—"

"Lily's been your sister for a long time. Why're you here *now?*"

Because I have nowhere else to go. Because I am run to earth.

She was furious! frightened! backed into a corner like a fucking rat! "Starr Bright" clutching the sequined purse and feeling the nudge, the impulse, how she might turn as if to leave and feign an attack of dizziness and when the man laid his hands on her slide the razor-sharp blade into his gut easy as you'd pierce a melon. A man, any man, daring to lay his hot beefy hands on "Starr Bright"!

But "Starr Bright" guided her in another direction. How much more strategic instead to go weak, or weak-seeming in the man's accusing eyes. Many times "Starr Bright" had humbled herself even bleeding in the mouth opening herself to a man's mercy. And this man she seemed to know having pillaged, raped, killed helpless women and girls in Vietnam in the guise of American soldiery and would surely do so still to this very day if granted immunity, and anonymity. So she was gripping his arm tighter and leaning on him for support and saying, her voice breaking, "Wes, if I didn't always tell you one hundred percent of the truth it's because I—I'm waiting to tell you. Just you. When we get to be better friends, when I can trust you."

Guardedly he asked, "Yes? And when's that?"

"I've been through some hard times—Lily knows. She's been so wonderful—generous—taking me in like this. And never a word of reproach."

"Right. I'd say, yes, she has."

She ignored his sarcasm. If you ignored a guy's sarcasm he sometimes dropped it.

Eyeing the amber liquid in that glass on his desk. Jesus, she needed a drink!

"When—can we get to be better friends? Oh, Wes, it's tonight I've got to live through somehow. I'm not looking beyond tonight."

Covering her face with the fingers of one hand. Her skin burning, feverish. It came over her like a wave of nausea, she wasn't wearing eyeliner or mascara, no dark glasses, her venous eyes and the soft crepey skin beneath them exposed, and he was standing close, she could feel his warm breath, this man peering into her very soul or seeming-so except "Starr Bright's" soul was one of those freaky distorting mirrors you looked into and saw your own mangled face.

He must've relented. There was the glass in his hand raised to her lips as you'd raise a glass to a small child's lips urging her to drink and she drank—bourbon. Sighing with relief.

"Oh God, Wes—thanks. I needed that."

She'd closed her fingers over his. Gazing up at him with hurt-swimming eyes.

He said, "It goes down smoothest after midnight, I've found."

"Yes."

She was liking this now. She was loving this. Loving *him*.

He opened a lower drawer of the desk and took out a bottle

and splashed more liquid into the glass, filling it halfway and sipping himself and again offering it to her and again she drank and felt the wonderful warm liquid in her mouth, burning down her throat and coursing through her blood. *Love me! You're crazy for me, you know it.*

The sequined purse was awkward by this time in her grip, she laid it on the edge of his desk within reach, she was breathing quickly feeling the charge between them like the air before an electric storm and there she was saying, in the same soft, broken voice, the voice that was exciting this guy pouring blood into his cock like a faucet she'd turned on with her deft manicured fingers, how since she'd been a girl a minister's daughter but not the minister's favored daughter she'd always figured she was being punished ahead of time for whatever sins she might commit—"Like God's giving me a promise. Next time it's my turn."

Wes frowned. Like he was seriously trying to understand. "What's that mean? I don't get it."

"If you're hurt bad enough, Wes, God lets you know the reason for it will be clear someday soon. So it isn't, you know"—pausing, knitting her forehead as if the words were painful to shape—"just for nothing. No *purpose.*"

Again Wes surprised her, smiling. "Hell, Sharon. You believe that?"

"Of course I believe that. It's been my life."

"More bullshit."

"What? Now this is getting insulting, Wes—"

Don't you want me to confide in you? Open my heart to you?

He was saying, almost as if it embarrassed him, spelling out such elementary truths, "Look. The purpose of life is—more life. No purpose beyond that. No more plan to it than the species trying to keep going, reproducing all they can so some individuals survive. I wouldn't say 'God' has much of a hand in it."

"Why, Wes, that's a terrible heartless thing to say! And you the father of a child."

"Why? Why's it terrible and heartless?"

"It's—atheism."

"So? I'm an atheist."

"In the war? In Vietnam? Were you an atheist there?"

Wes's eyes clouded over. He'd been liking this and maybe it was a mistake to break the mood but she was pissed at him, the guy's cocksureness and it was scaring her, too—how casually he'd dismissed God like you'd dismiss some damn dumb embarrassing old nonsense you used to believe when you were a kid. "Sure," he said. "Vietnam. That's where I picked it up. That, and a heroin habit."

"Heroin!" She'd had a habit some years ago but maybe better not tell him, not yet. "So—what did you do in Vietnam? Lily tells me you've never told *her.*"

Wes shrugged. "Let's drop it, Sharon. For now."

"You were liking it there, were you? Lots of guys did."

Wes drank bourbon. Wasn't going to say, was he. She laughed.

"You were just a young guy when you went in, weren't you? I bet you were hotheaded."

Again he said nothing. But just possibly he was liking this, too—some special memory he could play over in his mind. Like a scene in a movie he'd rerun lots of times.

"And the women, there? The girls? They all look so young, and the girls would've really been young. Twelve years old, ten . . ."

Stubbornly he stood mute, ungiving. As if by accident she nudged against him, the front of his trousers, Jesus he was hard, he was—*hard.* And laughed regaining her balance, clutching at his arm. Her long bare polished-looking legs in the sexy high-heeled shoes.

"Or, look"—she was giving him an out as if she'd just now thought of it, —"maybe you don't actually remember? Maybe it's all kind of blank. Like some things you'd dreamt and what was real mixed in together and—you've given up trying to sort them."

He frowned, and shrugged. "Maybe."

"You never would've hurt anyone except you were made to. You were there and what happened could only happen there. And only that way, at that time. *I know.*"

He wasn't looking at her but at the glass in his hands, and again he drank, and she'd closed her fingers around his holding the glass and she, too, drank; and the warmth of the bourbon passed between them, delicious.

He said, not angrily, but bluntly, "In fact you don't know shit about me, Sharon. So let's drop the subject."

"Anyway it happened a long time ago. You weren't anybody's husband or father then, lots of things don't count then."

If you touch me, try to fuck me, I'll kill you.

Hey no, look: big guy, I'm hot for you. Try me!

He was asking her again why, why'd she come to Yewville, why at this time? Not when her father died, or her mother? What's the story? And she listened, nodding and trying to think, what had she been telling Lily, obviously Lily had confided in this man, Lily was her sister but had betrayed her. Saying she'd been missing Lily of course—for years. For all of her life away from Lily. But now, these past few months, now the dance troupe was broken up owing her money almost $10,000 she was resigned she'd never receive unless she hired a lawyer and brought a civil suit and the sons of bitches would declare bankruptcy and she'd be left having to pay the lawyer's bills—now also she had some personal problems, these past few months— she'd come home to Lily hoping to be taken in.

Wes was regarding her doubtfully. As if he wanted to believe but couldn't quite.

She said, tears starting in her eyes, "The truth is, Wes, I'm about run to earth. That first night you saw me—how panicked I was, when one of your workers knocked on the back door? I was scared of my life. I *am* scared of my life. There's a person after me who wants to—hurt me."

"Who?"

"A man. Someone I knew in Vegas and L.A. I can't talk about it."

"Have you reported him to the police?"

"No. I mean—yes. In L.A., he'd beaten me and I had to be taken to a hospital and the police were called, that's their policy. But I couldn't press charges. He'd threatened he would kill me if I did."

"Which hospital was this, Sharon?"

"Somewhere in L.A., I said! I don't remember the name, I was taken there by some friends, *bodily*. I—"

"Why's this person want to hurt you?"

"He thinks he's in love with me! He's jealous and possessive and has always had his way with women and I was the first to walk away from him, he says he'll make me pay for that, the insult. He'd threatened to throw acid in my face and he black-ened both my eyes and—" She was wiping tears from her cheeks, startled at how feverish her face was. She hoped it wasn't flushed and unattractive, and this man standing so close.

"Does he know you're here?"

She saw where this was going and said quickly, "He has no idea where I am. He's looking for me, probably, in California. He doesn't know where my home was—*is*. As long as I'm here, I'm safe."

Wes was frowning. "But we should notify the police any-way. If he's threatened you."

"No! I can't."

"Why not?"

"I *can't*."

Her eyes were hurt, helpless; a wave of dizziness rose in her and how natural it was for the man to catch her, steady her. And suddenly they were kissing.

Yes. Like this. At last.

A man's arms around her and she was clutching blindly at him, clinging to him; slipping her hand inside his shirt, greedily caressing his warm, muscled back. And he was moving his hands over her, moaning softly, his hands hard and deft and his weight pressed against her pressing her against the edge of the desk and she was thinking *He will force me now, he will rape me as he has raped children* and the thought was both terrifying and exciting; exciting and terrifying; "Starr Bright" stood a little apart seeing the man's hunger, and the woman's, how her arms were closed desperately around his neck, her parched lips aching pressed so hard against his, and her tongue seeking his; and the sequined purse pushed back into a pile of papers atop the desk, nudged by her thigh. *Pig! Like any pig! Adulterer and fornicator!*

But he'd ceased kissing her. He'd ceased, and stepped away.

Turned from her adjusting his clothing. She heard his labored breath and saw a flush in his throat, rising into his face; he would not look at her even as she tugged at his arm, frantically—"Wes, what's wrong? Be my friend!"

"Sharon, I—can't. Not this."

She pushed into his arms again, baring her teeth in a smile; she kissed him again, or tried to; but the man stood stiffly, his shoulders raised so she had to lift herself against him. "Wes, don't reject me!" she heard herself plead. "I love you."

Wes gripped her hands, gently detached her from him. It was impossible that this was happening—wasn't it? His face was terribly flushed, and his eyes were averted in embarrassment, shame.

He was murmuring, "This isn't a—good idea, Sharon. We'd better say goodnight now."

"But why?"

"You know why."

"Wes, I'm so lonely! So unhappy. The first time I laid eyes on *you*—"

"No. That's bullshit."

"—it's the truth, I swear! My feeling for you, Wes—"

"There's Lily. It isn't just you and me."

"But—Lily wouldn't know."

"*I* would know. And you."

"Wes, please—"

Don't make me beg, "Starr Bright" will not beg any man.

It could not be happening but it was: the man backed off from her, eluded her grasping hands, mumbling an apology she couldn't decipher for the blood roaring in her ears deafening her and dizzying her and she could not comprehend he'd walked out! Walked out of the room, and left her staring after him! This good man, this good, decent man her sister had married, a man "Starr Bright" had no power over, could not touch.

"Fucking *husband!*"

In disgust pouring the remainder of the bourbon into the glass, and raising it to her parched lips.

10

Revelations

I t would have seemed at the outset the most ordinary of days—a Thursday in mid-April. Yet it would be the day of Lily's life she would never forget.

What a strange dream, or a jumble of dreams, she'd had the previous night. She'd been left exhausted! Waiting in line with her sister and other children to enter the TV studio theater in Buffalo where *The Starr Bright Hour* was broadcast. It didn't seem to matter if anyone had tickets—they had to wait, wait, wait. And at last they were allowed inside—forced to crawl on hands and knees through a tunnel of shiny tile that opened out into a cramped, low-ceilinged room of hurtful blinding lights and strange shadows harshly black as crevices in the very air. (Where were Mr. and Mrs. Donner? The sisters were alone, unaccompanied. There appeared to be no parents anywhere.) Overexcited, fretting children herded into rows of seats. A smell of wet wool, urine. Now began more waiting, waiting, waiting. Now began the confusion. The TV camera lights made their eyes ache. More children were being herded into seats that were already taken. Pieces of candy were tossed out into the audience and the children shrieked and scrambled for them. At last there came Bessie the Cow on stage—in a baggy spotted cow-costume with a silly cow-mask and lopsided horns. And

Louie the Lion with an unconvincing mane and drooping tail. "They aren't even trying to fool us," Lily complained to Sharon, on the verge of tears. A seven-year-old knows such things! Yet the other children were in an ecstasy of excitement and anticipation. The chanting song began so loudly Lily's ears pounded with it *Starr Bright will be with you so-oon! Starr Bright will be with you so-oon!*

But "Starr Bright" never arrived. Lily woke with a headache, breathless and nauseated and exhausted as if she hadn't slept at all. But what relief to be out of that terrible, airless place! What joy, to be not seven years old but thirty-seven! She felt guilty, though, at leaving her sister behind.

And then there was the quarrel with Deedee at breakfast.

Mom please. Will you stop trying to monitor my life. Biting back tears Deedee had pushed past Lily and hurried from the house; on her way to school, having had only two cups of black coffee, not a morsel of food. In three weeks she'd lost twelve pounds and it was true the weight loss was attractive, the girl's round face now slimmer, prettier, and her eyes larger but bright with agitation, nerves. And her skin sickly pale. What could Lily who was her mother do except plead with her gently, reason with her, provide all the low-calorie foods she wanted, plan menus around her obsessive diet. (Lily had called friends who'd been in her predicament over the years, had been given good, if limited, advice.)

Lily said, "Deedee, you can diet, but you can do it reasonably, healthily. Try!" and Deedee said, sighing, too jumpy to sit at the table, "Mom, I hate that name 'Deedee.' Can't you call me 'Deirdre'!" and Lily said, smiling, "Well, then, 'Deirdre'— you can diet, of course, but can't you approach it more *calmly?*" and Deedee said, looking at her as if she'd uttered the most bizarre nonsense, "Mom, I haven't got *forever.* I'm already *fif-teen.*"

As if fifteen were a tragic advanced age. As if time were running rapidly out.

Though she was desperate to escape, Deedee paused to take two cans of Diet Pepsi from the refrigerator to slip into her backpack.

Oddly, the name "Sharon" had not passed between them.

I can't blame my sister for what must be a weakness, a failing of my own.

★   ★   ★

"Excuse me, but will I be receiving a contract for next year?"

"Lily, what? A contract?"—as if he'd never heard of such a thing.

"A contract. A formal contract. For next year."

Entering the office of the art department chairman who was "Rob" to everyone on the staff Lily had felt sick with apprehension, nerves; out of nowhere, it seemed, she'd summoned up strength to make such a move, formulate such a request, at last; yet, once in Rob's office, invited to shift a stack of canvases (Rob was a painter with a controversial local reputation), she felt rather more anger, aggression. *You have no right to exploit me. To trade on my goodwill.* Rob's normally relaxed, somewhat condescending smile in Lily's presence had faded; he was rubbing at his nose, blinking at her as if wondering whether he'd heard correctly. Was this his most good-natured, self-effacing and dependable faculty member?—the wife of Wes Merrick? Lily had been teaching at Yewville Community College for years seemingly grateful to be hired at all, at any salary no matter how modest, and under any circumstances no matter how hasty, last-minute.

Lily Merrick's student evaluations were consistently the highest of any instructor in the small department, and Lily had frequently explained the fact away, as if embarrassed by it, "Well—my students are women, mainly. They get to be my friends." And the other instructors, most of them men, though liking Lily well enough and possibly even admiring her pottery, were quick to agree with her. *Women stick together. Can't trust women's judgment.*

Of course, Lily's occasional male students gave her very high ratings, too. But they liked her, it was presumed, because she was "so nice, kind."

There were two "stars" in the department: Rob, who was an action painter in the Pollock mode, thus expected to be absentminded, or temperamental; and a two-hundred-twenty-pound bewhiskered scrap-metal sculptor from Buffalo who was notorious for canceling his once-weekly studio class, or showing up hungover, morose and sullen. Both "stars" routinely received uneven, if not frankly low evaluations from their students; yet it seemed not to matter, their positions at Yewville Community College, and their salaries, were assured by generous contracts year following year. Lily had not wished to think of the injustice here, the unfairness; and so for years she hadn't thought of it; until, abruptly, it seemed only the other day after a conversation with Sharon about entirely different matters she'd begun to think about it; and to think about it seriously, practicably.

Saying now, "I was thinking, Rob, I'd like to apply to teach in Port Oriskany, if there isn't a position here. Lloyd Morgan"—Lloyd was chair of the department at the college there—"has told me he likes my work." This was true: Lloyd Morgan had been kind enough to send Lily a card, not long ago; but Lily hadn't been thinking of applying to teach at his college, a sixty-mile one-way trip, until this moment. *You see? I have other options. You mustn't take Lily Merrick for granted.* Rob was frowning, and tugging at his skimpy pewter-colored beard, which grew without a mustache on his upper lip and so looked oddly pasted-on, temporary. Clearly Lily's words were a total surprise

to him; he'd perhaps expected her to have dropped into his
office to invite him to dinner. But Rob was an affable individual, and he'd always liked Lily, her warmth, her reliable smile,
her enthusiasm, certainly he understood her practical value to
the department, and so finally, with a sigh, he nodded, and
agreed, yes it might be a good thing for the college to offer her
a formal contract, within the week—"Wouldn't want anyone
to steal you from us, eh?"

Lily said, "I was thinking of a three-year contract, actually."

"*Three*-year—?"

"More or less what other adjunct instructors have."

"Yes, but—well, our budget—" Rob squirmed in his seat,
tugged at his beard.

"And I think it's time for a raise, Rob, don't you? Approximately the same raise others have received."

"A—raise?"

And Lily smilingly improvised, naming a sum.

And so she left the Yewville Community College campus, driving her car out of the parking lot amid a festive glittering of
chrome and windshields in the bright April sunshine. Smiling
to herself, pleased, excited, a little frightened at her audacity.

About time, Lily of the Valley. What've I been telling you?
All these years!

★   ★   ★

When Lily arrived home it was 4:20 P.M. and there to her
surprise was Sharon awaiting her just inside the door, in the
kitchen, smiling but impatient; obviously Sharon had been
smoking, for the air smelled of it, but she'd gotten rid of the
cigarette, and had made an attempt to air out the kitchen by
opening windows, switching on the fan above the stove.
Sharon was oddly dressed, in the rumpled old trench coat of

Lily's she'd been wearing in wet, chilly weather; a black scarf
tied tight around her head hiding every strand of hair, as if she
were bald; ordinary stockings, flat-heeled shoes. Beneath the
trench coat Sharon was wearing a dress but what it was, Lily
couldn't see. The glamorous smoke-tinted sunglasses hid Sharon's eyes and her face had been artfully transformed into a model's flawless cosmetic mask. Before Lily could share with her
sister the good news of her three-year contract and raise at the
college, virtually before Lily could draw breath to speak, Sharon
informed her excitedly that, at last, she'd gotten over her ridiculous shyness and called an old friend—"And Marnie's invited
me over for dinner tonight, isn't that sweet of her?"

Lily said, "Marnie Spohn? I didn't—"

"May I borrow your car, Lily? Marnie lives just in—" naming a suburb of Yewville, "—it isn't far. Gosh, I'm so excited
it's like a *date*. I haven't seen Marnie in—" Sharon's voice did
not trail off so much as halt, as if she'd leave it to Lily to fill in
the precise number of years.

Lily said, "Well, I suppose so, Sharon. But—"

Not knowing why she was faltering in her sister's exuber-
ant, elated presence; why she felt almost childishly hurt; yes, it
was hurt she felt—as in those painful days when her pretty sister
would swing into the high school cafeteria with Marnie's
crowd, an older crowd, cheerleaders predominantly, totally
oblivious of Lily who often sat alone eating her lunch, or trying
to.

(And on the school bus going home Sharon would take
note of Lily's sullen silence, and ask her what was wrong, as if
she didn't know; and Lily would complain dolefully, "When
other people are around, you look through me like I'm not
even there"; and Sharon exclaimed with sly, cruel wit, keeping
her expression deadpan, "But I looked everywhere for you,
Lily—I did. Are you sure you *were* there?")

Lily smiled now, recalling. If that was what it was, no more than adolescent hurt feelings surfacing after so many years, sheer sisterly jealousy, Lily would survive.

She said, though knowing Wes didn't approve of Sharon borrowing the Toyota, "Of course, Sharon. Take the car. And remember me to Marnie—if she remembers me."

"I will, Lily! I will!"

It was an odd, almost manic response. And Sharon hugged Lily with a strange urgency, as if she were embarking on a dangerous mission, and not simply to dinner a few miles away; as if she and Lily might never see each other again. Sharon's thin, beringed fingers were disconcertingly strong, as Lily had noted in the past. She wore a sweet, piercing perfume; though much of her head was hidden by the black scarf, her earlobes were exposed, and golden earrings dangled from them as in a cascade of coins; around her neck, just visibly glinting inside the trench coat, was the striking gold chain Lily gathered had a sentimental value to her sister. Sharon said, breathless, triumphant, "Don't wait up for me, any of you. I might be late."

Sharon hurried outside, gripping her tote bag. Lily wondered what she might be bringing Marnie. A gift? Lily had made no special effort to glance into the bag but had noted its contents appeared to be covered by a scarf or shawl.

Since the other day, when Sharon had behaved so defiantly, with such actressy exaggeration, draping a man's brass-buckled belt around her hips and moving in a lewd, suggestive dance, a mockery of an erotic dance, Lily had felt uncomfortable in her sister's presence. Never could you predict when that other Sharon—"Sherrill"—or was it "Starr Bright"—might emerge, cruel and funny.

She'll be leaving me soon, she's become bored with me.

Lily watched as Sharon backed the Toyota around to drive out onto the street, in tight, anxious little jerks, foot on the brake, as if fearful of moving too quickly. Feeling again a small stab of almost pleasurable hurt, jealousy. She wouldn't have guessed that Marnie Spohn was anyone special to Sharon, no more than Sharon Donner was special to Marnie; and if Marnie had invited Sharon to dinner, why hadn't she invited Lily, too? She would know that Sharon was staying with Lily. And Lily hadn't seen, nor even heard of, Marnie Spohn in years.

Odd, Lily had the vague idea that Marnie Spohn had married and moved away from Yewville a long time ago.

She checked the telephone directory out of curiosity—no "M. Spohn." Of course, Marnie must be married. And Sharon had known Marnie's married name?

★   ★   ★

"Lily, last night I had a—talk with your sister."

"Yes? What about?"

Lily tried to smile. Seeing that Wes wasn't smiling. Her heart tripped absurdly. *He has fallen in love with her. He's finished with Lily now.*

"Different things."

Wes had startled Lily by returning home unnaturally early— only just 5:30 P.M. Not in recent memory had Wes Merrick come home so early even when, a few years previous, he'd been sick with flu. Now he stood awkwardly in the doorway of Lily's workroom, breathing harshly. His eyes snatched at Lily's, then shifted away; he was the kind of man who expects his wife to complete his thoughts for him; to articulate what he himself isn't quite able to comprehend.

Deedee had gone to a friend's house after school and Sharon was at Marnie's and Lily had been elated by the prospect of a free hour or more in which to explore a design for a large angular ceramic bowl, or sculpture; she wasn't yet sure which it would be; always in the past Lily's work had had a pragmatic function, it was a pot, or a vase, or a bowl, and could be justified as *serving a purpose*; but this design might be entirely different, and not at all "attractive"—she would wait and see. And now Wes stood in her doorway all but wringing his hands, clearly troubled and not knowing how to begin.

Lily said helpfully, "Sharon is out, visiting a friend from high school. I'm surprised—but relieved. Until today she hasn't contacted anyone in Yewville but us."

"Who? Who's she visiting?"

"A woman named Marnie Spohn. We went to school together."

Wes looked blank, the name meant nothing to him. "She's out, now? In your car?"

"Yes."

Lily steeled herself for the next of Wes's queries, for this was uncomfortably like an interrogation. But Wes said, instead, coming forward to touch Lily's arm, "Honey, it's hard to say this, but—I don't think your sister should stay with us any longer. I'd like you to ask her to leave as soon as possible."

"Oh Wes, why?"

This was not at all what Lily had expected. Yet she felt more stunned than relieved.

"She isn't a presence we want here. Especially with Deedee."

"You mean—the dieting? I've been talking to Deedee, I think she'll be more reasonable. This morning—"

"That, sure. But other things. The woman's general conduct—influence."

"Sharon has always been—flamboyant. A nonconformist. But she's good-hearted, so generous—"

"No, Lily. You're good-hearted, you're generous. Sharon is an opportunist and a liar."

"Wes! How can you say such things?"

"All day today, all last night—I've been thinking about her," Wes said slowly. He was caressing Lily's arm as if begging forgiveness. His skin was tired, coarse and sallow; his eyes were faintly bloodshot; his breath smelled just perceptibly of alcohol, and a flush as of guilt, or shame, suffused his face. "Last night Sharon came into my office around two. I was working on accounts. She was dressed to go out, she said she couldn't sleep, she wanted a drink, but I—discouraged her. From going out." Wes paused, looking anxiously at Lily. "She didn't tell you any of this?"

Lily said, "I didn't see much of Sharon today. She kept her door shut all morning and then I was out." Lily swallowed hard, frightened. "When she left for Marnie's about an hour ago she seemed very—excited. Hopeful."

"No matter what she seemed," Wes said impatiently, "you can be sure it isn't what she *is*. That woman has been lying to us all along. About the teaching position in Pasadena and the 'dance troupe' she claimed to be with and something so simple as where she's living now and why she's here."

"But—how do you know?"

"I know."

"The dance troupe—the school in Pasadena—"

"I *know*, I checked. And I asked her point-blank."

"I don't believe this. Sharon wouldn't lie to me."

"Well, she's been lying to *me*," Wes said angrily. "Maybe you and your sister share secrets I don't know about?"

Lily was alarmed at Wes's emotion; rarely in their marriage had he spoken to her in such a way, the way of a strong-willed, physically dominating man bullying a woman; agitated, confused, and taking it out on a woman. Lily said, "Of course, Sharon has confided in me over the years. I suppose you could say we have—secrets. We're sisters . . ."

"When it suits *her*."

"Wes, why are you so hard on Sharon? Why are you so angry? You've been saying you like Sharon, she wasn't what you'd expected."

"Because she's been lying to me, playing me for a fool. What is there between you that I don't know?"

Lily felt her face burn. She was angry, too.

"Wes Merrick, I will not be bullied."

"No one's bullying you, Lily. Just tell me is there something I should know, and I don't?"

Lily hesitated, hardly trusting her voice. She was so angry!

Pulling away from Wes, and when he gripped her arm pulling more decisively from him. And she'd been so happy! So pleased with herself, for once! Proud to anticipate Wes's response when she told him of her conversation with Rob. Thinking *I can respect myself now, I needn't cringe and apologize for my very existence.*

Wes said, exasperated, "Lily, God damn it!—I'm not accustomed to not knowing what's going on in my own house. I want your sister to leave."

Lily held back tears. "Wes, I've invited Sharon to stay for as long as—she needs to stay. You can see how she's been recovering, how much healthier she is. And she's been paying expenses. She would pay more, except I won't hear of it. She's our guest. She's my *sister*. She needs me, and I need her. I've been missing her for years. I've been—incomplete without her. Life hasn't seemed whole."

Wes said, "Lily, that's ridiculous. You sound like your sister now—exaggerating."

Was it true? Lily felt a suffocating wildness in her chest; in her throat and mouth; words not her own, yet clamoring to be uttered. *I hate you. I love her. No one is so close as Sharon and I. You don't know us. Leave us alone!*

More calmly Lily said, "I think, in fact, Sharon will be leaving soon," and Wes said, "Yes, but when?" and Lily said, recoiling from him, "Wes, your face, your eyes—you look so hateful. This isn't like you," and Wes said, flushing, "This isn't like *you*, and it's all her fault," and Lily laughed incredulously, saying, "We're adults—we don't blame other people for our problems," and Wes said, "Well, I do blame her. *I want her out of my house,*" and Lily said, "It's my house, too," and Wes said, "And I want her out of Deedee's life, completely," and Lily said, "But Deedee likes Sharon—so much. You haven't seen them together the way I have. I mean—the three of us, together. It's so important for Deedee to have an aunt." Lily was speaking rapidly, excitedly. She scarcely knew what she said. Her tongue was oddly numb as if losing sensation, becoming paralyzed. "It's wonderful for our daughter to have a *family*."

Wes was staring at Lily. "You and I are Deedee's family, Lily. We're all the family she needs."

"Wes, that's ridiculous. We're all related by blood—"

"Except me, yes?"

"What?"

"The three of you are related by 'blood'—Donner 'blood'—but not me?"

This was so: Wes was Deedee's adoptive father. But Lily had not meant it.

Yet she stood trembling, unable to protest.

Wes fumbled for a pack of cigarettes in his pocket and to Lily's dismay extracted one and lit it without apology. Lily could see the man's hands shaking.

After a moment Wes said, in a calmer voice, "Has your sister told you about this person who's stalking her?"

Lily said hesitantly, "Yes. But—"

"But you don't believe her?"

"Of course I believe her."

"*Do* you? I don't."

"I believe Sharon has had a difficult life. Her career might not be going so well as she says. It must be so competitive, so cruel! But she has her pride, she doesn't require our pity. She's still a beautiful woman and a gifted dancer and singer . . ." Lily's voice trailed off weakly.

Wes said, exhaling smoke in an abrupt, impatient gesture, "Last night Sharon told me that someone, a man, an ex-lover in California, has vowed to kill her. She fled him and she's hiding from him, is the story."

Lily said, defensively, "Sharon has always attracted men,

not always the best kind of men. She's lived dangerously—
sometimes. But—"

"But if she's in trouble, she should go to the police, Lily.
We can't protect her."

"Of course we can protect her! How can you say such a
heartless thing! Whoever this person is—he doesn't know she's
here. She's safe *here*." Lily paused, feeling the odd sensation in
her tongue of cold, numbness. She could barely look at her
husband; the acrid smell of his burning cigarette made her eyes
sting. "Wes, did anything happen last night? Between you and
Sharon?"

For Lily had to ask.

Wes sighed audibly. Pacing about Lily's workroom colliding
with things, not noticing where he blundered; a large blind
sweating animal in this unfamiliar, confining space. He said quietly, "I came close to—making a mistake with her, Lily. But I
didn't, and I don't want to talk about it."

Lily heard. Through a roaring in her ears, Lily heard.

Of course she'd known, known something, had sensed
something in Wes that morning when he'd risen earlier than
usual and was out of the house while she was still upstairs;
sensed something was wrong when Sharon kept her door shut
through the morning replying in vague monosyllables to Lily's
entreaties. *Sharon? Are you all right? Aren't you hungry? Sharon?*

How many entreaties, through a lifetime. Offering food,
drink, solace, love to others. Risking rebuff, or simply silence.

"Lily? I'm sorry. I don't know what to say—I'm sorry."

Still Lily could not reply. She was faint, leaning against her
workbench. The shattered pieces of the bowl she'd loved, the
bowl Sharon had knocked to the floor, were still on the workbench, on a sheet of newspaper, as if Lily hoped to reassemble
them; of course she could not, what a futile notion, she smiled
sadly at such a futile notion, yet she hadn't been able to throw
the pieces out just yet.

Lily said, "You've been so angry, Wes. I've never seen you like this."

"I'm not angry, Lily. I'm—scared."

"You! Scared . . ."

Wes said, "Since Sharon came into this house, things have been out of control. She's a disturbed woman. Very charming when she wants to be but it doesn't last. I think she's dangerous, and I want her out of here."

Lily tried to laugh. "Dangerous! Sharon . . ."

"She's crazy—in her soul. I've known people like that—not many—in Vietnam."

"Wes, what a thing to say, what an—accusation. Sharon is my sister—"

"Like I said, when it suits *her*. You hardly count in her life."

Lily drew breath to protest. *No!*

But it was true, probably. A simple fact. Anyone but Lily could see.

With deliberate fingers, Lily had been pushing pieces of the broken bowl into a heap in the center of the newspaper page; now she carefully lifted the corners of the page to secure the unwieldy, surprisingly heavy debris inside, and carried it to her wastebasket. She must have decided to clean up after all. Her next work, the ceramic bowl-sculpture, would be much more interesting than this had been. Perhaps a bit ungainly, even ugly. Beauty of a less harmonious kind.

Lily said, evenly, "You're attracted to Sharon, Wes. As a man would be. Any man. Of course." It was not a provocative statement but simply another statement of fact. But Wes responded hotly, "No. It was Sharon who sought me out, Lily. In one of her tight, sexy dresses and nothing beneath—*that* was obvious. Saying she couldn't sleep, she was lonely—" Wes paused, breathing harshly. It went against the grain of the man's temperament, to be informing on another; to be telling tales of another; alleviating his own compromised position by accusing another. Yet what choice had he? How otherwise could he explain? Lily saw with a rush of love for him, and sympathy, the helplessness in her husband's face: that her sister was making of Wes Merrick a person of the kind he himself despised. He said, in disgust, "Never mind. It's over. Nothing happened between us and nothing will. But I want the woman out of this house, Lily—or I'll have to leave, myself."

Lily cried as if stabbed to the heart. "No!"

It was then that the idea came to Wes. Lily saw it in his face, a look of fury and decisiveness, childish rancor yet adult rectitude.

I will cleanse my house of this pollutant. I will reclaim my family.

Striding to Sharon's room, pushing the door open (the guest-room door couldn't be locked except from the inside)—as Lily followed after, mortified, protesting, No! no! this is wrong, this is an invasion of Sharon's privacy!—but Wes in his wild mood paid her not the slightest heed. Impatient, muttering to himself, he threw open the closet door, pawed through Sharon's clothes on hangers and examined the floor, where pairs of shoes were arranged in rows; he inspected the bathroom, which badly needed cleaning; examined the glittering miscellany of items on the bureau top; yanked open drawers, rummaging inside—all the while Lily tried to restrain him, catching at his hands. No! how could he! Oh, Wes! On Sharon's bedside table was a Bible and this, too, Wes snatched up, leafed through, set down again; the floral-print comforter had been pulled up crookedly to the pillows on Sharon's bed, and this Wes pulled brutally aside, staring at rumpled bedclothes beneath as if he expected his sister-in-law to be hiding there; he checked beneath the pillows, and, as far as he could reach, between the mattress and the box springs; he bent to peer beneath the bed—hauling out Sharon's blue canvas suitcase, which was locked.

Lily was pulling at his hands, pleading. "Wes, no. Please let's leave now."

Wes struggled with the lock, might have broken it with his bare hands, recalled then a Swiss army knife in the hall cupboard and went to fetch it and forced the suitcase lock as Lily looked on helplessly, blinking back tears. "Look." Wes was lifting from the suitcase a remarkable assortment of things: several men's wallets, each empty; a man's platinum-gold digital wristwatch (flashing the exact time—5:49 P.M.), a man's gold signet ring, an Italian silk checked ascot scarf; and another Bible, smaller, cheaper, with tissue-thin pages; and, wrapped in a red rayon slip, what appeared to be a policeman's badge, gleaming as if it had been just recently polished.

Again Wes said, excitedly, "Look."

Lily stared at the gleaming object in her husband's fingers. "What—is it? Wes, I don't understand."

" 'Sumner County, Nebraska, Deputy Sheriff.' My God."

Lily whispered, "But how could Sharon have gotten that?"

"How could she have gotten any of these things? She's some kind of thief."

"Oh, Wes! We don't have any right to violate her privacy—even if—"

"Yes, we have the right. *I* have the right."

Now Wes had discovered newspaper clippings, tabloid pages that had been carefully folded and placed inside the suitcase lining. He whistled thinly, holding these out for Lily to read; but Lily could not read the lurid banner headlines, her vision swam in a panic. Wes read aloud, haltingly, " 'STAR' KILLER STRIKES 2ND TIME, VEGAS MOTEL, VICTIM 43, NEBRASKA SHERIFF'S DEPUTY'—my God. And here—the *Los Angeles Times*—'POLICE LINK SOUTHWEST MOTEL KILLINGS 'GORGEOUS' RED-HAIRED WOMAN SOUGHT.' Oh, Lily, Jesus . . . your sister must have killed these men. Killed them, stole from them." He read from another paper, " 'A star, crudely drawn in blood, was left on walls in the victims' rooms.' . . . Look, here's the *Yewville Journal*—Stanley Reigel!—"

Lily began to faint, and Wes jumped up to steady her; he

held her, and she clutched at him, terrified, unable to breathe; there was a violent pounding in her head as if an artery were about to burst; Lily was whispering, weeping, "We shouldn't have come in here. We shouldn't have looked. I knew, oh Wes I knew—we shouldn't have looked."

11

At the Starlite Motel, Yewville, New York

When, over the phone, he told her the name of the motel, she smiled happily—*A sign!*

You are sending "Starr Bright" a sign, thank you God.

That evening preparing for "MRS M DWYER" an envelope containing among other items the print of the angry-eyed girl. By this time half-convinced the girl was in fact Mack Dwyer's lover mistreated by him and vengeful as "Starr Bright" herself.

And the page carefully removed from the Book of John.

And hairs from the trash behind Rita's Beauty Salon.

These items to be left in the motel room, in the presence of the bleeding pig.

The letter she would mail afterward. Gloved hands always, no fingerprints to be traced.

And with this final sacrifice your destiny is fulfilled.

The man—"B. Decker" he would call himself—had made arrangements at the Starlite Motel on Route 209 North. Approximately four miles from Washington Street.

Pig-justice, he'd made the arrangements himself. She would be invisible. A shimmering upright flame, but invisible.

Arriving quietly at 6:05 P.M., parking at the rear. The room was 48 of the double-tiered mustard-yellow stucco building so of course she parked the Toyota elsewhere; partly hidden by an overflowing Dumpster, facing a canvas-covered swimming pool.

(Had she been here before? In summer? The swimming pool reminded her. There'd been a plastic mattress floating there, American flag colors. A sharp stink of chlorine and a woman's shrill sexy giggling that might have been her own.)

Crossing the oil-specked pavement to the sidewalk running beside the motel, making her way limping slightly, favoring her left leg, to room 48 at the far end. If anyone observed he would see a woman of possible middle age in a shapeless trench coat, head covered with a dark scarf and face obscured by dark glasses and her shoulders slumped; despite the limp, she wore high-heeled shoes. And carried a tote bag.

If anyone observed.

And no one did.

The desk clerk on duty at the Starlite that evening would not have seen this individual at all. The desk clerk would have seen and spoken with and taken payment (cash: $55.75 with tax) from only "B. Decker" who'd telephoned the motel that morning to reserve a double room for one night.

For "Mr. & Mrs. B. Decker" of Utica, New York.

The desk clerk would claim to have heard no sounds—shouts, cries, screams. If there were such. For room 48 was at the farther end of the building, a very private room.

"B. Decker" had specifically requested a "very private, quiet room."

Not peace but a sword!—she'd wakened that morning with Jesus' voice ringing in her ears.

She had honed the knife carefully in the Macy's knife-sharpener in Lily's attractive kitchen. This was a ritual of love, even tenderness. Never any haste. Never hesitation.

At the rear of the Starlite there was a smell of garbage and diesel oil. Insecticide and disinfectant. "Starr Bright's" sensitive nostrils pinched. The pig's habitat, the pig's lair. For a confused moment she could not recall which of them would be awaiting her inside, with a bottle: the one named Cobb, the one named Fenke, the one named Marr, the one named Hughlings, the one named Salaman . . .

Not peace her pulsebeat urged *but a sword. Not peace not peace but a sword.*

For there had begun in Sharon's soul a counter-urging, a small pleading voice to which she dared not listen. Urging forgiveness, forgetfulness. What would Lily do in her place, what would Lily think? What would Deedee think? And the man, what was the man's name?—the man her sister had married not a pig but a good, decent man a faithful husband—what would he think of her, how would he judge her?

But no, she dared not listen. It was too late, "Starr Bright" had honed the knife, all was prepared as in an act before a live impatient audience amid dazzling blinding lights and sexy-throbbing drums.

Not peace! not peace but a sword. Amen.

Within an hour they were happily drunk, couldn't keep their hands off each other; or so it seemed. "Mack Dwyer"—the thick-waisted thick-bodied middle-aged man with graying hair combed in silly, hopeful strands across the flushed dome of his head, and "Sherrill"—as she'd asked him to call her—with glossy burnished red curls spilling to her shoulders, large mascara-rimmed eyes glowing with pale green eyeshade, beautiful glistening crimson-kissable mouth.

"Sherrill" poured drinks from Dwyer's bottle of Seagram's with the skill and poise of a cocktail hostess. Sipping very discreetly herself, urging the man on to more, more. And more. Cooing to him, soothing, murmuring, nodding enthusiastically. Listening with rapt attention. For Dwyer, like most men, had a lot to say. Oh yes, a lot to say. His fleshy mouth worked, his hands gestured. He had opinions, he had memories. He had hopes, plans. You listened, and you nodded, and you filled the guy's glass.

The pig does 99 percent of the work actually. You just sit back, wait.

"Starr Bright" would boast laughing to the cops.

It had been a mild shock, though—Mack Dwyer. So much older. Hardly the same guy. Looking like Mr. Dwyer—his father. He was still good-looking in a jowly way, women would be attracted to him, that air of confidence, swagger. But his face was starting to sag and his skin was of the hue and texture of cooked oatmeal. Now he'd removed his sport coat you could see the fistfuls of flesh at his waist spilling over his belt. Where once Mack Dwyer had been lean, muscle-hard, quick hands and feet, a panther.

Smiling she swooped to kiss him on the lips. Not a sensuous tongue-prodding kiss, not yet. More of a light teasing peck of a kiss.

"Wow! What's that for?"

" 'Cause it's so great to see you again, Mack. And looking so handsome like always."

Dwyer laughed grunting and reached over for her, as if to swing her onto his lap or onto the bed beside him; but quick-silver Sherrill eluded him, patting the back of his hand with her gloved fingers. It was a turn-on, tight red lace gloves with the red jersey sheath-dress hiked up to her thighs as she coiled herself in a chair; crossed her long lovely dancer's legs, gleaming in smoke-colored diamond-patterned stockings. *Take a good look, fella. Take an eyeful. 'Cause that's all you're gonna get of "Sherrill."* Thinking how strange that driving to the Starlite Motel, parking the Toyota and approaching room 48 she'd been feeling jumpy, anxious; wondering if maybe, this time, she should turn back. Lily's voice urging *Forgive him! Forget the past! Come home to us, Rose of Sharon!* But then at the door she'd pulled off the scarf and fluffed out her shiny red curls and removed the tacky trench coat to stuff into the tote bag and straightened her shoulders so her breasts emerged and wetted her lips and stepped into the light ready to see herself reflected in the pig's glistening-admiring eyes—Jesus, it felt so *right. "Starr Bright" in the right place at the right time and the rest of life is so boring.*

Noting how Mack Dwyer was breathing hard, staring at her in a slow-blinking way. Boyish, but dirty-minded. Sure. You could tell this guy was a small-town politician—even now, trying to figure out how he can fuck her, he's making gassy speeches.

And wearing a showy expensive wristwatch. Another digital with ebony face and flashing numerals exactly like—whose? The name was gone and the face except the "cabana" in Joshua Tree, the way the walls had shone afterward.

Sure she'd laugh telling the cops *I just liked to kill, it's a real rush. You should try it.*

Mack Dwyer was saying, phony-sincere, "Hell, I certainly did try to keep track of you, Sharon. I mean—'Sherrill.' People said you'd gone away, you were a famous model. Saw some pictures of you in a fashion magazine—fantastic! *I* went to Bucknell and flunked out first semester and my dad said he'd give me a second chance on the condition—" How earnestly the man talked as if Sherrill gave a damn, complaining of his marriage which wasn't "what I'd been looking forward to, frankly" and his kids who were "self-centered taking their father for granted" and his career as a Republican that was "on the upswing again after some rotten luck in the last election." Here was a man aggrieved, maudlin, in urgent need of female consolation. Here was a man deserving of a whole lot better than he had. Staring at Sherrill like she was a trick that might vanish. And tugging at his necktie, slick shiny red-striped tie selected for this special occasion. Saying, "It's terrific, Sharon, I mean 'Sherrill,' you called me like this. I was crazy for you, honey, back then, I really was; why we broke up *I* sure don't know," and she laughed and said, "You don't, huh, Mack?" and he said emphatically, shaking his head so his jowls quivered, "I *don't.* But I have this feeling you blame me, right? It was something I did or said, right? Shit, I know I was an s.o.b. my

last couple years of high school, you girls shouldn't have spoiled
me so I lost perspective—you know?" and she laughed saying,
"So I guess it was our fault, huh?" and he reached for her again
playfully and clumsily and not yet dangerous and she was able
to elude him leaving him panting. "Jesus, Sherrill! You're so
beautiful. Your eyes, your skin—hair—that dress—you do forgive me, don't you?" and she said, in a sexy-throaty-teasing
voice, "Now why would I need to 'forgive' you, Mack? You
got a guilty conscience?" and he said, with boyish contrition,
"It *was* my fault, wasn't it? What'd I do? Was it—oh, Christ I
remember: this girl from Stillwater was going out with Budd
Petco and she and I sort of traded dates—at Wolf's Head
Lake?—and you hid in the girls' changing room crying I guess
and wouldn't come out, Budd said—" and she said, smiling
sharply, "No, Mack. Sure wasn't me," and he said, "It wasn't?"
and she said coolly, "Some other girl of yours, hon," and he
said, sipping at his drink, "Could've sworn. Pretty girl with red
hair, freckles all over . . ." and she said, bemused, "You remember 'Sharon Donner' with red hair and freckles?" and he said
cagily, "Hmmm, sweetheart, the age I'm getting to, I don't
know what the hell I *do* remember," and she said, smiling, lazily
stroking the shining calf of one of her legs as if unaware of how
provocative a gesture it was, the perspiring man only a few
inches away staring at her, "You remember your senior prom.
I was your date," and Dwyer smiled again in his sheepish-
boyish-lewd way murmuring, "Mmmm, yeah, I guess I do—
sure," and she said, "You and your football team buddies got
me drunk and—you know," and he said, shifting his shoulders
excitedly, " 'Got you drunk'—I don't remember that, Sharon.
Hell, I got pretty smashed myself," and she said, teasing, playful,
poking him in the thigh, "What you guys did to me in your
father's van, remember that van?—wasn't so nice," and he said,
frowning, staring into his glass for a moment before drinking,
"Look, I don't remember that, I was smashed out of my skull,"
and she said, shaking a forefinger at him, close by his flushed

face, "Piggy-piggy! *Was* Mack naughty? 'Big Mack' and his team buddies?" and he said, defensively, "I don't remember anybody doing anything they didn't want to do," and she said slyly, "It was statutory rape, Big Mack," and he repeated, doggedly, "*I* don't remember anybody doing anything they didn't want to do," and she said, " 'Statutory rape'—rape by the statute," and he said, "There sure as hell wasn't any *rape*, that's a laugh," and she said, "Because I was only fifteen," and he said, making a snorting noise like laughter, "Hell, *I* was only seventeen, or—" and she said, "Eighteen, actually," and he said, "Well—whatever. We were kids," and she said, lightly, in a kind of singsong, "And I didn't say yes, Big Mack, not yes to five guys," and he said, "Yes, but you did say yes—you didn't say no," and she said, "Maybe you didn't hear," and he said, "In fact I was smashed out of my skull, that's the fact, I don't remember any of this," and she said, laughing, "Oh, well—boys will be boys, eh?" and he said, with a heavy sigh, tugging at his necktie, "I guess. Now I got kids of my own, sons, who don't listen to me," and she was laughing at his look of physical discomfort, an aroused, sweating male, an upright thick-bodied pig in clothes too tight; and playfully she raised her leg, and drew the instep of her high-heeled shoe against his thigh and side, poking, tickling, and he gaped at her in startled delight, and she leapt to her feet now displaying her slender body, stretching her arms, in a pretense of kittenish yawning, showing the tip of her pink tongue between crimson lips.

As if the musical tempo had been quickened, now the action would begin.

"O.K., Big Mack, strip."

"Huh?"

"Strip."

Running her tight-gloved fingers through the man's disheveled hair and, when he lunged for her, leaping back agile as a dancer or a gymnast. "Hey! Whew!" He'd exploded in laughter, spilling whiskey on his trousers.

She, too, was panting. And perspiring. But loved the feeling, like a cocaine high. Commanding, " 'Starr Bright' says *strip*, fella."

Laughing, eager, Dwyer stumbled to his feet. She danced away, keeping him at arm's length. She was snapping her fingers and moving her eel-like body in tight, erotic contortions, laughing at his dazed expression, commanding, "Strip! It's time—strip for 'Starr Bright'!" and Dwyer said, blinking, "Who's 'Starr Bright'?" and she was pivoting away, keeping the room's sole chair between them, singing, "—'gonna be with you soon! Gonna be with you so-oon!' " and he tried to fall in with her mood, swaying-drunk, saying, "If I strip—you, too, sweetheart? You're gonna strip, too?" and she said, "Right! Just turn your back, honey," and he said, with babyish inflection, "Don't wanna turn my back, wanna watch," and she darted at him to run a quick-caressing hand down the front of his thick body to his bulging groin and he shuddered as if struck by a current of electricity, his eyes lost focus, and she laughed saying, " 'Starr Bright' will teach you tricks she learned in New York—L.A.—Acapulco—Paris—Tangier—*Hong Kong*!—but Big Mack's got to turn his back first," and she was dancing, shaking shoulders, hips, pelvis, "—then there's gonna be a nice sur*prise*."

So Mack Dwyer trustingly turned his back on her, muttering and laughing to himself; panting as if he'd run up a flight of stairs; fumbling to remove his white cotton dress shirt that was sweated through under the arms and across the back, tossing his tie into the air, undoing his belt, his trousers. Nor slackening the beat though regarding him now with a look of loathing, she reached for the blue-sequined purse and removed the knife; her protection; pearl-handled stainless steel carving knife remarkably light in the hand with a five-inch blade honed to razor-sharpness that afternoon; the knife that fitted her right hand perfectly; the knife that steadied her hand so it ceased to tremble; the knife that thrilled her like a baptism, it felt so *right*.

Every time, so *right*.

Dwyer clumsily stripped to his shorts, cotton boxer shorts, she noted with disdain the flaccid fat at his waist, the pocked thighs, pallid legs. The boy Mack was gone, a stranger had taken his place yet must be punished. She hid the knife behind her back as he turned to face her expectantly.

His heated face sagged in disappointment.

"Eh, Sharon honey? What's wrong?"

She was smiling at him, shining. An upright flame, a woman clothed in the sun and upon her proud head a crown of twelve blazing stars. And in her sexy high-heeled shoes, her supple legs as far apart as the tight sheath dress would allow, a dancer's or an athlete's pose, poised in readiness.

The wild music pounding between them faster and faster had ceased now, abruptly. Whatever mood, rudely shattered.

Dwyer's bloodshot eyes lowered, to his own body. He said, mumbling in chagrin, "Guess I—I'm changed some, eh? Not like eighteen."

Still she said nothing, smiling; poised in readiness. At a short distance a car door slammed, a car was driven noisily away. The man was abashed and apologetic but beginning to be annoyed, a sullen droop to his mouth. "Sharon, you're not changing your mind, are you? Because if you are this is a helluva time to—"

Now bringing the glittering knife around so he could see it, moving deft and unhesitating and bent slightly at the knees, feinting the blade toward him as he stared, astonished, backing off, eyes widened as in a caricature of incredulity and alarm. He was gasping for breath, "—wait, no, what—is this?—what the hell—oh my God, wait, Sharon—" as astounded as if the very earth had opened up before him about to suck him down to oblivion. He backed clumsily away, aside, shaking his head murmuring no, no, no and she discerned in his dazed eyes how he would make a desperate swipe at her, hoping to send the knife flying from her fingers, imagining her fingers weak, imagining her a weak woman easily intimidated by a man's superior strength; and so seeming to invite him, taunting him; and he

did move, but so clumsily, stiffly, his athlete's reflexes long since
blunted, she had no difficulty leaping to one side like a cat, and
swinging the blade in a swift powerful arc even as the man's
arm was moving in an arc of its own so the blade caught him in
the palm of his hand slicing the skin in a deep four-inch laceration from which bright blood at once erupted, and as he whim-
pered in pain clutching the wrist of that arm she drew the blade
swiftly along his forearm, this time in a deep six-inch laceration,
beautiful to her eye—"There, pig! Now you know 'Starr
Bright.'"

     She paused to switch on the TV. Network evening news in
too-vivid color.

     Dwyer stumbled backward in panic, against the edge of the
double bed, nearly falling; blood flowed in two streams down
his uplifted arm, dripping to the carpet. She did not give him
time to recover from the shock of the assault nor even to
breathe but advanced upon him, smiling, "No, I haven't
changed my mind, Mack, 'Starr Bright' never changes her
mind," and he was begging, pleading, "Wait, no—Sharon,
please you don't mean—can't mean—help me I'm bleeding,
my arm—I swear to God I'm so sorry—" and a thought came
to her, it was perhaps not a thought of her own but one sent to
her from God for *in these days shall men seek death, and shall not
find it; and death shall flee from them* so she circled the trembling
man urging "On your knees! Pray to God to save you!" and
Dwyer sank to his knees on the bloodied carpet staring at her,
trembling with terror staring like a transfixed animal, and she
was speaking calmly to be heard over the animated TV voices,
"Yes, pray! Pig-rapist, pray! 'Our Father who art—' *Pray!* 'Starr
Bright' didn't do this for Stan Reigel but she will do it for you,
Big Mack, remember Stan-the-Man your team buddy?" and
Dwyer failed to comprehend so she repeated her words and this
time a sick comprehension dawned in his eyes, his body
stricken with grief for its own mortality, so she commanded
him again, pointing the bloodied tip of the knife at his throat,

"Pray, pig! If God has mercy, 'Starr Bright' has mercy, if God has no mercy, how can 'Starr Bright' have mercy? 'Our Father who art—' "

At once the terrified man began, " 'Our F-Father who art—in H-Heaven'—"

So Mack Dwyer, forty years old, naked except for sweat-dampened boxer shorts, knelt on the soiled carpet of room 48 of the Starlite Motel, Route 209, Yewville, New York, in the early evening of a Thursday in April, praying for his life. As "Starr Bright" looked on, an empty vessel to be filled with God's will.

12

Rose of Sharon,
Lily of the Valley

*T*here *is evil that takes hold of people, that isn't born in them; the way a thistle seed takes hold in soil. There is evil that is allowed into the heart, invited in.*

In a suspension of dread Lily awaited Sharon's return. In the pretty lavender-and-cream bedroom that had been Sharon's. She sat on the edge of the bed, she stood, paced about, gazed worriedly out the window into darkness; sat again, weak, sick with anticipation of what was to come. Spread out on the floral-print comforter were a dozen or more newspaper clippings and pages, a *Newsweek* feature with the lurid title "First 'Big League' Female Serial Killer Strikes in Southwest, California," at which she couldn't bring herself to look; and the wallets, the wristwatches, the leather belt with the brass buckle, the Nebraska sheriff's deputy badge. Wes had opened both windows to dilute the stale odor of strong perfumes, cigarette smoke. Lily wondered whether the odor would ever entirely fade from the room.

She'd been crying, and there was a choked, constricting sensation in her chest. In her fist she held a damp, shredded tissue. In another part of the house Wes was pacing, smoking. From time to time she heard his footsteps approach—he returned to stand in the doorway, looking at her. He'd wanted to call the police immediately but Lily had pleaded with him,

"Wes, no. Please. Let me speak with Sharon first. Just the two of us."

Wes had said, almost angrily, "Lily, your sister is insane! She's a homicidal maniac."

Lily had pressed her fingertips against her eyelids. Her head swam. Wanting to protest *I can't believe that. There must be some explanation. It can't be as it seems!* But she said nothing.

At least, Deedee wasn't home for this. She was staying overnight with a girlfriend—fortunately.

Lily began to cry again, Wes knelt beside her and held her and in a gentler voice said, "The woman might be dangerous, Lily. She is dangerous," and Lily said, "Not to us, Wes," and Wes said, "To anyone! She's insane." But Wes relented, and agreed to let Lily speak with her sister alone, for a short while. Assuming Sharon returned at all.

He would remain, he said, downstairs, in his office with the lights out. Never far from a telephone.

How she loved him, Wes Merrick, her husband! Foreseeing that, when this nightmare ended, when Sharon was gone from them, and their happiness restored, she would never tell him who Deedee's mother was, she would never confess she had no idea who Deedee's father was. For such "truth," though factual, was not the truth of the heart. Such "truth" was not worth a moment's pain suffered by another.

To live with a secret, secrets—and to live happily.

What is this but the human condition?

So Lily told herself, tears like acid scalding her cheeks.

It was at 8:40 P.M. that Lily saw a car's headlights turn into the drive.

Sharon returning home from—wherever she'd been.

Lily steeled herself. Rising to stand beside the bed, clasping her hands together in an unconscious attitude of prayer, then dropping them at her sides. She knew that, in his darkened office, Wes stood rigid as well, waiting.

Sharon must have seen the lighted windows of her room, must have seen Lily inside, hesitated for a moment before opening the door and stepping into the room. And in that instant seeing Lily's expression, and the items spread out onto the bed; her eyes locking with Lily's in the full force of recognition.

"So, Lily. You know."

"I—don't, Sharon. I don't understand."

"Yes. You do."

Lily would recall afterward the flatness of her sister's voice. The look almost of relief in her blood-veined eyes.

Sharon came into the room, breathless, stumbling in her high-heeled shoes as if she were drunk, or dazed by a drug; the tote bag slipped from her fingers and fell to the floor, and Lily could see inside what appeared to be, among other things, a curly red glamor wig and a blue-sequined purse. Sharon was wearing Lily's old trench coat, unbuttoned; beneath, slacks and a sweater; the flawless cosmetic mask looked like crust on her strained face, her crimson lipstick was eaten partly away and her mascara was smeared. Her hair, visibly thin in the direct overhead light, was damp, as if she'd only recently showered. She moved slowly as if her joints ached.

Lily said, faltering, "But—what? What should I know, Sharon?"

Sharon said, shrugging, "It's true. What the papers say. I'm the one. I killed those men."

"Sharon, no! My God . . ."

"Who broke the lock on my suitcase? Wes? Good. I'm glad. I'm tired of running, I'm run to earth." Sharon glanced around, squinting, as if seeking Wes out; but Wes was not visible; she laughed, and raised her voice, "Wes! Good! Call the police! *I'm so tired.*"

Lily would have gone to Sharon to take hold of her hands but Sharon brought her hands up close to her body in an odd shrinking gesture, shutting them into fists; as one might do not wanting to be touched; not wanting another to be contaminated by one's touch; as if her hands were soiled. It was an unmistakable gesture and though Lily could see that her sister's hands were clean, perhaps scrubbed clean, the thought came to her *She has killed someone, tonight. She has just killed.*

Lily was crying, "Sharon, my God, why?" and Sharon said, as if confused, "*You* didn't know, Lily? Didn't guess?" and Lily said, "How could I guess—such a horror! It can't be true, can it?" and Sharon said, flatly, "Eleven men. Pigs, not men. God guided my hand, Lily. And another," drawing from the trench-coat pocket a man's digital wristwatch to toss onto the bed amid the others. Lily stared at first uncomprehending. "Sharon, who?"

"Guess, Lily of the Valley."

"Mack Dwyer—?"

"A pig who used to be 'Mack Dwyer.' "

Sharon tried to smile, wanly. Lily was appalled, even at such a time disbelieving. "No! Sharon, I can't—"

"Where's Wes? Has he called the police?"

"No!"

"No?"

Sharon was peering toward the doorway, the darkened hall. She seemed confused. Her bloodshot eyes were shiny yet unfocused. Her damp pale blond hair had been expertly fastened at the back of her head in an elegant French twist from which a few tendrils had escaped. In the high-heeled shoes she stood swaying, shivering.

Now Lily took her sister's hands, gently pried open the fists; held her hands tightly in both her own; Sharon's hands were icy-cold, tremulous. There was only a faint fragrance of perfume about Sharon, a smell rather of soap, shampoo. *She has showered off his blood. She has washed herself clean.* Lily pleaded, "Sharon, tell me there's some—mistake?"

"No. No mistake."

"But—why?"

Sharon said, with sudden passion, "Why? You know why,

Lily! They were pigs who didn't deserve to live! 'Starr Bright'—her revenge."

" 'Starr Bright'—?"

"God guided my hand, Lily. Now God is done with me. This"—indicating the things on the bed—"you—and Wes— it's a sign, God is done. It's over."

"But, Sharon—"

Moving still in that slow, arthritic way, blinking rapidly as if to get her vision into sharper focus, Sharon went to the tote bag and took from it the blue-sequined purse and opened it and held out for Lily's horrified examination a knife, a kitchen carving knife with a gleaming blade, and Lily recoiled, and Sharon laughed saying, "No, no, it's washed clean, the pig's blood is gone." This, too, she dropped onto the bed with the other items.

Going then like a sleepwalker to the telephone on the bedside table, to Lily's amazement fumblingly dialing a number and saying in a husky, hoarse voice, "H-hello? Police—?" and Lily cried, "Sharon, no!" and snatched the receiver from her, and put it back.

"Why did you do that, Lily?"

"Sharon, not yet! Not yet! It's too soon."

"No, it's time, Lily. God has abandoned me and I'm so tired, it's time."

Lily pleaded, "No, no, no," pulling Sharon into her arms, sinking onto the edge of the bed, and Sharon swayed, stumbled, sank to her knees beside her, limp and unresisting and beginning at last to sob, as she'd done when they were girls, in the identical posture years ago in the farmhouse in Shaheen in their shared bedroom on the second floor beneath the wind-ravaged eaves, begging forgiveness of Lily of the Valley, for she was Rose of Sharon who'd wronged her, or had wronged someone, or had been wronged by someone, insulted, injured, cut to the heart, trembling with rage, indignation, sheer unnameable passion. Lily was stroking her sister's head, her sister's thin shoulders, Lily whispering, "Thank you for coming to me, Sharon, for coming back to me," and Sharon said, "Help me, Lily? Don't stop loving me?" and Lily said, "I'll never stop loving you, Sharon," and Sharon began to pray, " 'Though I walk through the valley of the shadow of death . . .' " and Lily joined her, " '. . . I will fear no evil: for thou art with me: thy rod and thy staff they comfort me. . .' " and that was how Wes discovered them, a few minutes later.

13

"Deirdre"

It wasn't at Ali's house they had supper but at the mall where Ali's mother let them off. They ate at Pepe's Pizzeria or rather Ali ate and Deirdre drank two large diet Cokes saying that's all she wanted, she wasn't hungry. And at Pepe's there were three guys eyeing them, older guys from another high school who followed them into the movies sitting in the row behind them and cracking jokes, laughing and when the movie ended they asked the girls if they'd like something to eat, the girls said O.K. but they couldn't leave the mall because Ali's mother was picking them up at nine, and Ali and Deirdre went to the women's room whispering and giggling together, and Deirdre was feeling just a little light-headed, nothing serious but that weird thing with her eyes like she was seeing double and needed to blink hard to clear her vision, but Ali gave her another diet pill and that helped, actually she felt terrific, both of them felt terrific giggling about the guys whose last names they didn't know but they'd seen them around the mall, sure. The girls lit up a single cigarette for a quick smoke to share and Deirdre's gaze kept drifting to the mirror, not knowing if she liked what she saw there, or whether it scared her, her hair in the new way, the face that was hers yet not exactly, the slimmer cheeks, large startled-looking eyes outlined in black like eyes in a drawing. She was excited, maybe nervous a little, her fingers trembling as she approached the mirror gravely to smear Plum Moon maroon lipstick on her mouth, her wound of a mouth, raw and hungry.